ABOUT THE AUTHOR

When Chris Behrsin isn't out exploring the world, he's behind a keyboard writing tales of dragons and magical lands. Born into the genre through a steady diet of Terry Pratchett, his fiction fuses a love for fantasy and whimsical plots with philosophy and voyages into the worlds of dreams.

You can learn more about his fiction and download two free books at his website, chrisbehrsin.com.

facebook.com/chrisbehrsin

twitter.com/chrisbehrsin

goodreads.com/cbehrsin

bookbub.com/authors/chris-behrsin

DRAGONSEERS AND EVOLUTION

SECICAO BLIGHT BOOK FOUR

CHRIS BEHRSIN

WORLDWALKERS PUBLISHING

Cover Design Layout by Chris Behrsin
Copyediting by Wayne M. Scace
Proofreading by Carol Brandon

ISBN: 978-1-915866-32-3 (paperback)
ISBN: 978-1-915866-41-5 (hardcover)
ISBN: 978-1-915886-27-9 (e-book)

Published by Worldwalkers Publishing

For my sister, Joanna, with fond memories of the adventures we've shared

EAST
CADIGAN
ISLAND
CADIGAN
Pinnatu Crater
Paradise Reef
Oahastin
Bamfordo
SOUTHERN APPROACH
SOUTHERN BARR
Soora
Gahl
S
PALLANDI
OCEAN
0   100

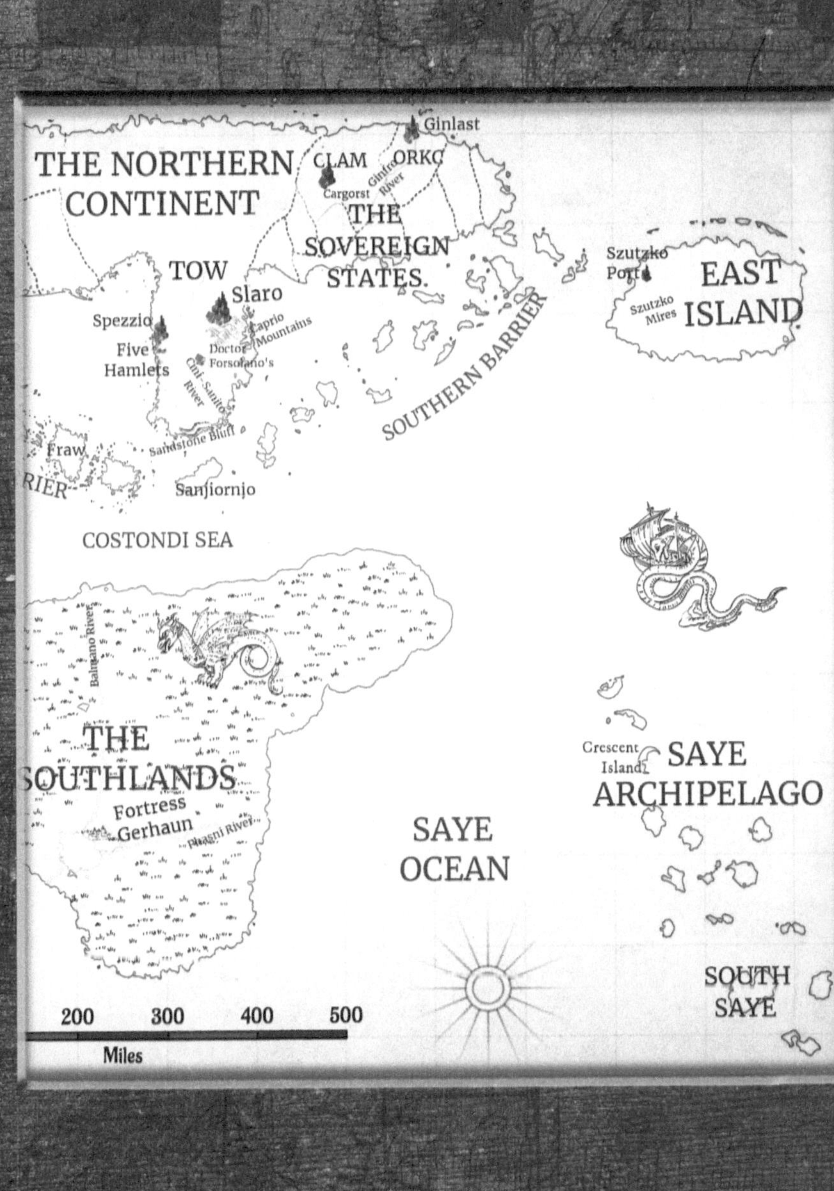
THE NORTHERN CONTINENT
Ginlast
CLAM
ORKO
Cargorst
Gintro River
THE SOVEREIGN STATES.
TOW
Slaro
Spezzio
Caprio Mountains
Five Hamlets
Doctor Forsolano's
Cini-Sanito River
SOUTHERN BARRIER
Szutzko Port
Szutzko Mires
EAST ISLAND
Sandstone Bluff
Fraw
RIER
Sanjiornjo
COSTONDI SEA
Balmano River
THE SOUTHLANDS
Fortress Gerhaun
Phasni River
Crescent Island
SAYE ARCHIPELAGO
SAYE OCEAN
SOUTH SAYE
200   300   400   500
Miles

PART I

"Hierarchies are essential to the proper running of an organization, and they must be adhered to no matter what the personal costs."

— BASSALHAN CAGARI, DRAGON QUEEN

SECICAO IS the destiny of the world I have inhabited. Here, there is no need for any life other than the two species Finesia has deemed worthy – secicao and black dragons like myself.

The clouds produced by it now hang off me like a shroud. Once, their eggy smell would have disgusted me. But the gas clings to my skin as water droplets might when I emerge from a crystal pool. I stand naked and tall as I admire the land that will one day become mine.

Wiggea, my former dragonelite and now my servant, stands beside me, his hand in mine. I give him a confident smile. He smiles back from beneath his slicked back hair. His expression is subservient, and he looks at me as if I'm the only person of importance in the world.

Which will soon be true. Now, all I need to do is plant my roots in the soil here. To become the Tree Immortal, the destiny that has been handed down through legacy.

"That's it, my acolyte, embrace your destiny." Finesia's voice sounds as pure as the clouds feel. I stand on a rise overlooking my subjects below. The shades – the dark forms, the spirits of those we left behind, who can twist and form into anything they

please. They weave their way between the secicao, the thorny plants that have consumed the world.

Here, I have claimed my dominion.

"Not yet," says a shrill voice from behind me. Alsie Fioreletta. She's a part of the equation too. "We have not yet fought our final battle."

I turn to her. She has a wicked grin framed by raven hair falling over slender, yet muscular shoulders. She's naked, just like I am. Yet she stands with confidence, as if she was wearing the richest clothes in the world.

"Then we shall fight it now," I say, and I push Wiggea away. In this place, I can summon anything I will, as I need it.

I'm no longer naked, now wearing a coat of radiant silver armour. Yet, I feel no weight in the attire or the five-foot claymore that has suddenly appeared in a sheath on my back. I draw it and Alsie, now in full splendid golden armour, also draws hers.

"We shall fight again, but you are destined to lose," she says. "Finesia has her own purpose for you, but you shall never claim your ultimate prize."

I grit my teeth and point my sword at her. "She would never lie to me..."

"Oh, these aren't lies. It's only that you've failed to learn of your destiny, Dragonseer Wells. You've not yet come to examine your fate for what it is. You don't have the determination, the grit to see it through."

Every time I've met her in this place, and I never learn anything new. "Just shut up and fight," I say. I raise my claymore to the sky, clutching it tightly in both hands. Such a sword would have once felt heavy to me. But I'm no longer a product of my old world, and Finesia's gift has granted me superhuman strength.

"Gladly." Alsie performs a mocking half-curtsey, not taking her eyes off me as I charge forwards.

I scream out, my voice gaining such power that it deepens

into a bellowing roar. The brown clouds, part slightly as my sword cuts a path through them. I narrow my eyes. My feet carry me quickly down the hill.

Our swords clang; sparks fly. The impact sends me barrelling backwards. Alsie remains rooted to the ground.

She displays a sneer, comes in with three long strikes of her glistening sword, which I barely dodge. I backwards roll, and then I lift myself into a defensive stance.

"Attack, wench," Alsie says. "Isn't this what you want, to prove that you can kill me? Yet, not once have you done this, in this world or reality."

"I want to claim Finesia's prize. She has promised me an ultimate destiny. She has promised me eternal life."

Alsie lets out a cackling laugh. "Eternal life. Oh, that you shall have, my dear. There's so much yet that you have to learn."

"Shut up," I scream. "I don't have to listen to this."

"No, you—" Alsie's words get cut off by my sudden lunge towards her. She pirouettes out of the way, as if she was born for this kind of swordplay. I follow my lunge with an uppercut, and then I bring my sword down in a downward sweep.

But it isn't Alsie I hit. She's already started to transform, a black cloud billowing around her. My sword meets hard dragon scales. Out of the growing miasma comes a deafening roar.

I stumble backwards as Alsie's dragon head lunges out of the cloud, snapping its jaws. She tears into the soil and tosses up several secicao branches, which she throws into my path. I swipe the branches away with my sword before they land. Alsie pulls back her hind legs and launches into the air.

She roars out again, calling out for all who can hear the extent of her challenge. I squint at her, and I ram the blade of my claymore into the ground, sending a shudder up my spine.

Then I transform.

The scales tear through my skin, a pain that has become more recently a pleasure. In dragon form, I launch into the sky.

We meet in a tangle of scales and flesh, our claws tearing into each other's wings. I try to get on top, to push Alsie down toward the ground. But she's stronger than me. She always has been. The brown clouds part from us, as if afraid of this sacred battle.

I feel myself falling, and so I pull away just before I hit the ground. A roar comes out from the base of my stomach into the sky, and the ground shudders beneath me. I turn back to Alsie, and hover there in the air, and she stays there, watching me from a distance.

"*You are getting stronger, wench,*" Alsie said in my mind, her voice resounding through the collective unconscious into my head. "*But you still can never win.*"

"*One day, I shall. That is what Finesia has promised to me.*"

"*Really? And why do you think you deserve Finesia? You give her nothing and expect everything in return. She's grown disappointed with you, and that is why the ultimate prize will be my own.*"

She cuts through the sky like a spear, and I try to dive out of the way. Now the sky is too heavy. The clouds, which had felt airy, now feel like treacle. I hover, helpless in the air, as if my legs and wings have been nailed to an invisible board.

A green light fills the surrounding sky, pulling the clouds back towards me like a vortex. All I can do is watch paralysed as Alsie's snout tears right towards my throat.

Time seems to slow, and I watch in horror at the sharp teeth that will rip the life out of me. Her breath is putrescent, and mucosal fluid drips slowly from her thin, leathery lips. This now, is my time to die, failed by Finesia. Or have I failed her?

Her voice comes in my head, as resolute and sure as the first day I'd heard her. "*This is how it will be, my acolyte, unless you finally learn to let me in...*"

Yet Finesia's words aren't the last I hear, but Alsie's, cutting through the collective unconscious like poisoned darts. "*Our ultimate battle is drawing closer, Dragonseer Wells, and soon you shall learn what you are truly made of."*

Time speeds up once more. A sudden pain comes to my throat, as if just hit with a hammer.

Brightness fills my vision and I awaken into a world more brutal than the one I've just dreamed.

I JERKED up on the single bed, cold sweat clinging to my skin and terror beating in my heart. My throat felt raw, and I wondered for a moment if I'd screamed out. That might have sent Hastina running into the room, checking that Finesia hadn't taken over my mind.

Only the faint eggy scent of secicao remained from my dreams. This mixed with the mould and mildew created a cocktail of pungent smells that it had admittedly taken a while to get used to.

Fortunately, the toxic secicao clouds were safely distant. We now had Bassalhan Cagari, the despot dragon queen who had replaced Gerhaun Forsi as ruler of Fortress Gerhaun. Like Gerhaun, the new dragon queen created a protective bubble of the collective unconscious that pushed the secicao clouds away.

I reached out to take a glass of water, the coolness of it washing away a grittiness that lingered on my tongue. A dim light shone through the high but narrow window from where came the soft crooning sounds of the dragons in their stables outside.

I put my hands to my throat. The skin felt tender there, but the pain soon subsided, as if my hands had some kind of healing properties. I realised I'd left my mind open. Hastina was out there in the complex somewhere, and she nor Bassalhan would appreciate my dreams.

Hastina was a dragonseer, just like me, who also inhabited the fortress, pounding order in with the butt of her spear. I reached out with my mind for any sense of anyone prying into my thoughts. I couldn't sense her, but I could sense Bassalhan.

I grabbed my handkerchief from the bedside table to wipe the sweat away. The post-sleep blurs in my vision faded to reveal the sparse room. I'd tossed my blanket off in my sleep and the sheets had also bunched up at the bottom of the bed, revealing a mattress stained brown by stale sweat.

I made the bed, and then I lifted my mattress and pried out a deerskin-bound notebook from underneath it, resting next to a second book, which I ignored. Using a silver pen I had placed on the bedside table, I scratched pictures frantically in the first notebook, recalling the visions I'd seen in my dream. The shades. Wiggea standing beside me, Alsie naked and then covered in resplendent shining armour, the stench of secicao all around me.

That was what scared me the most. In the dreams, I basked in the smell of secicao. There, it had seeped up my nostrils and lingered on the back of my tongue as if it was all I needed to survive in this world. Then I had once again battled Alsie, and she said the same thing she always said – that we hadn't yet reached our final battle, whatever that meant.

The dreams always seemed the same, but I scoured my mind looking for something new. Something that could help me understand what Finesia was trying to do to me. An edge I could use to push her out of my mind.

I kept my thoughts masked as I drew, making sure that neither Bassalhan nor Hastina could hear how I'd still see these visions through their connection to the collective unconscious. It was no secret to her and Bassalhan what I'd done at the factory – how I'd unknowingly massacred thousands of slaves there in one of these dreams. When they first arrived here at Fortress

Gerhaun, they'd clarified that if I showed any sign of Finesia taking control of my mind, then they'd kill me. More recently, they'd posted several guards outside my door every night and forced Faso to install a quick-access alarm there, should I unwillingly transform into dragon form.

There was a chance I'd be able to escape if I transformed quick enough – just as I had when Travast Indorm tried to execute me via firing squad at the factory at Ginlast. But I'd have nowhere to go in exile except into the open arms of Finesia. That thought scared me more than anything else.

I finished scribbling, and then I leafed through the pages of my book, examining the sketches I'd drawn in indigo ink. I wasn't much of an artist, admittedly, and to the untrained eye I'm sure these would look little more than childlike scratchings. Still, they incited vivid memories of my dreams, and I ran through the images in my head, remembering all these terrifying visions.

I caught another strong whiff of the secicao outside Fortress Gerhaun. That was strange, as Bassalhan was an even greater source of the collective unconscious than Gerhaun Forsi ever was. I thought nothing of it until I sensed motion in the corner of my eye.

I swung around to see that a tendril of brown secicao gas had somehow snaked through the window. It stretched out towards me as if part of a great beast searching for an intruder in its territory. My heart stopped in my chest, and my mouth felt suddenly dry.

"That's right, my acolyte," Finesia said in my mind. *"The more you exist in this place, the more I can infiltrate even the strongest barriers. Soon, there will be nothing that can stop me. Then we will rule together as one."*

I wasted no time and searched around for the nearest possible weapon. Hastina would let me hold no arms in my bedroom in case I lost control in the middle of the night.

But I had my pillow, which seemed an adequate defence

against an unwitting tendril of gas. I took hold of it, and I wafted away the gas with as much ferocity as I could muster. I swiped it around in a frenzy, only stopping once the stench of secicao had faded. By the end of it, I was breathing heavily, and I tasted bile at the back of my throat. Around me, feathers fluttered to the floor.

"What the dragonheats are you doing?" Hastina's voice floated over from the doorway, and I spun around to see her framed there, one hand on her hip, the other clutched around the rope wrapped around the shaft of her incredibly sharp-looking spear. She had an artificial metal leg which she'd lived with so long that it did nothing to impede her movement.

"I—" I spotted the notebook in my periphery vision, open at a double-paged amateur depiction of two black dragons fighting in the air. It would be an even bigger disaster if she noticed that, so keeping my gaze on her, I strolled over so my hips blocked her view of it.

I kept facing her, with my pillow folded horizontally in front of my thighs, to further obstruct her chances of seeing the book. "What do you mean, what am I doing? I should ask what are you are doing, charging into my room like this. Can't I have at least a bit of privacy in this new dictatorship that you've created in my old mentor's resting place?"

"Just answer the question, Dragonseer!"

I sighed and clutched around inside my mind for a fast answer. Anything would do. "I'm airing the room. It gets a little musty in here from time to time. It's good to add a little airflow sometimes... Starve the mildew."

Hastina didn't even offer a scowl. Instead, she studied me with her hazel eyes, her heart-shaped face framed by a fiery mass of wavy red hair. "You look like you've just been caught in the act of something, Dragonseer Wells. What are you hiding behind you?"

She tried to peer around me, long enough to see the book on the bed. She twisted her spear slightly, as if to warn me she could impale me in one thrust. I often wondered how I would fare against her in dragon form.

She noticed the book on the bed. "A journal?" she asked. "Is that it?"

"I—I like to write down my thoughts sometimes. It's lonely here, being separated from Taka, and nothing to do except talk to Doctor Forsolano and my parents."

"Taka was never your son," Hastina snapped back.

"Nor is he yours. But Sukina entrusted *me* with the task of looking after him."

"I'm sure she would have seen things quite differently if she knew how Finesia inhabits your mind. Now hand over the diary." She lowered her spear slightly to make room for me to move towards her outstretched arm.

"Flaming wellies, you have to be kidding me," I said, and I placed my hands on my hips. "This contains my most personal thoughts. My affairs... Can't I have any privacy in this place?"

Hastina's expression didn't waver. "If it contains thoughts, some of which might belong to Finesia, it will give us a little idea of what's going on inside your mind."

I tried my hardest not to show any unnecessary fear. But I could see how tightly Hastina's hand was clutched around the shaft of the spear. It would take her only one swift movement to impale me in the gut, should she feel she had the incentive.

I grimaced, and I turned around, blocking the diary from her view again. A bead of sweat trickled down my temple, but I didn't wipe it away. I licked the dryness off my lips.

I didn't pick up this journal. I instead covertly placed the diary in my left hand, slid this hand under the mattress, switched the journal with an almost identical book. I passed this into my other hand, making sure that it looked like I'd lifted the original copy off the bed.

The replacement contained some incredibly personal stories. Grievances sometimes about living in the same fortress as my parents, because sometimes, even though I had to go to war, they could be overprotective.

I'd also written into it some romantic fantasies and accounts of Rastano Wiggea, and myself – from before he was turned to Finesia's side. I'd recounted our kiss underneath the Pinnatu Crater, when the magma had danced around us, sending up black plumes of sulphur in the heat. I'd also written about exactly what I'd wanted to do next.

This was my personal diary, which I'd neglected it lately in favour of the sketchbook I was using to record my dreams. Still, it was the best I had, and hopefully Hastina wouldn't question why I hadn't updated the diary for several months.

"Here," I said. "And please, once you realise that this has nothing to do with Finesia, start respecting my privacy and don't read everything I write."

I didn't know if she knew anything about the affair I'd had with her former husband. If not, she was about to find out, and dragonheats knows what the consequences of that would be.

Somehow, this seemed smarter than letting Hastina and Bassalhan know of the dreams I feared the most.

"I'll leave that to Bassalhan to judge," Hastina said, and without offering me another glance, she raised her spear back to a safe position and turned towards the door. Before she left, she looked back over her shoulder at me. "By the way, she wants to meet with you in ten minutes sharp, about a matter of utmost importance."

"I'll be there," I said, silently letting out a breath of relief. Hastina walked out the door, and I closed it behind her.

I sat on the bed, and another bead of sweat dropped off the side of my brow. After another deep breath and an opportunity to re-centre myself, I vowed I would find a better hiding place for that dream journal.

But first, I needed to attend this meeting and find out what it was about, because I knew it couldn't be anything good.

3

INSIDE THE TREASURE CHAMBER, Bassalhan, the fearsome golden dragon queen – who the other six remaining queens saw as their leader – lay over the treasures that Fortress Gerhaun held to fund the military operations abroad. She was curled around the golden dragon queen egg that Velos and Gerhaun had created together. As Bassalhan shifted, a coin tinkled down the treasure pile and landed spinning on the floor.

Because she was a good head taller and much bulkier than Gerhaun had been, Bassalhan had ordered some of the surrounding stables of the Greys to be removed so she could have a little more space in there. This meant tearing the tapestries off the walls, and the dust created by the renovations had always lingered.

The enlargement meant there was much more room here for meetings, and Hastina stood by the empty presentation area, where General Sako would often bawl about military tactics, to the apparent disinterest of the dragon queen.

As I stepped forward, Bassalhan lifted her head and pushed her massive snout towards me, sniffing me as if she were blind. She snorted, letting out a sulphurous breath that tossed back my hair. I ran my tongue over my bottom lip to moisten it a little, then bit down on it to remind myself not to express fear.

Hastina stepped forward on her good leg, keeping her stare affixed on me and her grip even more secure on her spear than before, ready to defend her dragon queen, just in case I tried anything. Even if I transformed into my dragon form, I had no idea how I'd go about bringing such a massive beast down.

I ignored Hastina and faced Bassalhan. "*You called me, ma'am,*" I said in the collective unconscious.

"*I did,*" the dragon queen replied. "*But before I tell you my news, have you got anything you want to express to me?*"

I looked at Hastina, whose expression was blank. Clearly, she'd reported everything that she'd seen in my chambers but, given there was no sign of aggravation in her face, I guessed that she'd read none of the more revealing passages yet. Either that, or she'd completely forgotten her love for Rastano Wiggea, her former husband, if it ever existed. Honestly, the way she behaved, it often seemed that she was incapable of love.

"*Yes, I do,*" I said with my hands on my hips. "*I've said it before, and I'll say it again. I really don't appreciate having my privacy invaded like that.*"

Bassalhan let off a low and deep growl. "*Dragonseer Wiggea entered your room for a good reason. She heard strange noises, and you were talking to yourself, saying things about a final battle. Do you remember any of that?*"

I shook my head and clutched my hands to my temples. I had screamed out in my dream, after all. "*No... None of that happened. There was this secicao gas, a tendril of it pushing through the window, and I couldn't let the secicao creep in. You have to understand, Bassalhan, I had to keep it out. It's my duty as a dragonseer, isn't it? To erase secicao from this world?*"

"*But that's folly. Secicao can't pass through a powerful source of the collective unconscious.*"

"*How would you know? Just because you haven't seen it happen a thousand times before, doesn't mean it can't happen once. What if secicao has found a way to infiltrate the fortress?"* I also almost added the implied follow-up question, 'What if Finesia has found a way in?' but I stopped myself, judging it wiser to keep that nascent thought away from prying minds.

"*That's what I mean,*" Hastina said. "*More and more fabrications. We can't trust leaving her alone without me. You must lock her up, Bassalhan.*"

"*No,*" the dragon queen snapped back, and a snort came out of her nostrils, sending out a plume of black bitter smoke with it. "*Dragonseer Wiggea, should you cross the realm of the inhumane, you will become no better than Alsie Fioreletta and her cohorts. You must train the troops to watch her and ensure she's locked up if there's any sign of her turning. But a vivid dream or a nightmare isn't enough evidence. All men and women have them, particularly in a place where secicao is so close.*"

"*Even if letting her roam free might mean the destruction of the dragon egg?*" Hastina asked. "*She could even become powerful enough to destroy you, Bassalhan.*"

"*I will let no such thing happen,*" Bassalhan said, and she looked behind her at the massive nest woven from gold thread that contained the egg which held Gerhaun's and Velos' child, the young queen. "*If Alsie Fioreletta could kill the dragon queens, then we'd all be dead by now.*"

"*Or perhaps there's a reason she wants you to live,*" I said.

Bassalhan snapped her head back to me and studied me with her huge yellow eyes. "*What do you know?*"

"*Nothing,*" I said, and I tugged at the lapel of my shirt. It was wet, coated in cold sweat. I could feel my heart thumping just beneath it, and I centred myself and reminded me not to be intimidated by the situation. Sukina would have advised me much the same if she were present in this situation, and so would Gerhaun. "*You called me here. But if there's no reason for this meeting but to try to trick me into revealing something I don't know, then I've got better things to be doing.*"

I turned on my heel, ready to leave.

"Stop!" Bassalhan roared out loud, with such ferocity that it caused me to freeze in my tracks on sheer instinct. I heard some guards shuffle from outside the double doors. But they didn't dare enter the room. I turned back to Bassalhan, slowly.

"Such insolence," Hastina muttered, and I saw her twist her spear out of the corner of my eye.

Bassalhan ignored her and continued to speak in the collective unconscious in a gentler voice, as if her display of anger was just for show. *"Dragonseer Wells, you know the importance of obedience. You observed it with Gerhaun, and you shall observe it with me."*

"Perhaps if you'd let me continue my life as normal here and see Taka. Then I'd feel more of an urge to show that respect."

Since that afternoon when the dragon queens and Hastina had arrived in Fortress, Bassalhan and Hastina had blocked all contact between Taka and me. At the start, I could have conversations with him in the collective unconscious. But we communicated less and less as he settled into his regimen. At first, I'd try reaching out to him, and he would say that he needed to focus on something. Then we simply fell out of touch.

I could wander Fortress Gerhaun freely, although Bassalhan's guards were always posed in the corridors near where Taka was, because I couldn't visit him. The reason, Bassalhan had explained to me, was that they couldn't risk me corrupting his mind and strengthening his connection to Finesia. I suspected that they'd brainwashed him into thinking I wasn't a good influence on him. If he saw me now, I worried he'd look upon me as a stranger or an enemy and not the dragonseer he once admired.

Bassalhan lowered her great snout towards the ground and rested it on a massive, faceted ruby. The gem shifted a little, sending up a thin trail of blue dust.

"Taka is exactly whom I wish to speak to you about," Bassalhan said in the collective unconscious. *"I trust you've been keeping in touch with the news of abroad."*

I nodded. *"Candalmo Segora still visits to deliver the weekly run of the Tow Observer magazines."*

"Then you know about the developments in the palace? We've not talked much about affairs outside the fortress."

I recalled a double page feature in one of Papo's most recent issues of the Tow Observer. It showed Cini's throne room, much as it looked when I had visited there several years ago, right before Alsie killed Sukina with a poison dart delivered straight to her throat. But now, the only thing that remained from my memory in that picture was Taka, playing with a model airship. Besides him was a mysterious woman dressed in black with a mask that looked like an incredibly ugly dragon. The mask was also black, polished to shine, and had tendrils dangling from the top of it that looked like strands of liquorice. They called that woman the 'Masked Regent', appointed the task of guarding the new king, namely Taka.

"Fortunately," I said. *"I know that you've not sent Taka back to Cini's old palace. Though whoever they've posted to pose as him bears a striking resemblance."*

"They must have searched far and wide for a good lookalike."

"Then they've done the job well," I said. *"But who is the Masked Regent? Do you know?"*

Bassalhan lowered her massive head. *"I don't..."*

"So it's not Alsie? Or Indira?"

"No, Alsie has been sighted in other places. Meanwhile, though Indira hasn't been seen since the battle of Ginlast, our sources have confirmed that it can't be her either."

I clenched my teeth, remembering. It hadn't been much of a battle, but a massacre, and I had performed the killing. I could still taste the fire passing through my mouth. I could still smell the ash and char from the slaughter. I could still feel the wet stickiness of blood on my face, and I could still remember waking, completely innocent, on a warm sickbed as if nothing had happened. Yet I hadn't been in control of myself then; Finesia had taken control of my mind.

"So why did you call me here?" I asked. They were taking an

awful long time to get to the point.

"*Because we've decided to send Taka to the palace, and we thought you should know.*"

"*What? You'll be sending him right into the jaws of the enemy.*"

"*No, we won't,*" Hastina said with a grimace. "*We wouldn't dare go into such a situation without a plan.*"

"*But what if the Masked Regent is Indira? Or it could be any one of Alsie's minions…*"

"*The Masked Regent isn't Alsie Fioreletta,*" Hastina snapped back. "*Nor is it my mother, and we know from their appearance that it isn't Charth.*"

"*But any three of those could be at the palace,*" I pointed out. "*And how do you know it isn't Alsie or Indira, anyway?*"

"*Silence!*" Bassalhan snapped. "*We don't need to explain ourselves to you, Dragonseer Wells. We just wanted you to give you one moment to see the boy before he leaves. If you would want to, that is…*"

"*Though be warned, I'll be keeping a close eye on you as you do,*" Hastina added.

I lowered my head, knowing I really didn't have a choice in the matter. At least I'd be able to meet with Taka, so I could express to him that I still cared. I bit my tongue hard to suppress my rage. Another outbreak would do me no good in this situation and would give Bassalhan every excuse to revoke her offer. "*When can I see him?*" I asked.

"*Later this morning,*" Bassalhan said. "*In around twenty minutes at your parents' tearoom shall be fine.*"

I nodded. "*Then that's that. Is there anything else?*"

"*No, that will be all,*" Bassalhan said, and she opened her mouth into a cavernous yawn. Bassalhan did not differ from Gerhaun in that respect – she really appreciated her sleep.

I left the treasure chamber feeling ever so slightly divided. I was content that I was going to see Taka, but I feared it might be the last time I ever did.

4

Once I passed back through the oak double doors of Gerhaun's former treasure chamber, the rage that I'd kept bottled up during the conversation with Bassalhan and Hastina finally exploded within me.

How dare they make such a crucial decision on Taka's future without including me. Dragonheats, had they even asked Faso's permission? Taka was still a child after all.

I stormed past the two guards in pale-blue attire standing outside. Hastina had brought them in from outside Fortress Gerhaun, and she'd scouted for them personally across the Sovereign States. They wore a different uniform to the standard olive colours of this fortress, their attire this time pale-blue with thin scarves around their necks that hid the corded muscles underneath. They each wielded a halberd with a particularly sharp looking blade.

I hurried down the corridor to the place I most wanted to be when I wanted to escape humankind. It was only a few turns to Velos' stable, which fortunately hadn't been denied to me during my imprisonment at Fortress Gerhaun.

My dragon stood in the stone room in front of me – Velos, my oldest and still my best friend in this world. He lowered his blue scaled head to me, crooning. His warm breath brushing against my belly soothed me a little. I reached out, and I stroked him under the jaw. Behind his head, his bronze mechanical armour reflected some of the thin light, giving it a dull green colour.

"Pontopa," a voice came from beside me. Startled, I stood up, swivelled around into a blast of cologne, and raised my fists towards the smarmy looking face belonging to Faso – one of the last people I wanted to see here. "Whoa, easy tiger. It's not me you want to be fighting."

"I'm not sure about that," I said, and noticed a red unopened toolbox positioned next to Velos' helmet that lay on the floor. "What the dragonheats are you up to now, Faso?"

He shook his head and placed his hands out in front of him, backing up against the wall. The first time I'd caught him making modifications to Faso was when he'd installed the armour on Velos, without Velos' or my prior permission. The resulting black eye I'd given him was well deserved, in my opinion.

"I'm merely admiring my handiwork," Faso said. "It's been quite a while since this miraculous invention saved us from those automaton sharks."

I squinted my eyes and pinched my lips together. "Go on..."

"Well, I was just considering some modifications. I thought that—"

"Whatever it is, no," I said.

"You're not going to hear me out?"

"Oh, for wellies' sake. No, Faso. I've bigger fish to fry right now..."

"Please, just—"

"I said no! Whatever you're planning, Velos doesn't need any more modifications." I looked up at Velos, half wanting him to roast Faso on the spot. But despite all the unwarranted changes he'd made to Velos, my dragon seemed quite taken to the pompous inventor.

Then I remembered. Faso was Taka's blood father and, as unsympathetic as he was, he wouldn't be here considering a new project if he knew Bassalhan was about to send Taka into King Cini's former lair. "Faso, you probably should—"

"Not now, Pontopa," he said, as he turned up his nose. "I've bigger fish to fry..." He brushed past me and towards the doorway, where he stopped and then looked back at me. "I'll get Hastina's permission for this. Stern as she is, she seems to have a much more level head on her. Then I'll talk to the general himself as well. You won't stop me making the necessary changes to win the war this time."

I wasn't going to let him get away that easily. "Hastina is about to send Taka to Slaro."

Faso froze in his tracks as if he'd just heard a wolf. He turned around slowly. "Say that again..."

"I was just in a meeting with Hastina and Bassalhan. They're sending Taka over to Cini's former palace so that he can ascend to the throne as king. The boy's become a tool, Faso. A tool in their stupid plans..."

Faso raised his eyebrows, as if he didn't believe me. Hastina and Bassalhan weren't the only ones in the fortress who thought I was mad. "Why would they do that? They'll just end up getting captured. Isn't it obvious that the Masked Regent is one of Alsie Fioreletta's own?"

"I suspect so too. Oh, it's just so stupid, Faso. I can't believe they haven't told you this. I mean, you're Taka's father."

Faso's face went still, and he stepped up so close that I could smell the mint on his breath. He studied my eyes for a moment, not blinking once. Eventually, he took a deep breath and turned his head towards Velos.

"I can't believe this... Why would they do such a thing? Think, Faso..." He tapped his fingers to his forehead.

"It's unacceptable," I said through clenched teeth. "I only just heard myself."

Faso didn't seem to hear me, instead seeming lost in his train of thoughts. "I guess they didn't want me stopping them. But we can't let them do it. What can we do to keep Taka safe?"

"I don't know. There's nothing we can do."

Faso looked towards the helmet. "Are you going to go with them?"

"I still don't think they'll let me leave the palace."

"Unless..." Faso said. "Even my dragon armour doesn't have a chance in full-on combat against all the Greys we have available, if it comes to that. Besides, we don't want to destroy those that are protecting us from the dragonmen. But there are other ways."

I raised an eyebrow. "And what are they?"

"That's what you didn't give me a chance to explain. Have you ever heard of stealth technology?"

"I'm guessing it's something to do with staying unseen."

"Exactly," Faso said with a smirk. He walked back to the helmet and cradled it in his hands. It looked slightly different than when I'd last worn it. Before, there'd been nothing to see through except a screen that saw through Velos' eyes, but now, a glass full-face visor cover the front of the helmet. An arrangement of brass slats like those belonging to shutters formed another layer above the glass. The slats were open.

Faso opened his toolbox and produced from it a brass boxy contraption with a display screen at the front, behind which a red needle hovered above a grey semicircle with marks at the circumference of this designating some kind of measurement.

"What's that?" I asked. I ran my finger over the cool metalwork.

Faso flicked a switch at the bottom of the device, and it started beeping slowly. He pointed it at me, and the frequency of the beeps picked up a little. He turned it in the direction of the treasure room, and the beeps sped up even more.

"This, I called a Gordoni-counter. It allows me to detect levels of a special kind of radiation, because interestingly there's a lot here and we're being exposed to it every day."

"Radiation?"

"I've been doing a little research into the collective unconscious on my own. You know, it took me a long time to acknowledge it exists. But I've picked up certain rays in the vicinity. I mean, there are these rays around us all the time. But the Gordoni-counter picks up more when you dragonseers and the dragon queen speak to each other in the collective unconscious, or when you sing dragonsongs to talk to your dragons."

"So, you mean they're like ultraviolet or visible light?"

"They're similar, but not completely the same… And since I discovered them, I decided to call them Gordoni Rays. Quite fitting, don't you think?"

I snorted, then the cogs started to spin in my head. "Wait, so what you're saying is…" I put my hand to my chin. As soon as I realised what this was about, I made sure to mask any information Faso gave me from Hastina and Bassalhan. If there was a way of measuring the collective unconscious, I didn't want them to know about it – if they didn't know it already. "So, you're now telling me that the collective unconscious exists?"

"I'm saying I'm not going to discount its possibility anymore. But the thing is, I can keep the Gordoni Rays from leaving your head, as well as Velos', and stop you from being detected by other dragons or those who can detect their presence. I just need to make some modifications to Velos' helmet."

My blood suddenly started to boil, as I realised the implications of this. "That would block my connection to Velos. How could I possibly guide him then?"

Faso nodded. "It will, and he got disgruntled when I first tested a prototype on him. But then he seemed to get used to it. It seems that he quite enjoyed his moments of peace."

I glared at him. I wasn't sure I liked where this was going. "What are you saying?"

"I'm saying that once Hastina's dragons leave, you already know that many of the guards here are loyal to you and won't report you leaving. Bassalhan will usually know if Velos flies out of the fortress, but Bassalhan won't be able to detect if we block off the physical – or should I say electromagnetic – connection between the emitters, namely you and Velos, and the dragon queen. It also means that we'll be a lot harder to detect by Alsie's dragonmen."

I took a deep breath as my chest tightened. "You mean to say you've already installed this on Velos' helmet?"

Faso nodded and gave me a meek smile.

"Dragonheats, Faso, you've made another modification without my permission."

"But once again, it's for the greater good, don't you think? I don't know when you're going to see this, but I'm on your side, Pontopa."

I huffed. He never even thought to ask. Some things never changed.

"Let's see how this plays out over the next few hours," I said with a sigh. I really didn't have the energy to take a swing at him this time. Besides, doing so would only make things worse for me here.

Faso clenched his jaw. "Fine..." He bent down and started examining the helmet again. "But just in case, I'll make sure the modifications are working as planned."

"Just one more thing, Faso..."

"Go on..."

"What are the slats for?" I touched one of them on the underside, noticing that the surface was slightly smoother than above.

Faso batted my finger away. "You'll mark the screen with your fingerprints. Oh, never mind." He pointed to a small bulbous dial at the side of the helmet. "You see this knob? This allows you to open and close the screen. You'll need to do that to see through Velos' helmet as you did before."

I nodded. "I understand."

"Well I'm glad you're behind me on this one." He turned back to his work.

Velos had already fallen asleep underneath my arm, and I stroked his head a second time, then I decided it was better to leave him to his reverie. I had that meeting with Taka to attend to. Before I left, I looked once more at Faso, and I considered telling him about this meeting.

But I decided it better not to have Faso there. Besides, I hadn't seen Taka in ages, and I wanted to make sure I had some time with him without Faso bumbling into the conversation every minute. Surely, Bassalhan would tell Faso her plans soon and also give Faso some time to spend with Taka. Even if she didn't, we weren't going to let Taka be used as a pawn in this stupid game.

I'd promised Sukina, and so I'd find a way to keep Taka safe, even if I had to steal him away from Fortress Gerhaun. Really, I had no other choice.

THE CURRENT POLITICAL climate had forced Mamo and Papo to downsize their little tearoom business. Gone were the rich aromas of teas from far and wide places that seemed to soften the tongue, spiced with bergamot and different varieties of pepper and anise.

Instead, the room smelled of those stuffy tea bags containing crushed bitter leaves, the tea from which I used to drink during the secicao harvesting runs sometimes, when my stomach felt too rough for a cup of secicao.

The tearoom was almost empty, as was usual this time of the morning. Papo was the only customer, sitting at one of the round tables, made of the heavy teak wood imported from Cadigan by Candalmo Segora and carpentered by Papo's rough workman's hands. He sat propped up on a foldable chair with his legs crossed, cradling a copy of the Tow Observer in his hands. He must have read the magazine five times today already. It was as if he wanted to cling on to the news, when I knew he'd rather be out helping fight the wars.

But that was the thing. Right now, there were no wars to fight. Everything was happening under a veil. We knew the drag-onmen were becoming more prevalent in the Northern Continent, and that some of them had also crossed the Saye Ocean to the southeast, scorching the islands of the Saye Archipelago to a crisp, and putting the merchant traders who relied on those islands out of business.

With the supplies of a rich variety of teas wiped out from the Saye Archipelago, Candalmo instead sourced the tea for the tearoom, and various materials from the continent of Cadigan – the southern part of it, where secicao hadn't yet spread its roots deep beneath the soil.

Across the rest of the world, farmers were finding it increasingly harder to grow crops, livestock were getting skinnier, and the Tow Observer claimed it was only a matter of time until the world starved itself to death.

In Slaro, the capital of Tow, the secicao houses had completely closed down. Gerhaun Forsi's book 'Dragonseers and Ecology' had been reprinted in bookstores across the city as, since the disaster at Ginlast, the population had started to educate themselves on how dangerous secicao was. Still, they'd come to the realisation far too late.

It wasn't just the Masked Regent we had to worry about when sending Taka to Cini's Palace. The blight hadn't yet reached Tow, but it had quickly spread across the Sovereign States, and experts thought it would be a matter of months before it hit the capital.

Thus, the Tow Observer did nothing but make Papo increasingly anxious that our home village of the Five Hamlets, where he had built a life for himself, would soon be annihilated, and there was nothing anyone could do.

That didn't stop him reading it, though, over and over again.

Mamo stood behind the counter, cleaning the pots and pans with a worn metal scourer. She came over to join me when I sat down opposite Papo, who put down the magazine and looked up at me with an unconvincing smile.

"Have you had breakfast yet, darling?" Mamo asked, as she reached out to brush a strand of hair away from my face. "We wondered where you were this morning... Did you go to the canteen?"

"Not yet... I got busy with things."

Mamo shook her head. "Well, that won't do... What have I told you about eating at regular times, Pontopa?"

She stood up, walked back to the bar, and scooped up some dry bacon and stale bread onto a plate. She brought this back with a glass of water and placed both on the table, together with a knife and fork. "I know things are tough, but we've got to make do with what we've got here."

I stared down at it, and inhaled the smokiness, letting it cleanse my lungs. I cut off a small piece of bacon and chewed slowly. It was a little dry, so I washed it down with a swig of water, then I cut straight to the chase. "I guess neither of you have heard about Taka."

"Gracious, no, we've not heard anything from him for weeks." Mamo said. "I wish Hastina would let him visit here more. It's so cruel to cut off a boy from his connections like that." Mamo had been complaining about this all week.

Papo slowly shook his head as he glanced back at the magazine. "What are they up to now?" he asked, and he took a sip of his tea.

"They're sending him to Slaro. Hastina and Bassalhan want him to take the place of the lookalike on the throne."

"You've got to be kidding..." Mamo said, her eyes wide.

"Well, it makes a lot of sense when you think about it..." Papo said. "From a strategic perspective, I mean..."

Mamo glared back at him.

"But not Taka," Papo said. "No, that boy is far too young."

"Exactly," I said. "I understand extra troops in Slaro might be useful to help fight the spread of secicao. But whoever the Masked Regent is, she must be working for Alsie Fioreletta, and we're sending Taka right into the lion's den."

"So, what are you going to do about it?" Papo asked.

"I don't know. I wish I had a plan." I leaned in closer,

checked over my shoulder to see if any of Bassalhan's guards were close and watching. "Faso has something… He's worked out a way to follow them without them knowing we're there. A way to shield my connection to the collective unconscious."

"Trust that boy to think of a solution before the problem even arises," Papo said with a smirk. Often, I wondered if he was prouder of Faso than he was of me.

Meanwhile, Mamo was studying me with a frown on her face. "Don't you need the collective unconscious to steer Velos, dear? I mean, if you run into one of those dragonmen, I don't think Velos would fare well using his instincts alone."

"He's got the dragon armour," Papo pointed out. "Just turn the dial and he'll augment."

"But without Pontopa's connection to the collective unconscious, neither Velos nor Pontopa might see the threat coming."

"Which is exactly why I'm not sure it's the best idea," I said. "But then, what choice do we have?"

Papo closed his magazine and pushed it away. "Why don't I go to the palace with Taka and Hastina? You can talk to them and demand that I also stay there to oversee matters. That way, I can help steer Taka away from any danger."

"No, Papo," I said. "We're not sending you into the fray after your injury. Risking Taka is one thing, but risking you too…"

"That injury was years ago. Besides, this might be the best solution here. You need someone in there who can get Taka out at the first sign of any trouble. I can do that."

Mamo saw my frustration, and she reached out and squeezed my hand with a clammy grip. She turned to Papo. "Cipao, you know what they've been saying in the Tow Observer. The Masked Regent might be one of Alsie's own."

"Exactly," I said. "You'd be putting yourself at risk unnecessarily. I know you're bored, Papo. But I'm sorry, you're just not equipped to handle this."

"It's better than—"

Mamo again glared daggers at Papo. "Cipao, that's enough. This isn't the time for this."

"Fine," Papo said, and he turned his head towards the sounds of heavy footsteps coming from the entrance.

Two pale-blue suited guards with halberds entered the room. They took positions at each side of the doorway and stood there at attention, the sharp point of their halberds pointing directly up.

Hastina followed them in with Taka trailing slightly behind her. "What did I tell you about looking smart," she said to him. "Straighten up for wellies' sake."

He wore clothes, made of the same velvety material as when I'd first met him. They hung loosely off him as if his body had been made for them.

I took another bite of my bacon, washed it down with the water, then I stood to greet Taka.

IT WASN'T the fact I probably wouldn't see Taka again that hurt the most, as after all, I hadn't seen him for an awfully long time. Rather, it was the expression of contempt and mistrust on his face as I approached him. He looked at me as if I was some kind of monster.

He was wearing the kind of perfume that only royalty could afford, of crushed flowers that would be extinct by now if they weren't cultivated in the courtyards of royal palaces and in specially treated soil.

"Taka," I said, and I reached out to touch his arm, but he backed away. I tried to probe him in the collective unconscious, but he'd blocked me off from him.

Hastina turned to Taka. "Come on, Dragonseer Sako," she said. "At least say something to your aunt."

Dragonseer Sako... The name echoed around my head. Dragonseer Sako was still Sukina in my mind, and Taka was far too young to assume that title.

"She's not my auntie," Taka said. "She's... She's a dragonwoman. An agent of Finesia."

The words hit me like a sledgehammer to my heart. At the factory massacre, Taka had turned into a dragonman too. Really,

I should be no different from him. The wind from outside whistled through the corridors and the eggy smell of secicao replaced the aromas of tea. For a moment, I imagined I saw a tendril of that brown gas creeping around Taka's chest, but I only had to blink, and it was gone.

"Taka, what have they done to you?" I asked him.

Hastina gave me a scornful look. "Tell her, Taka. Remember what we talked about. You'll have to make tougher decisions in Slaro Palace."

Taka, who had started to slouch, straightened his posture. He looked at me. "Fortunately, my benefactor, Bassalhan Cagari, reached me when I had a supple mind. She and Dragonseer Wiggea have taught me how to keep Finesia out, and I managed to build a fortress to stop her coming in again. It's a shame, Dragonseer Wells, that you have also not learned to do the same."

Dragonheats, they had completely brainwashed him. I couldn't even imagine what lies they'd told him about me.

"Taka," I said. "I've been fighting her. I promise... Since what happened at Ginlast, I haven't let her take control."

Taka's eyebrows furrowed, and he turned his head up towards Hastina as if looking for approval. Her eyes were focused on Papo's copy of the Tow observer, and she didn't seem to notice the boy's hesitation.

Papo had the magazine angled in such a way as to show the picture of the Masked Regent and the lookalike boy standing side by side on the cover. The masked figure had a black gloved hand placed on the boy's sandy hair, and that was when I realised – Taka had been dressed and had his hair done in the exact same way as the boy on the cover, waves applied to the style to give it a look of fluidity. It wasn't just his perfume I could smell, but the thick hair gel required to accomplish such a feat.

"Dragonseer Wiggea, what shall I say next?" Taka asked, and Hastina turned slowly towards her.

"Remember our lessons on diplomacy, Dragonseer Sako.

What did you learn? You need to start speaking that way, if you are going to assume the new role."

Taka turned back to me. Gone was the coldness in his eyes. But his expression wasn't warm either. Rather, he looked at me in the same way nobles look at you when they want to convince you of their apparent kindness. You just had to serve royalty long enough to know that such looks were fake.

"Dragonseer Wells," he said, and I clenched my jaw to hear him address me in such a way for the second time. He sounded so unlike the little boy I had helped raise after Sukina's death. "I will be absent from Fortress Gerhaun due to a mission of great import. I will reclaim my position on the throne at King Cini's former palace. You may, no doubt, be grieved by this, because of our former relationship. Rest assured, this is the best place for you now, given the circumstances."

My head was spinning in confusion. My hands and feet tingled, and I could feel the blood pumping through the veins in my arms and legs. It just wasn't right. He shouldn't have his childhood confiscated from him so early.

"Is this really the world you want him to grow up in?" Finesia said in my mind. *"You know, my acolyte, that there are better ways."*

I grimaced and pushed Finesia away. I'd learned from experience that it was better not to answer her. Perhaps if I continued to do so, my subconscious could eventually pretend she wasn't there. Really, she seemed to find ways in at the most inconvenient moments.

"The boy has travelled too far away from us," Finesia continued. *"It is your duty to bring him back to us. That, my acolyte, is your next task..."* Her last words drifted out into stillness, and I managed to leash her at the back of my mind for now.

Yet, Taka must have noticed her disturbance, because his gaze penetrated even deeper as he studied me. It was as if he could see into my mind. "You must understand, Dragonseer Wells, that Bassalhan Cagari hasn't made this decision lightly. And though it will be your instinct to accompany me, it is much safer for everyone if you stay at Fortress Gerhaun."

Mamo shuffled over, and soon was standing next to me. "Taka, this is no way to treat your auntie," she said. "She's looked after you for many years. Treat her with a little compassion for dragonheats sake."

"Stay out of this, Versalina Wells," Hastina snapped. "You are a civilian here, and this is a military matter."

"As Pontopa's mother, I feel I do have the right to say at least something here. You can't raise him like this, Dragonseer Wiggea. Plus, this scheme to send him into the palace is stupidity."

"As I said, this is a military matter," Hastina said. "While you are taking asylum under a dragon queen's roof, I strongly advise you not to demean her authority."

"But Taka is only a child," Mamo said. "He's not old enough yet to deal with military matters. You know this isn't right..."

"Desperate times call for desperate measures," Hastina said, tilting her head upwards slightly.

This time, it was Mamo I could see fuming, and I reached out to touch her shoulder. "It's okay, Mamo... Leave it."

She sighed, and she looked as though she wanted to say something else. But Hastina butted in first. "I think we've done what we needed to today. Dragonseer Sako, is there anything else you want to say to Dragonseer Wells?"

Taka glanced towards the doorway. "I think that's enough," he said. "We should continue our preparations."

"Yes we shall," Hastina said. She gave me the once-over, then turned and walked towards the door.

Taka glanced once more at me, and I thought at that moment I saw a trace of compassion in his expression. But it quickly faded, and he turned and followed Hastina. The trail of rich perfume he left behind soon dissipated, to let back in the aromas of dry bacon and stuffy tea.

PART II

"There are two types of creatures. Those who embrace evolution's ultimate goal, and those who shy away from it. Only the first will ultimately survive."

— *ALSIE FIORELETTA*

THE WIND HAD PICKED up so much now that it howled, buffeting the tapestries on the corridor walls, and kicking up little eddies of grey dust from the floor. It was the kind of wind that would precede a thunderstorm. Or at least it might if we were anywhere else but the Southlands. It never rained here as secicao soaked up all the water vapour from the surroundings for its own nefarious deeds, making the air outside the fortress desert dry.

Fortunately, in addition to helping the fortress retain a natural level of humidity, the collective unconscious kept most of the secicao gas out of here despite the wind – if it didn't, we wouldn't be able to breathe here. Still, traces of it got carried in upon the gusts, creating an acrid, nausea-inducing stench. Though I'd never seen a visual indication of this before, like the tendril I'd seen before in my bedroom. If, that was, I'd actually seen it and it hadn't been a figment of my imagination.

Mamo was loitering nearby, studying me underneath a concerned frown. She stepped forwards and touched me gently on the arm. I let her embrace me in a warm hug, the scent of her lavender shampoo providing a little comfort. Yet my mouth tasted sour, my chest was tight, and I could feel my heartbeat in my chest.

"We'll work this out, dear," she said, stroking my hair. "There's a way out of this."

Papo's hand touched my shoulder. "I'll talk to Faso. I'll see what he can do."

I broke Mamo's hug, then I spun around, a little frustration starting to bubble in the pit of my stomach. Common sense, fortunately, prevailed. We simply didn't have a better option than Faso. He'd have the technology to help sneak me and Velos out, so I could do what I could to help, even if I was forced to do so undercover and from a distance.

Papo turned towards the doorway, but before he managed to take a step, Doctor Forsolano strolled through the door. The doctor was about five years older than Papo, and his thin face showed off his wrinkles. Despite this, he still had a look of vitality to him, as he applied all his good health advice to his own life. Looking over his horn-rimmed glasses, he scanned the room, first seeing Papo whom he nodded to, then he saw me.

"Pontopa," he said. "Gracious heavens, I thought I'd find you here. I've been looking for you all over the fortress."

The muscles in my face slackened. They said that bad news always came in threes, and I'd already received two pieces of it.

"What is it?" I asked. "Something to do with the tests?" Doctor Forsolano had sent me to take these tests after discovering some unexpected murmurs in my heart.

The doctor shook his head. "No, nothing like that. I came to let you know that we've managed to acquire more cyagora. A farm in southern Cadigan managed to store some seeds and they have now grown a whole field of it. I thought it might come in useful, but..."

"But?"

Doctor Forsolano looked around the room for a second time. His gaze fell on Mamo, whose eyes were red around the rims as if she'd been crying.

"Wellies, what's going on in here?" Doctor Forsolano asked.

I shook my head. "It's about Taka. I probably shouldn't go into. But Doctor, you said about the cyagora. I might need it."

After how that anti-depressant drug had made me feel before, I dreaded having to take it again. It numbed my connection to the collective unconscious and to Velos. Yet, it seemed I might have no other choice.

Doctor Forsolano nodded, took a small jar out of his pocket, containing around ten large pills, and handed it to me. I opened it and looked inside, the astringent smell of it reminding me of the vivid dreams I'd had when I had first come off these. I suspected that a dry spell following prolonged exposure to this drug might cause Finesia to come back even stronger. But I had shared this theory with no one.

Finesia meanwhile was churning out insults inside my mind. But I didn't let her words register. I wasn't going to use it yet, anyway. Somehow, I thought it better to put on Faso's helmet than to have to push all my emotions away.

"Pontopa," Doctor Forsolano said. "Did you let anyone in your room?"

I frowned, as I stuffed the jar of cyagora in my jerkin pocket. "No..."

"It's just I checked there for you first, and two guards were already inside there. They were Hastina's guards. You know, with the neck scarves..."

My heart skipped a beat. "What?" I asked. "What the dragonheats were they doing there?"

"I saw them at the wardrobe, searching through it."

My eyelids tightened. "Dragonheats! Did they get near the bed?"

"I don't know..."

I took a step towards the door, but Mamo grasped my arm stopping me. "Dear, Hastina told you to stay here. You know you shouldn't be aggravating her."

"This is too important, Mamo," I said, and I broke free from her grasp.

"Why? What have you done? What's in the bed?"

"It doesn't matter," I said, and I hurried out of the tearoom.

I recall little from my walk to the bedroom. I vaguely remember having the strange sensation of tendrils of secicao gas wrapping around me as I walked, forming a protective sheath around my muscles. But I was in such a fit of rage I didn't care.

The next thing I remember was reaching the bedroom, the door closed, and the two guards in pale-blue uniform standing outside, nothing different about them. I turned to the one I liked the least, the guard with rough stubble, buck teeth, and a cleft lip who always stank of the kind of cologne Papo might have worn thirty years ago.

"You searched my room," I said through my teeth.

The guard shook his head. "Not me. Besides, if I did it would be none of your business, *Dragonseer*." The honorific came out in an acerbic tone.

"Then, you," I said to the other guard, pointing at him. He was younger looking with a clean-shaven face and a feminine, almost button, nose. "Tell me what happened. Did you search it? I know someone was in here."

"You aren't at liberty to give us orders, ma'am," he said in a softer voice. "And you know I can't report any military matters to you. Sorry, that's just how it is."

The first guard gave the second a cold stare. The second guard shrugged, then offered me a meek smile.

I pushed past the first guard and opened the door. On the other side, the room looked completely undisturbed. The bedsheet was still at the foot of my bed, the blanket still strewn across the floor, and the air still had that thick mustiness to it, with that eggy secicao smell growing stronger as the wind raged.

I closed the door, and lowered myself against it, with my back blocking off any access. Dragonheats, if anyone tried to come in right now, I could swear I'd turn into a black dragon and eat them on the spot. I sank down to the floor, where I remained for a moment, breathing heavily.

My eyes focused on the mattress, on one of the brown sweat stains there, which I imagined for a moment looked like one of the shades from my dreams. I should have picked a better hiding place. Hiding it inside the mattress, perhaps. Or maybe I shouldn't even have been jotting down sketches in it at all.

I lifted myself up on heavy legs and tramped over to the mattress, dreading what I would soon discover. I lifted the mattress slightly and, the smell of fresh ink assaulted my nostrils.

Heart pounding, I raised the mattress onto its side. Written there, in thin red wiry writing were the words: "Next time, do not take me for a fool."

Dragonheats! I wanted to kill that woman. I stormed out the door, ready to hunt down Hastina and give her a piece of my mind. My former trusted dragonelite, Lieutenant Gereve Talato stood outside talking to the guards, and her presence stopped me dead in my tracks. I turned to her.

She gave me a kind look that told me I still had her allegiance if I needed it. I'd seen her around the fortress these last two years, but we hadn't had much chance to have a talk.

"What is it, Talato?" I asked. I didn't mean to be so abrupt, but she'd unfortunately caught me in a sour mood.

She lowered her head. "Our scouts spotted dragonmen approaching the fortress, hundreds of them. General Sako asked me to send for you at once, because he thinks we're going to need all the help we can get."

8

As Talato and I hurried towards the central courtyard, I tasted blood on my tongue through biting it so hard, and I wanted blood as well. I didn't know quite how I planned to get it yet. At that moment, I didn't care.

The wind was now roaring, as if the secicao was hurling tonnes of air across the Southlands. The tapestries whipped with such force that it seemed they might tear apart. It sounded like I was surrounded by beating drums. A heady scent of ozone had mixed with the secicao, the cocktail of the two becoming increasingly repulsive.

"*Is this your work?*" I asked Finesia in my mind. "*Are you causing the wind?*"

"*You know, in all this time you've had me in your head, this is the first time you've reached out to ask me something.*"

"*Just answer the question...*"

"*So much more of what you see in the world is of my work than you can imagine. Maybe the wind is mine, or maybe it's a natural phenomenon. How would you know the difference?*"

"*Because nature is good, and you are evil.*"

"*But that's exactly what I'm telling you. The line between nature and I isn't so well defined as you suppose. In time, I will*" *turn the planet into a much stronger version of itself. This is evolu-tion, my acolyte, where only the fittest survive."*

Really, I didn't know why I was entertaining her like this. I tried my hardest to push her away. If I let her into my mind every time I felt any strong emotions, then I had no chance of winning my battle against her.

I put my hand into my jerkin pocket and ran my fingers over the cool jar of cyagora, considering. But right now I needed my emotion, and I might also need my connection to the dragons as well.

The central courtyard was already set up for a briefing, in an arrangement I knew all too well. The screen at the front displayed an image of a dragonman standing on its two hind legs, a circle around its throat indicating the weak spot. Two burly pale-blue suited guards stood on either side of the screen, and they were straining to keep it in place.

Usually, General Sako would present these briefing, but this time it seemed like Hastina was running the show. With her spear clutched in her right hand, she bawled out orders in an incredibly loud voice, and no one in the audience dared inter-rupt her.

The troops had arranged rows of deck chairs across the courtyard, where they sat in ranks. Hastina's pale-blue uniformed guards sat at the front, with General Sako's lieu-tenants, including Lieutenant Talato and Lieutenant Candiorno behind them, and then the rest of the guards in olive-coloured uniform sat towards the back. Strong gusts of wind swept through the courtyard, coats flapped, and the troops leant forwards as if afraid they might get blown away.

Faso stood at the very back, next to his mousey-haired girl-friend Asinal Winda, near the projector. His oiled hair seemed unaffected by the wind, and Winda had hers tied up so that only the ponytail danced like a flickering flame.

I marched to the front where Hastina stood on one side of the projection screen. On the other side stood the ruddy-faced

General Sako, Sukina's father. He had his hands folded underneath his chest, and his grey handlebar moustache twitched with every step I took. The smell of stale secicao on his breath assaulted me as I moved forward.

I had my fists clenched so tightly by my sides I could swear my nails almost drew blood from my palms. Hastina stopped speaking as I approached and watched me with disdain. She raised her spear with both hands and crossed it across her chest. The wind tossed her fiery hair to the side, displaying a small ear with a large piercing at the lobe.

She glanced down at my fists, then studied my face with narrowed eyes. "I hope you've not come looking for a fight."

I opened my mouth to give her a piece of my mind, still so furious that I would have done anything. But General Sako got in there first.

"Blunders and dragonheats," he called out from beside her. "Dragonseer Wells, are you here to join us? I thought you told us before, Dragonseer Wiggea, that she wouldn't fly with us on any missions."

"That was before," she studied me with a frown, her jaw tight. "You are here to help, aren't you, Dragonseer Wells?"

I bit my tongue to stop myself making this situation worse. They needed me out there to help control the Greys in battle. Doing anything to convince them otherwise wouldn't do anyone any favours right now. "I won't let you down," I said.

General Sako looked at his pocket watch, then he took a draw of his pipe, and looked anxiously towards the ramparts. "Splendid, Dragonseer Wells," he said, and he propped his pipe in his breast pocket. "I thank you for your camaraderie. Lieutenant Talato, you will accompany your old commander on Velos. Candiorno, I want you with Mr Gordoni and Ms Winda on the dragon automaton."

The bugle call came, and with it a rush of wind. This carried with it a terrible ear-splitting roar of what must have been thousands of black dragons.

Static pulled at the hairs on my arm, and above us, lightning raged at the threshold between the collective unconscious and the brown, bilious secicao clouds. Another roar came from within the fortress, and I felt a sense of agony in the collective unconscious. Bassalhan, it seemed, was struggling to keep the secicao clouds out.

More murmurs came from the crowd, everyone probably wondering the same as I: 'how long could our protective barrier hold?'

Hastina was looking at me with narrowed eyes. "I'll be watching you, Dragonseer Wells," she said. "If you try anything you shouldn't, I warn you that your life will be forfeit on the field."

"I understand," I replied with a curtsy. "I will do Bassalhan proud."

I nodded, working to keep the rage tamped down within my chest. "I'll show you that I'm loyal to you today, Hastina, and that you have nothing to fear."

9

Lieutenant Talato and I emerged from the roaring corridors into Velos' stables. Velos saw us come in, and he lowered his head, letting out a plume of black smoke. He crooned as he pushed his warm head into my chest, then he turned to Talato and let her stroke him under his muzzle. Talato laughed vigorously, heaving her shoulders and tossing her short blonde bob around a little.

"I guess he's missed you," I said to her.

"I've missed him too, Ma'am," she said. "And it's good to be serving under you again."

"Does that make you a dragonelite now?"

"I don't care for titles anymore... I just want to help you out."

Above us, flashes of green lightning streaked through the clouds and again came that billowing roar of the black dragons somewhere beyond the thickening murk.

It suddenly dawned on me that I had forgotten to ask Hastina for my secicao flask back. One of the restrictions that Bassalhan had imposed on me was that I wasn't allowed access to secicao in any form. I glanced down at Talato's hip, where she had her own silver hip flask secured to her bandolier.

"Do you have secicao oil?" I asked.

"Yes, Ma'am. Since Ginlast, I've been using Dragonseer Sako's blend."

"May I?" I asked reaching out. She'd already removed the flask from her hip.

My hand was clammy as I took the flask in it, and saliva moistened my mouth. I hadn't realised how much I craved it until this moment.

I unscrewed the cap, and as I inhaled the sweet aroma of the oil, I took down a double swig. The smooth liquid rolled over my tongue, bitter at first, until that bitterness faded into a pleasant warmth at the back of my throat.

The world ghosted into speckled green, and I could see the outline of everything around me. I watched in slow motion as the wind blew a small stone off the wall. I caught this, then I tossed it over the wall.

"*Well done, my acolyte,*" Finesia said. "*You draw me closer to you when you behave in such a way.*"

"*I need secicao to battle Alsie Fioreletta and her minions,*" I said.

"*You need it because you crave it. But you know full well that with me you need crave secicao no more.*"

Talato regarded me. I couldn't see her face, only the heat signature it emitted, but I could imagine her expression, particularly her furrowed eyebrows. She took the flask from me and took a swig herself, then she took a deep breath and stretched her hands out wide.

"Lieutenant Talato."

"What is it, ma'am?"

I reached into my pocket and handed Talato the jar of cyagora. "You know what this is. Doctor Forsolano managed to secure some, and I have a feeling that I might need it. Do you remember what we talked about last time I put these drugs in your care? Do you remember what I might need you to do?"

Talato nodded and pocketed the cyagora. "I'll do my best

Ma'am… Oh, and another soldier gave me a spare rifle, I thought you might want it."

She took a Pattersoni rifle from her shoulder, leaving a second one on her other shoulder for her. I'd been focusing so much on getting out there again, I hadn't even noticed she'd been carrying two. I accepted it and slung it over my shoulder.

"I've been holding on to these for you too," she said, and she reached into the inside pocket of her jacket and produced a pouch, which she opened to reveal my two knives in their sheaths. Admittedly, I hadn't used them for a while.

"Thank you," I said, and I took the knives and stuffed them into my garters.

Velos lowered himself to the ground, so Talato could walk over and climb the ladder on his flank. He kept his head lowered, so I could vault onto it. I tightroped up the ridge of his nose, careful not to kick his eyes, then I crawled around his steering fin towards the front seat.

"Gas masks," I hollered back, once I was seated. But I didn't have to, because from behind came the sucking sound of Talato securing hers in place.

I stood up slightly so I could reach under my seat for my own bit and clip device. The 'bit' was a family nickname for the mouthpiece that divers used, and the clip on the nose was to stop me breathing the secicao gas.

Faso had installed an oxygen tank behind my seat, and I plugged the hose from this into the bit and turned the valve. I pegged the clip onto the secure part of my nose, and I placed the bit in my mouth.

"You don't need that anymore, you know," Finesia said in my mind. *"You can breathe the secicao."*

That may have been true, but I certainly didn't want to show this to the troops, or to Hastina, for that matter. I clamped down on the bit, and sucked in my first breath of oxygen, elated not just from the sudden rush to the head, but also to finally be flying again after so long. The oxygen combined with the aftertaste of the secicao sent a cool freshness through my mouth, as if I just eaten an entire packet of mints.

I pulled back on Velos' steering fin, and he roared, lowered himself to squat on his hind legs, and used them to launch into the air. He stretched his wings and lifted himself with steady, yet slow flaps.

I could feel the elation in him, not just in the way that he rumbled under my legs, but I could also sense his emotions in the collective unconscious. He tossed back his head and let out a second huge roar to express his joy in our reunion.

Admittedly, it was great to be flying again, but I know we also both feared we were heading towards our doom.

IT WAS cold amidst the secicao clouds, and their acidity scratched at my skin. Despite the clip on my nose, their sulphurous stench seemed to filter through everything.

I could just make out the outlines of the writhing secicao branches below, everything coloured in green due to the secicao oil I'd just taken. The fortress was now a distant blob on the horizon I'd left behind.

The cool wind beat against us, and Velos strained to keep a straight path through it. If it weren't for my harness, I probably would have also struggled to stay astride. The dragonmen had certainly picked a good time for an attack.

A flapping sound came from beside me, and Hastina levelled her dragon, Bellroot, next to Velos. Bellroot was citrine in colour, but he was green in my augmented vision. He wore no armour – I'm guessing Faso hadn't dared even trying to install it on him. Hastina pointed to where her eyes would be and then pointed to me as if to say she was watching me. Her metal leg dangled off the side of Bellroot, swaying in the wind.

I ignored her, and I sang a song to call up some grey dragons from the fortress. I felt the tug of another song – Hastina calling to another flock, and we were soon both surrounded by two flocks, which curled away from each other in flight.

Each of the Greys had a soldier on top of them, with their Pattersoni rifles drawn and ready to try and shoot dragonmen from the sky. Not all of them were with us. I reckoned only half of them had been sent from Fortress Gerhuan. What the dragon queen planned to do with the rest of them, I had no idea.

"Shall I augment Velos, Ma'am?" Talato called out.

Velos trilled at the idea.

"Do it," I called back. "Against these dragonmen we'll need all the help we can get."

Talato reached down and turned the dial at the back of Velos' flank. The armour under the seat felt suddenly warm. Its bronze exterior glowed faint green, as the fans in its side tanks pumped secicao through it.

Velos sped up a little, but I pushed down on the steering fin to remind him not to fly too far ahead – the Greys wouldn't be able to keep up. Now augmented, he flew much steadier against the wind.

Secicao also coursed through my veins, giving me an enhanced awareness of the surroundings. If I needed to, I could focus on details, slowing time in my head so that I could react faster.

The aftertaste of the oil still tingled at the edges of my tongue, and I craved more, though I knew I didn't need it. Around me, the other soldiers and their dragons battled the wind to stay aloft, and still the dragonmen were nowhere to be seen.

Faso's voice crackled from beneath me, startling me for a moment, before I remembered the speaker system that was installed on the armour.

"Dragon automaton coming through," he called out, sounding incredibly excited about it. "Inventor extraordinaire and his glamorous assistant can take the centre."

Then, another voice came out of the speaker – a feminine

one with a staccato bite to it. "Took your time setting things up, Gordoni," Hastina said. "But I'm glad to see we can all communicate. This way, Dragonseer Wells, I can keep you in check."

"You know," I said. "I've run plenty of operations like this before. You have no reason to micromanage me."

There came a huff from the other end, muted due to Hastina's mask. "I'm taking enough of a risk letting you control the dragons. Be warned, any sign of trouble, Bassalhan has ordered your dragons to turn on you."

I swallowed hard. "As I said, I won't let you down. Now where are Alsie's dragons? I would have thought we'd have seen them by now."

"The wind must have carried their voices further than they seemed," Hastina said.

"Yes, my sensors detect they're still a mile or so away," Faso said. "With the speed we're flying, we should reach them in a few minutes."

My teeth clenched down on the mouthpiece, and I could taste the rubber mingling with sweat. Some sweat rolled down my nose, and the clip started to slip. So, I adjusted it to keep it in place and stop the secicao gas seeping through my nostrils into my lungs.

The wind tugged on my hair, and I wished I had taken a moment to tie it down as Winda had. I leaned forwards in the seat, and I drew the Pattersoni rifle off my back and readied it.

10

"*I SEE both of you wenches are here,*" Alsie Fioreletta said in the collective unconscious, and we heard her long before we actually spotted her. "*Though I only need one of you today. Where is the boy?*"

"*Alsie Fioreletta,*" I said. "*I will kill you.*"

"*Dragonseer Wells, let me do the parlaying,*" Hastina said, then she addressed Alsie. "*We are not stupid enough to send Taka into battle. We heard about some of the trouble he was allowed to get in during Gerhaun Forsi's rule, but now under Bassalhan Cagari we are more careful.*"

"*So careful that you have sent half your entire fortress into a massacre,*" Alsie said. "*You must realise you cannot win this.*"

"*You are not invincible,*" Hastina replied. "*Given your vulnerabilities, you know well that our best bet is in numbers.*"

"*So, pray tell me, what happened to the other half of your forces?*" Alsie asked.

There was a pregnant pause, and I gathered the sense of something building in the distance. I didn't sense it physically, I sensed it in the collective unconscious. Green lightning flashed around us from the clouds, each spark sending shudders through Velos.

"We had a deal, Dragonseer Wiggea," Alsie said. *"And it looks like you haven't honoured it."*

That caused my breath to catch in my throat. *"What deal?"* I asked.

"She was meant to bring us Taka in exchange for our word not to destroy you," Alsie said.

"Hastina? What the dragonheats!"

"Shut up," Hastina said. *"When I want your opinion, I'll ask for it. Meanwhile, you were not meant to come so early, Alsie Fioreletta."*

"Why? Did you have something else planned?"

"The deal was for us to deliver Taka to you in one day's time."

"Well, it's a good thing that we arrived early, because it looks like you were planning to deceive us all along. What were you and Bassalhan up to, Dragonseer Wiggea?"

My heart skipped in my chest, just as another gust of wind came, stronger than the others, and which knocked Velos sideways for a moment. I had exactly the same question. What the dragonheats was going on here? In my augmented vision, I saw shapes through the clouds. It was the dragonmen, and there were so many of them that they seemed less of a flock and more of a swarm.

I sucked oxygen through my teeth, and blood rushed to my brain, helping me think a little more clearly. Another gust tried to knock Velos off course, so I tightened my grip on his steering fin to keep him steady.

The Greys under my command didn't manage to hold their position so well, and they were scattered by the wind. I sang out a dragonsong in my mind to bring them closer together.

It was then that I noticed that our conversation in the collective unconscious had gone awfully silent. Dragonheats, Hastina must have cut me out of the channel. I opened up a new one directly to her so I could confront her head on.

I didn't care about her negotiations. Right now, it should have been *me* shooting *her* out of the sky.

"*Dragonseer Wiggea,*" I said in the collective unconscious, "*you better tell me what the wellies is going on, and you better start explaining fast before I start taking matters in my own hands.*"

"*Not now! I'm trying to address a delicate situation.*"

At that moment, I didn't care. "*You and Bassalhan have been bargaining Taka away behind my back. Do you know how valuable the boy is to us? And even if he wasn't, he's a child, not a game piece to be played with on a board.*"

"*You have no idea what you're talking about...*"

"*Yeah? Try me.*"

Another channel opened up. "*You should really not cut your dragonseer comrade out of important conversations like that,*" Alsie Fioreletta said. "*And you forget that I have the power to bypass these channels. So, let's all be civil and talk like adults should.*"

"*Then maybe you can tell me what's going on here,*" I said back to her.

"*Gladly,*" Alsie Fioreletta said. "*Finesia's dragonmen and dragonwomen aren't here to destroy. The destruction of the dragons on this continent will happen naturally soon enough without us having to interfere. This is a migration, and we are here to take Taka to our new home. I believe that Finesia hoped that you would join us too. Or didn't she extend an invitation?*"

"*Migration? Hastina, what have you agreed to?*"

"*This is none of your business, Dragonseer Wells,*" Hastina said. "*Given what you are, you have no right to interfere in these negotiations.*"

"*I wholeheartedly disagree,*" Alsie said. "*The young dragonseer plays a huge part in Finesia's plans. Now, Dragonseer Wells, given your dragon queen has clearly been hiding things from you and you've failed to listen to our honoured Empress, I'm forced to explain myself. We're migrating to the Saye Archipelago. The reason for this, you will discover soon enough. Now, as to the boy, Dragonseer Wiggea. Where is he?*"

"Well, as you can see, Taka is not here," Hastina said. *"Even if you manage to destroy us today, you will not reach him."*

"Destroy us..." I said. *"You mean to say that you expected this, Hastina? You meant to sacrifice us all?"*

"You don't understand. The boy must survive. And who's to say that I'm sacrificing you? Alsie Fioreletta does not know the cards I have to play." She sounded confident about it, and I wondered if she was bluffing or if somehow she'd called for help.

"And what about the troops – the Greys, Talato, Faso, Winda, Doctor Forsolano, my parents... Are you telling me that after all this time, after how valuable they've proven, that they're expendable?"

"This is for the greater good," Hastina said. *"Now, speak no more, and that is an order. As for you, Alsie Fioreletta, you must turn back if you want to see the light of tomorrow. I will not hand you the boy, and I will not let you through to Fortress Gerhaun."*

"You can't win," Alsie said, sounding slightly entertained. *"Don't you understand? If you fight us, you die. Bring us the boy and you survive."*

I was only half listening. At the same time, I was trying to work out what they might have done with Taka. I didn't think I would get the answer out of Hastina, no matter how hard I tried.

My mouth was dry, and I longed for the taste of secicao on my tongue. The green glow in my vision was also starting to fade a little, and so I turned around and reached out towards Talato whose eyes regarded me through the glass of the mask.

"Could I take another swig?" I asked.

"Sure, Ma'am," she shouted back, her voice coming out muffled. She handed me the flask.

As I unscrewed the cap, again the sweet aroma wafted out, which I could smell, despite the clip on my nose. Somehow, I craved it even more.

I lifted my mouthpiece, so I could pour the smooth liquid down my throat. As I did, my muscles loosened. The slight sense of heaviness lifted from my eyes, and my vision strengthened. A sense of clarity washed over me.

My mind went blank, and my breath got caught in my throat. *"You want to know what's going on..."* Finesia said. *"I can show you the truth... I have that power..."*

Suddenly, a torrent of images cascaded through my mind...

Taka gazing out from the ramparts of Fortress Gerhaun towards the battle... Behind him, in the courtyard, Bassalhan lying with a massive saddle over her back... Clouds swirling around the dragon queen... Next to Bassalhan, the egg strapped up in a thick harness as if ready for travelling... Sparks of lightning plucking at the distant clouds.

This vision wasn't a figment of my imagination. It felt like one of those dreams I'd had, as if I belonged there with them and not here on what Hastina seemed to want to turn into a field of our own blood.

"They think they can hide this from me, but I have my own spies in the fortress. Which is why I sent Alsie here today."

"No... This is just an illusion."

"Oh, I don't think so. Search the clues. You know really what is happening here. They wanted to draw you out here."

"I don't believe you," I said, clenching my jaw. Tears started to well in my eyes. But it couldn't be true. It had to be a trick.

"Oh yes you do," Finesia said. *"Without you, they could steal the boy away. The perfect plan, an escape to Slaro. Bassalhan, the fool, she thinks she can inhabit King Cini's former palace, and push the secicao away from there. She thinks that she can use his old forces to defeat me. Build an army, stop the revolution. What she doesn't realise is that, as the only deity who hasn't abandoned this world, I'm always one step ahead."*

My breaths were heavy, and my heart was beating fast. I clenched my hands around Velos' steering fin so tightly that I caused him to buck. *"An evacuation,"* I said. *"Bassalhan would desert us... General Sako... Doctor Forsolano... My parents..."*

"What did I tell you, my acolyte? There is no good or evil in

this world. There is only the fight for survival. In the end only the strongest survive."

Her words coursed right through me, as strong as the secicao that was building in power in my veins. Hastina now was slightly in front of me, and it would be a trifle to turn my rifle and shoot her out of the sky.

"Not yet, my acolyte," Finesia said. *"You have more important tasks to complete... Now, go after the dragon queen and give her what she deserves for how she's treated you."*

My blood was pumping so fast now that I could feel its pulse in every inch of my body. I lowered my rifle.

"Bassalhan," I said, and with the rage, fear also emerged in another part of me. Because I knew that I'd crossed the threshold. I'd let the rage and the secicao grow so strong, and now there was no going back.

I took the clip off my nose to take a breath of the heady air, as if I was inhaling the aroma of a good wine. My skin itched, and then I felt it tear as thousands of dragon scales pushed through from underneath the skin on my forearms and calves. My scream of pain transformed into a roar of ecstasy as more scales pushed out of the thinner skin on my face.

I hadn't transformed like this for so long now, and I'd missed it so much.

"That's it, my acolyte," Finesia said.

At the same time, Hastina's voice came over the speaker system. "Dragonseer Wells, what are you doing?"

But I wasn't listening. Black smoke swirled around me slightly, before it got carried away by the wind. The harness that had me pinned to the seat of the dragon armour tore out of its sockets.

"Dragonseer Wells," Talato shouted. "I'm here... Hold on to yourself..."

I turned to see her clambering over Velos' armour towards me. She had the jar of cyagora clutched in one hand and I felt her strong grip clutch my forearm. A gust of wind rocked Velos and pushed her back from me. Velos roared to the sky as if in pain, and I joined him with a second roar of delight.

A crack of rifle fire sounded from beside me and my augmented senses noticed a bullet whizzing passed me in slow motion, barely missing my throat. I snapped my head to the right to see Hastina with her rifle aimed right towards me.

She had taken a shot, and she'd been ready to kill.

Alsie's black dragons took that opportunity to close in. In the haze of my pre-transformation, I didn't see ugly creatures anymore, but remarkable works of nature. Indeed, they were the perfectly evolved beasts of evolution, and secicao was the perfectly evolved plant. Together we would rule the planet.

But for now, Alsie and her minions would deal with Hastina and her dragons.

Fully transformed, I launched into the sky, leaving Velos behind. Everything else seemed to happen in slow motion.

Hastina cycling her rifle ready for another shot, the spent brass falling to the ground. Velos tossing around in the air, and Talato struggling to get to the front seat of his armour to keep control of him in the wind. Faso somewhere in the distance screaming out something. A thousand voices hitting me at once, melding into a cocktail of confusion, but this quickly fades.

Only Finesia's smooth voice remains, as she sings praises and adulations inside my head.

Part of me wants to feel guilty, because I'd promised Gerhaun before she died I'd never transform again. That part of me soon sinks deep into the crevices of my mind, and in its place rises the monster I fear the most.

11

BRANCHES OF SECICAO writhe on the ground below, reaching up as if they want to draw me into their embrace. The secicao clouds roil around me, and everywhere I look, green sparks of lightning flare.

My former brethren – the Greys – roar out in protest at my sudden departure. I have betrayed them, and they now have no choice but to take me down.

But I am too fast for them, and I have a power that they've never seen in me before. The scream I cry out isn't vocal, but it pulses through the collective unconscious, deafening all in the vicinity who can hear it, namely the Greys and Hastina.

One by one, souls drop out of the collective unconscious, the racket there reducing with each fall, like strings snapping in a string ensemble. In another form, to lose the connection to the dragons would have jarred my spirit.

But now, I am not human. I am much better than any human. A marvel for this world to behold. The pinnacle of evolution, created by Finesia's hand.

It is time for me to progress towards the destiny humankind was meant to claim. King Cini II could never understand this when he started the dragonheats. Dragons in Finesia's chosen form are what we as a species are destined to become.

Secicao is the perfect form of plant life, and there is no need for any other flora to live upon this world. And I, like all the dragonmen and dragonwomen my blood has spawned, am a wonder of evolution. Finesia knows this, and once we rule the world, we will no longer need our human forms and shall shed them forever.

"I am proud of you, my acolyte," Finesia says. *"You may fight me often, but whenever you truly need to call on me, I am there. Together we shall rule the world unencumbered. You need nothing else in your life but my protection."*

"And Alsie?" I ask her back, drawing off one of the few cogent threads of thought that I have left.

"Alsie is nothing to me," Finesia says. *"She wants to be grand. She wants to become as powerful as a god. But I only need to use her for a specific purpose, and then I shall discard her, husk and all."*

I squeal in delight to know that I am Finesia's favourite. I have no reason not to believe her. After all, she has never lied to me before.

I suck in a great breath of secicao clouds through my massive nostrils. I let this build inside me, until I can taste the sulphur at the back of my throat. Then, I let out a searing jet of green flame. The air warms around me, and I feel satisfied that I'm working the way I should.

I lost the green temperature-sensitive vision during the transformation, and instead I see the world in much richer colours than a human can. Straight ahead, I can see the first traces of Fortress Gerhaun.

At first, it is only a blurry blob in the clouds. Soon this grows into a great towering structure, and then I am over the courtyard. Bassalhan has left, and all that remains in the open space is a single figure sitting down on the chair, placed on the multi-jewelled eye of the golden dragon mosaic.

I get a little closer to see General Sako has been trussed there, his mouth gagged. But my duty isn't to rescue him.

I turn my head and see Mamo and Papo standing by the doorway to the courtyard. They are arguing with some guard there, and by the animation in their gestures I can see that they are angry.

Something, deep at the back of my mind tells me I should feel something about this. Now Bassalhan has left, it won't be long before the secicao clouds engulf the fortress.

Then, there will be no breathable air. Those few remaining here will surely die. My parents... General Sako... they should mean something, shouldn't they?

But they do not matter anymore. My foolish ideas of love for them cannot get in my way. Their shapes coalesce in my own vision, and General Sako, my mother, and father, and even the guards become dark forms – shades from a once important past. They are nothing but remnants of a dying species. I need to leave them behind. It's my only way to survive in the new world.

All that matters now is Taka and his retrieval, and Bassalhan has already stolen him away. I don't care why he is so important to Finesia, only that she needs him at the Saye Archipelago, and that he plays a part in the Tree Immortal's rebirth.

The rest, I shall discover when Finesia chooses to reveal it to me.

THE JOURNEY CARRIES ME WESTWARDS, and for a while I know nothing of my mind. I only see dreams of shades looking up at me from the ground, visions of the future in the sky, the secicao worshipping me from below. Behind me, I wonder about the bloodshed. Will Alsie Fioreletta kill Hastina, or will she let her live?

Whatever she decides, Alsie will die at my hand soon. This is the destiny Finesia has promised me – that it is I who shall take her place.

The secicao clouds can tell me all. Wherever Bassalhan, goes she pushes the secicao away, leaving currents in her wake that are easy to trace for those evolved enough to sense them.

The path she had cut through is wide. Soon the clouds will close around it, leaving no trace. But for now, I can follow her. She hasn't gone far.

The wind howls around me, and the lightning from the clouds strikes me occasionally, filling me with power stronger than what I might receive through a hip flask of secicao oil. It sends a warm sensation through my body, and I trill in delight as the muscles tighten in my wings.

I AM FASTER THAN BASSALHAN, and I am faster than the Greys who accompany her. So, it isn't long until I reach them with dragonfire burning in my stomach and the craving for blood on my tongue.

A covey of them is arranged in a close-knit formation. Bassalhan is at their centre, with Taka on a saddle on her back. Bassalhan has the harness with the dragon queen egg in it clutched tightly in her fore claws. The Greys flutter around her, each with a pale-suited soldier on its back.

They have their rifles ready, as they scan the sky ahead. But none of them are watching their rear, so they do not know I'm here. I've kept my mind silent, my thoughts masked, and so Bassalhan has no way of detecting me in the collective unconscious either.

I don't believe in sneak attacks, nor does Finesia. So, I roar out to let the dragons know of my coming. I bring up a dense ball of green fire from the base of my stomach, letting it warm my windpipe. It brushes over my coarse tongue and then shoots out of my mouth. It whirls through the secicao clouds, gaining power from the static around it. Then, it hits one of the Grey dragons on the flank, sending it spiralling to the ground.

"That's it, my darling acolyte... Now you can release the power I've been harbouring within you all these years. Show our enemies what you're made of..."

The Greys are slow to react, and don't shift until the felled dragon hits the ground. They scream out in chorus, and Bassalhan ducks down as the dragons wheel towards me. They lash out like bats attacking a target.

But I only need to wrap my wings around me, narrowing my form, allowing me to shoot through their formation like a bullet. Their claws glance off my skin, which they cannot penetrate. My only weakness is at my throat, and that I won't let them anywhere near.

Rifle shots follow from behind me. Some graze my wings, and then more lightning streaks out from the sky – another of Finesia's gifts to help me claim my destiny. I let it wash over me, before I enter the bubble of the collective unconscious that Bassalhan is using to push away the secicao clouds.

"You are beautiful, my acolyte," Finesia tells me. *"A truly wondrous work of creation, and now you shall display your greatest performance yet."*

Taka is standing on Bassalhan's back, the dragon queen hunkering ever closer to the ground. If she gets down too low, secicao will take her in its embrace. Taka has nowhere to go, and so he curls into a ball on Bassalhan's back. I swoop down and I pick him up in my talons. But I don't steal him away, as my work here isn't yet complete.

Instead, I deposit him down in the secicao, allowing the branches to wrap around him.

He is at no risk since he's already a dragonman, and he can breathe the secicao. He belongs to Finesia now. I watch him writhe within the secicao's grasp for a moment. His struggles will just cause it to tighten its hold on him. No doubt Finesia is in his head, telling him the exact same thing.

"Dragonseer Wells," he calls out in the collective unconscious. Then, realising that won't work, he calls, *"Auntie Pontopa."*

I push him back to the place in my mind that I've been keeping Finesia up until now. He is nothing but an errant child, and he soon will learn to respect Empress Finesia as he should.

A thunderous roar comes from Bassalhan's throat, who has now turned around to face me. She is hovering there, the greys lumbering around her, waiting. I level myself out to meet her penetrating gaze.

"Identify yourself, filthy servant of Finesia," the dragon queen says. *"And I may honour your former name, before you die."*

"You know who I am. For you left me no choice but to accept Finesia's gifts."

"Pontopa Wells... You're a disgrace, and a weakling, and you no longer deserve the name Dragonseer."

"In the new world, I shall call myself what I like. I have no need to bow to dragon queens anymore."

She doesn't reply with words, but with a searing jet of blue flame that comes straight out of her mouth. It's hot enough to melt the heaviest of metal, and it's directed right at my throat, narrow and fast.

I dodge to the side slightly and block the missile with my wing. Then, I'm flapping hard, pushing myself upwards with broad, strong sweeps. I wait until I'm high enough – and I get to an altitude where the secicao clouds touch Bassalhan's protective barrier.

Another lightning streak grazes my head and fills me with new energy. Blood swells to my chest, my wings, and my limbs. My muscles expand, then pop, increasing my bulk even more.

Secicao fire raging through me, the hot tang of blood on my tongue, I enter a dive. I hit Bassalhan on her back with such force that I push her towards the ground.

She lands on her side, angling herself to protect Gerhuan's

and Velos' egg, which tumbles away from her. I wrench my claws into her bony ribs, and she roars out with such force that her body trembles underneath me.

She crashes against the secicao, flattening a broad swathe of foliage. For a moment, the surrounding secicao branches twist away from her, deterred by the source of the collective unconscious that she emits.

I can feel her rage in the collective unconscious, I can hear her maledictions of me as a traitor, and I can understand her fear of death, but I don't share this fear.

Soon, the secicao realises its purpose, and the branches sweep back towards Bassalhan. They wrap first around the great golden dragon's massive thighs, then grow upwards and entangle her neck. As they continue to creep around her, they extend their thorns, piercing Bassalhan's thick hide between the scales. Though the old form of dragons feed on secicao roasted by their own breath, they can only take a certain amount of raw sap in their blood before it poisons them.

Taka's voice is also there, and it momentarily draws Dragonseer Wells back to consciousness. *"Auntie Pontopa... If you won't stop for me, stop for my mother. Remember what you always told me Sukina said. Remember what you were fighting for."*

But he's incredibly naive to think this will work. *"I'll deal with you later, Taka,"* I say. *"Your rightful place is by Finesia's side."*

Bassalhan's Greys have turned around and are hurtling towards me to protect their queen. If I don't deal with them, one of them may pierce my weak spot with their claws or teeth. If I don't deal with them, I might never live to be there by Finesia's side as she stamps down her new order.

That won't do at all.

I leave Bassalhan struggling in the branches, as I tear through the sky towards one dragon. Its rider fires a rifle shot at me, and it glances off my shoulder. The sharp bite there stings for a moment, and I clench my maw as I ready myself for the kill.

As I speed closer, for a moment I recognise the face behind the glass of his mask, but I only need to blink, and that face becomes complete blackness. He is just a shade like all others who once served me – lost to a distant past.

I hit the Grey head on, and I wrap my thighs around its body, then I clamp down on its long neck, breaking the bones there and sending dragon and rider plummeting to the ground.

More dragons follow as I lead them upwards, then I turn suddenly at my peak, again surrounded by secicao clouds. My dive comes from even higher than before. The clouds are getting thicker and even more lightning is raging around me.

Again, I tighten up my body, and I twirl as I dive, gaining speed. Some dragons try to push me off course, but I have so much strength and momentum now that doing so is like trying to redirect an avalanche with a twig.

As I accelerate towards the ground, my target becomes clear. The dragons are now plucking at the ever-tightening secicao, trying to pull it off Bassalhan, but their efforts are futile. The secicao has now found its way around the dragon queen's neck and has fastened itself around her maw, stopping her from calling out or breathing fire, and revealing an open throat.

Her last words are laced with abject terror. *"Dragonseer Wells, stop this... There must be some some way back to yourself. There's always a way to redeem yourself."*

But there is no redemption. Not anymore...

I fasten my thick leathery lips around Bassalhan's throat, and I bite down with a crunch. My teeth slice through scales and flesh alike, as I tear into her thick hide with my teeth. Some of her silver blood courses down her neck, and more of it fills my mouth, and then trickles down the back of my throat. Mixed in with the secicao sap injected into her bloodstream, I am now drinking *Exalmpora* – the drug that first connected me to Finesia and that I've craved for so long. Strength surges to my thighs, and I use them to snap the bones in the dragon queen's neck.

Bassalhan's life passes from her, and a rift surges out through the collective unconscious. Somewhere nearby, Taka screams, and the surrounding dragons chirp in confusion. Bassalhan's protective bubble is still there, but it won't be long until the secicao digests the dead queen's body, her royal blood fortifying Finesia's power.

More rifles crack from around me. The riders have lost control of their mounts now, and no one has a chance of hitting their target. Just to be sure, I scream out once again in the collective unconscious to disorient the Greys.

I'm not sure if the boy's sobs are intended for Bassalhan, for Hastina, or for Sukina. But they allow me to locate him quickly. As I lower myself towards him, the secicao releases its grasp, allowing me to sweep him up in my claws.

The dragon egg remains behind me, still secured in its harness. It lets out a protective bubble of its own, that pushes the secicao clouds away slightly. The secicao will eventually break through the shell of that egg, and once it does the embryo inside will feed Finesia's plans.

As Taka writhes within my grasp, I continue northwards, and then I get ready to head east. *"Now join your brothers and sisters,"* Finesia says. *"You have served me well, my acolyte, and it is time to start your new life."*

Meanwhile, Taka is also saying something in my mind. *"Where are you taking me... Answer me! What are you planning?"*

"Just ask Finesia," I reply. *"She can tell you all."*

"No! I told you once. I'm not letting Finesia into my mind."

"Taka, do as I say. Once again, you are now my ward."

"But this isn't you, Auntie Pontopa... Remember my mother... Sukina wouldn't want this."

"Shut up!" I tighten my grip on his body.

Taka's muscles go limp, and it feels that if I drop him then he would fall apart in the sky before he even hits the ground. But it's his sobs that bring me back to reality. That, and the name, *Sukina*, spinning around my head.

I've failed her. She entrusted me with Taka, and instead here I am under Finesia's control, carrying him towards whatever fate lies in wait for him.

Finesia's voice starts to fade. Instead, the voice of Dragonseer Wells is back, and with it the dangerous question in my mind... *What have I done?*

The question weakens my resolve. The muscles in my body are becoming numb, and the power Finesia has gifted me with is slipping away.

"*Acolyte, you are not listening to me,*" Finesia says. "*You must go east now. That is where you destiny awaits.*"

"*You made me do this,*" Dragonseer Wells says, and for a moment I can't even hear my own thoughts.

"*You are not a dragonseer. You are my acolyte, and you have much to do. Take back control, my acolyte. You must not let the dragonseer back in.*"

Finesia's attempts are futile. I now have relinquished control of my mind, and Finesia's influence it on it is fading fast. My wings beat once more as my body turns to the west, and I send commands to them to do something else, but it's no good now.

The final words I hear, are Finesia's. "*Once again, you fail me,*" she says, just as we break through the secicao clouds into a clear blue sky, and for a while my mind goes blank.

PART III

"Once one discovers their calling, they must make a choice. Either they stick to it with an unbreakable sense of duty. Or, from the inside out, they choose to die."

— *HASTINA WIGGEA*

12

I woke up, human again, with the taste of bile, blood, and regret on my tongue, my eyes raw from the tears of horrifying dreams, my scalp itchy and my hair sticky with cold sweat.

A searing pain cut through my upper arms and chest. My muscles weren't just tingling but bound by some heavy material. I tried to lift my hands, but they were also bound to my knees, and a hard and rough surface pressed against my back, rubbing my back raw through my shirt.

Blurs coalesced in my vision, as I opened my eyes to assess my surroundings. I squinted against the light coming from the bright blue sky. The sun shone down from above, baking the scratches on my forehead. I called out something, but my voice came out hoarse and faint.

There was a blurry form on the ground in the distance – a person, a head shorter than I. It moved rapidly toward me, and it extended something towards my throat, nicking the skin there and creating a sharp stab of pain. My ears were pounding, and my voice came out muffled at first.

"Taka, is that you?" I don't know if I was comprehensible. My voice sounded slurred to me. My head felt hot with blood pounding through it, and I could still hear the rhythm of my heart, loud in my ears.

"What did you do?" Taka asked.

I grimaced. "I did it, didn't I? I killed Bassalhan... Taka, I'm a monster... I deserve to die."

The shapes in my vision had started to take definition. I saw Taka's scowl first, his eyes focused on whatever he pointed at my neck. It looked to be some kind of straightened branch from a tree. I felt something wet there, as if he had pricked out a few drops of blood.

"Dragonseer Wells," he said. "No, not even Dragonseer. I don't think you deserve to be called that. Is there any semblance of Dragonseer Wells left in there? Or are you completely lost to the darkness?"

"Taka, I didn't want to..." My voice trailed off as I realised I had no excuses. I was meant to be the one in control. When I had told Sukina on her deathbed at Doctor Forsolano's hut that I'd look after Taka, with that had come the implied promise that I'd become a role model to him. But I couldn't even look after myself.

I peered down without bending my head to see that, beneath Taka's makeshift spear, the boy had trussed me in the branches of a tangly shrub, with its short thorns pricking at my skin.

I knew this plant. *Calianai*, a hybrid of secicao and dandelion that could only be found in the Southern Approach. It had only just started growing here in the last year, and I often wondered if this was secicao's way of preparing the soil to spread into this archipelago. I could no longer smell the secicao from the Southlands, but instead the calianai's bitter pollen.

"We escaped the Southlands, Taka," I said. "Finesia wanted me to go east and follow Alsie's migration to the Saye Archipelago. But I didn't. I managed to recover myself from Finesia at the last minute, and I brought you here."

Taka's eyes narrowed. "You failed me. Don't try to justify your crimes, because right now, you aren't redeemable."

"So, kill me… I deserve it. End my life and put all this misery to rest."

Taka tightened his grip on his spear, and he lowered his head for a moment, as if considering. "If you turn back into a dragonwoman again, I will. And don't think I won't be fast enough… You know, I remember the old Auntie Pontopa, before you did what you did at Ginlast. But now, Hastina and Bassalhan have helped me realise what you've become."

"Taka, you turned at Ginlast too. You massacred Cini's airship, remember. Just, teach me what they taught you. Teach me how to keep Finesia out of my head to stop this happening again. Because it seems like you're a lot better at it than I am."

Taka kept his eyes focused on mine, but at the same time his bottom lip trembled, and his face was blanched of colour.

"That's the thing," he said. "Bassalhan and Hastina told me you were too far gone to save you from Finesia. Just like Charth was…. The more I observed your behaviour in Fortress Gerhaun, the more I believed it. Sometimes, at night, I would hear you wandering the corridors talking to yourself. Just as Bassalhan said, I'm really not sure you can be saved."

More tears welled at the corners of my eyes, and I tried to fight them back, but I couldn't. I let out a few sobs, and then a cough surfaced from the back of my throat. The cough caused the spear to scratch my neck. I yelped out, but Taka didn't move a millimetre.

I was just about ready to give up. If I ended this now, I wouldn't have to deal with the guilt of it anymore.

I opened my lips to tell Taka that he was right and that he should end my life, but then I felt something familiar in the collective unconscious. It was a weak thread, but Velos was out there somewhere, and my connection to him strengthened my resolve slightly. The connection didn't quite feel as it used to, as if Velos was resisting it. Still, it provided solace to know it was there.

"Taka, please. At least get me water. What I did was awful,

and I'll never forgive myself for it. But if you decide to end this now, let me die with a moistened throat."

Taka looked over his shoulder. The spear didn't move.

My heart was pounding in my chest. I half expected Finesia to intervene. For her to enter my mind and tell me exactly what to say to stop Taka. But she didn't.

"So, are you going to end this now?" I asked.

"I don't know..."

"What would Hastina do in this situation?"

"She'd kill you without a question."

"And what would Finesia do..."

"She'd spare your life. She'd want her servant to live."

"Would she? Even if killing me might bring you closer to her? Is it you she wants, or me? Because Alsie Fioreletta had brought her forces to Fortress Gerhaun for that reason. They wanted to take you away to the Saye Archipelago as part of Finesia's plans."

Taka's gaze rolled slowly back to me. "You're lying... They have no reason to need me there. I'm nothing to Finesia..."

"Taka, I'm merely telling you what Alsie Fioreletta and Hastina told me. Alsie demanded that Bassalhan handed you over in exchange for not destroying Fortress Gerhaun. But Bassalhan, it seemed, wanted to get you away before Alsie stole you away to the Saye Archipelago. They wanted to protect you, Taka... They probably realised they would have no chance of defending the fortress against Alsie. The rest, you probably know."

Taka studied me, his chest rising and falling slowly. The bottom of his eyes glistened with nascent tears. "You killed Bassalhan... That cannot be changed."

"Not me," I said. "There's another person inside me. Taka, I'm so sorry. Despite how Bassalhan treated me, the real me would never do such a thing. You have to believe me."

"So, you now want to live? You've decided you might still

have a chance of walking in the light?" He tightened his lips. "I'm not sure that's possible…"

I nodded as far as I could without pushing my windpipe too close against that spear tip. "A sip of water, Taka, and we can at least discuss it. I'm sorry, I know I need help. I just don't know where to find it."

A deep sigh came out of Taka. He lowered the spear. "Water, I can do. But I've still not decided what to do with you."

He turned around, but after a few steps he paused and raised his hand to peer up at a point just above the horizon. The sunlight glinted off something in the distance, then I saw two V-shaped winged forms flying straight towards us.

Velos, he was here with his armour. The only other metallic thing that flew like that was Faso's dragon automaton. I wasn't sure if their arrival was a good or bad thing.

13

As Velos winged closer, he let out a roar so loud that the ground rumbled beneath my feet. Through the roar and in the collective unconscious, I could sense his anger and contempt for me. I honestly thought that he was about to end my life here and now by dousing me in flame.

"*Velos, I'm sorry,*" I said in the collective unconscious, and I muttered it under my breath at the same time. He couldn't understand Towese, so I also sang a dragonsong in my mind to express the same sentiment.

Candiorno was sitting at the front of his armour, his hands firm upon his steering fin. Talato sat at her regular place at the back of the armour. The dragon automaton flew alongside Velos, with Faso and Winda on its back.

Both dragon and machine came down together, but Velos touched down first, churning up a massive plume of dust and dirt over the dragon automaton and plastering its riders. Faso shouted out something at Velos, and Velos drowned him out with another massive roar.

He was clearly angry. *Does he know what I've done?* I wondered. *Does he know that I've just killed a dragon queen?*

If he'd passed the Greys that had witnessed the murder on

the way here, they would no doubt have told him what I'd done. Dragonheats, I wouldn't blame him if he'd requested that they follow in his wake and exact revenge.

Or, he might have just been angry because I'd transformed on his back and deserted him. Either way, I didn't blame him.

Taka had left us to go and find some water. He returned with a gourd full of it, strolled up to me, and poured it into my mouth. It was full of grit, as if Taka had purposely dragged the gourd along the base of the river to make it as dirty as possible. Still, it moistened my throat, and for that I was grateful at least.

Faso had already dismounted from the dragon automaton, and he strolled over with his ferret automaton, Ratter, perched on his shoulder. The automaton looked at me unnervingly with its red glowing crystalline eyes.

Faso had a frown of confusion on his face. "Taka, why did you tie up your Auntie Pontopa like this? Is this the way you treat an old friend?"

Taka shook his head. "You should have seen what she did. She turned into a black dragon, and she... Bassalhan is dead, Papo. This woman, who you call Auntie Pontopa – and I don't know why because she isn't related by blood – she murdered Bassalhan. She tore out her throat, and I saw it with my own eyes."

Faso's jaw dropped. "You've got to be kidding? Pontopa, why would you—"

"I didn't choose to do so," I said with my head bowed. "Finesia... She took control."

"I see," Faso said, with his head cocked. "Is she there now? You know I brought the helmet. Maybe it can help, although I'm still not entirely convinced Finesia exists, and if she does, she has to be a construction of the mind."

A hand clasped Faso on the shoulder. He moved out of the way, to reveal Lieutenant Talato's burly frame standing behind him. She had the jar of cyagora in her other hand. "May I, Mr Gordoni?"

"Of course. Though I don't see how that will help in the long run. Pontopa, I really need some time to study you. Maybe I can take a blood sample..."

"Oh, shut up, Faso," I snapped. "Now really isn't the time."

"Fine." Faso crossed his arms

Talato stepped in front of him, a pill clutched in between two fingers of her right hand. "Dragonseer Sako, perhaps some more water?"

Taka nodded, and Talato stuffed the pill in my mouth. Taka poured some more water down with it, and there was less dirt this time. I let both down my throat, still raw presumably from breathing fire in my other form.

"You really think you'll be able to keep me out," Finesia said in my mind. *"I know where you are now, and when I need you again, I'll find a way back into your mind. Cyagora lasts for but a few days, while I have all the time in the world."*

I shuddered, and I don't know why I did so. Perhaps it was the implications of Finesia's words, or perhaps it was the cyagora taking its effect on me. That pill acted fast, and my muscles weakened even more until I could no longer feel my fingers and toes. An intense sensation of guilt for what I'd done also sank into my chest, but that feeling was soon washed away by the drug.

It was replaced by a mellow kind of feeling that knew not despair nor elation. My connection to the collective unconscious also got cut off, and with it, that bond I held with Velos. But he didn't seem to mind, as he rested his head against the ground and fell quickly asleep.

"She should be safe now," Lieutenant Talato said, looking at Taka.

Taka stepped forward, and studied me, his expression still twisted with anger. He lifted up the spear again, and pressed it to my throat as before.

"Taka," Faso said. "There's no need for such violence. Leave the woman alone."

Taka glared back at him. "I've been trained as a dragonseer, which gives me the right to use violence when the occasion fits."

"And now she's defenceless. Tell him, Pontopa..."

"I—" I lowered my head. "I deserve a lot more than that, as he said."

Faso shook his head. "That still doesn't make it right. Taka, we'll need to talk about your behaviour later. Violence is not okay unless absolutely necessary."

Taka huffed, and he stepped back, but kept the spear pointed high.

Faso took Ratter off his shoulder and placed him on the ground. Kneeling, he tapped the automaton on the back using a complex rhythm. It rushed forwards, its red eyes focused on me.

It clambered up my trouser leg, moving so fast and so lightly that it sent a shiver up my spine. In an instant, it was dangling off the vines at my stomach, and a hot pain flared at my navel followed by a snap before the bindings fell free. Ratter rushed up my arm and cut the vines at my chest. I gasped, suddenly realising how much my breathing had been constricted.

I stepped forwards slightly, my legs bandy. But Taka made a sudden movement with his spear. He swept it downwards, and he pointed it at my stomach rather than my throat. This time, though, it didn't touch me.

"Why did you free her, Papo? Do you know how dangerous she is?"

"Lieutenant Talato gave her the cyagora, for wellies' sake. So, put that spear down! While she has those pills, she's harmless. And you'll keep on them, Pontopa, won't you?"

"I'll try," I said, meekly.

After my participation in the Ginlast massacre, I had vowed to come off them. I had partly blamed the withdrawal symptoms of that drug, believing that the act of stopping taking them had given Finesia a greater opportunity to close in. Now, it seemed that Finesia found it easier to control my mind, withdrawal symptoms or not. I worried that eventually she'd weave her way around the drug too.

"How do you know that's going to be enough?" Taka asked me.

Faso studied Taka with a frown of concern. "You're becoming more like Hastina every day you know, Taka? Whatever happened to your childhood? Pontopa right now needs some rest, and—"

Faso looked over his shoulder at Winda, who was tightening a bolt on the dragon automaton's head. "Darling, could you bring me the helmet?"

Winda looked like she felt that Faso had been asking too much of her lately. She turned to Lieutenant Candiorno, who had been watching things unfold from a distance, with his rifle slung low beneath his hip. "Lieutenant, would you please do that for me?"

"At once, Ma'am," he said, sounding like he was happy to finally have something to do.

Lieutenant Candiorno jumped on to the back of the dragon automaton, and fetched the helmet from a compartment underneath Faso's seat.

Faso took it from Candiorno. "This, we can use to cut off Pontopa's connection to the collective unconscious," he said in an incredibly flat, dry voice, "once the cyagora has worn off, of course. I'm not completely sure if the Gordoni rays are what's causing this connection to Finesia. But I have a hypothesis."

Taka lowered his spear and placed its butt in the dirt by his feet. "Fine. But be aware, if I see any sign of her transforming, I'll end her life before we even see the black mist."

I swallowed hard. He was certainly becoming like Hastina.

"Fine," Faso said and stepped forward.

I had so many questions. We'd been so caught up in the moment that I hadn't even had a chance to ask what had happened at Fortress Gerhaun. My parents, for example... Were they okay? Clearly, there was more to this than anyone had explained because no one seemed panicked at all.

Before I could open my mouth to say another word, an overwhelming sense of tiredness wracked my muscles and sent my head spinning. The cyagora was taking effect, not to mention the post-exhaustion from turning into a dragon.

I fell to the ground, and I passed out.

14

I awoke to the aroma of mackerel wafting from an open fire. My head was stuffed into something soft and warm, and I raised my hand to feel the cold metal on the outside of the helmet.

A tight band ran around my head, just below my temples, and I could feel my pulse beating against it. I didn't dare try to adjust the helmet, because I couldn't sense anything in my mind at all. No Velos. No sense of a mad empress watching me. My thoughts, it seemed, were finally my own.

I was safe... For now.

My hip dug into the springy, yet firm ground beneath me, and my eyelids seemed to be glued shut. I forced them open, to see that Faso had fortunately not blocked off my vision and kept the slats open. It was like looking through a window, except this window was a pane of glass right in front of my face. The heat from the fire pricked at the skin on my forearms, and the amber glow of the setting sun cast prismatic reflections across the glass.

The whole party – Faso to my left, then Winda, then Candiorno, then Talato, and Taka closest to me – sat on a log behind the firepit, watching several fish roasting on a wooden spit. Only Taka kept glancing over at me, but I guessed with the reflection of the sun obscuring my face from him, he couldn't see whether or not I was awake.

I started to prop myself up with my elbow, but I stopped myself as Faso started to speak. I thought it would be to my advantage to learn a little of what was going on before I announced my entry back into the land of the living.

"So, what are we going to do now?" Faso asked.

Taka scraped at the ground with his heel. "I don't know," he said. "Bassalhan is dead... Maybe I should call out for some Greys and find my way back to Fortress Gerhaun. But if I do, I'll have to tell Dragonseer Wiggea what happened. Then she might fly back here and kill Dragonseer Wells."

"I thought you wanted that?"

"I don't want her to die..." Taka replied, his voice sounding strained. "I just... I want the old Auntie Pontopa back again. But how can we know we can trust her? I've seen her do awful things, Papo, and I'm not sure I'll ever meet the person she was again. She's crossed too far into the abyss..."

I had limited ability to feel emotion with the cyagora tamping mine down. Still, those words meant something to me. Taka still cared.

Faso opened his mouth to say something, then he closed it again and shrugged. Winda, who was holding Faso's hand, stood up and walked over to Taka. She put her hands on his shoulders and knelt down to his level.

"You know," she said. "I've seen a lot of dark stuff in life that you wouldn't even imagine. My parents... They did some terrible crimes in Slaro, and for a while I hated them. But you've always got to believe there's a way back with people. Everyone has some light, and you can either choose to help them discover it or leave them to sink into the darkness. The choice you make will govern who you are as person. Remember that."

Taka looked across at Winda. "I'm sorry, I didn't know," he said.

Winda nodded. "It was a long time ago."

"And what happened?"

"They died, in the end..." Winda lowered her head. "But I made peace with them before they did."

I'd never known this about Winda. I'd always thought of her as the mellow one. She certainly made Faso a better person, and that's how I'd seen her really – the kind of person who lifted people up.

She was also incredibly quiet about her own issues. Just because she didn't talk about her past much didn't mean that she didn't have one. I felt bad for never trying to connect to her. If the world ever returned to normal, perhaps I'd take her out for a drink sometime.

My stomach was rumbling like crazy, and I was desperate for water, so I knew I couldn't stay eavesdropping on their conversation for much longer. Besides, it didn't sound like they were going to talk about what happened at Fortress Gerhaun. I'd have to ask for myself. I just hoped my parents were okay, because if I'd left them for dead to kill Bassalhan – whether I'd been under Finesia's spell or not – I'd never forgive myself.

I coughed, gently, to make myself known, and I lifted myself up on a shaky forearm. I groaned as I stood, not sure if I had the strength to lift myself. A waft of smoke came from the firepit, and my mouth watered and drew me towards the fish. Taka stood up and watched me warily. I stopped before him, and I bowed my head.

"Taka, I want to change," I said. "What I did was awful, and if there's a way of getting Finesia out of my head, I'll take it. Even if it means wearing this thing for the rest of my life." I knocked on the helmet.

For a while, Taka said nothing, and we stood staring at each other as if we were on either side of an abyss. Eventually, Winda who was still kneeling where she had been talking to Taka beckoned me over. "Let's take it one step at a time," she said. "Would you like something to eat, Pontopa? You must be starving."

I nodded. "I would... Thank you."

I sat on the ground on the other side of the fire from the log. The heat from the firepit warmed my skin, which was still raw with cuts and scratches. I noticed a small pot with water and a ladle in it, resting on a tree trunk besides the fire. I crawled forwards, and tried to open the visor so I could drink.

Unfortunately, it wasn't a simple case of just swinging it open. Faso chuckled, and Winda shot Faso an angry look, then she looked at me with a softer expression. She stood up, stepped over and flipped a latch on my chin. The visor automatically sprung up and outwards. I nodded my thanks and scooped a couple of ladles into my mouth.

"You can keep that open if you like," Winda said. "It won't interfere with the cage that we designed to completely shield your skull. Though bear in mind that the glass is reinforced to offer protection from bullets and the like."

"Don't you mean that I designed?" Faso said with his hands on his hips.

"Faso, you know full well who drafted the blueprints for that invention. Just because you never told me what purpose you planned to use it for, doesn't mean you can claim credit..."

I smiled, although it felt a little forced with my emotions still suppressed. "You tell him, Winda. Stick up for yourself."

"I will," she said, and she sat down on the ground next to me. She'd now lost her ponytail, and the light from the fire coloured her loose straight hair in warm hues. She reached out and touched a point on the top left of the helmet. "By the way, if the helmet is too tight, you can turn this larger dial here. We've designed it as a one size fits all device, so others can use it too, if necessary."

"Thank you," I said, and I fiddled with the dial to make the helmet a little more comfortable.

Faso stood up and prodded a fish with a set of tongs. "By the way, Winda. Did Hastina ever tell you why she wanted those blueprints for the Roc missiles? Is General Sako having some of those automatons built for his arsenal? Because I don't know why I'm never included in these plans."

Winda shook her head. "I asked, but she said it was confidential."

"What did I tell you? More and more secrets with that woman..."

But this had piqued my interest. "What blueprints?"

"I'm sorry, she said I was to keep this top secret, and I've already said too much. I'll tell you one thing though, I designed a powerful weapon for her. Anyway, you said you were hungry, right?"

I nodded, and Faso used his tongs to remove a fish from the spit. He placed it on Ratter's back, who was already resting on the ground.

The automaton made a chirping sound, then it scooted over to me. I didn't care how hot the fish was, and the muscles in my hands were desensitised from the cyagora anyway. I took the fish in my palms, and I tore the salty flesh off the bones with my teeth.

After I was finally well nourished and hydrated, I quizzed everyone about what had happened in the battle with Alsie. How, in other words, had Faso escaped with the dragon automaton and Velos? Faso being Faso, was ever so willing to take the gauntlet and explain.

It turned out that Hastina had also been holding some cards close to her chest during the parlay, and the ball hadn't been completely in Alsie's court. Just before this, when Bassalhan had learned of Alsie Fioreletta's imminent arrival, she'd sent out a call to rally the other dragon queens. All six of them had left their fortresses at once, each with an army of Greys.

Then, during the meeting with Alsie, Hastina had simply needed to stall for time. Bassalhan was only meant to have been away from Fortress Gerhaun for a short while before her second in command Castlonth – who I guess was now leader of the dragon queens – would take her place. All this happened before the secicao gas could close in on Fortress Gerhaun, choking it of life.

"So that means that my parents are safe?" I asked. "I thought that Bassalhan had abandoned them there."

Faso looked at Taka, who shook his head. "They kicked up a fuss about us leaving. Particularly General Sako, who tried to stop me. So Bassalhan ordered her guards to restrain him just as we took off."

"But he was tied to a chair..." I said. "Why didn't you just lock him in the cells?"

"I don't know. We left Bassalhan's dragonelite to do it. Maybe they didn't have the key or something."

"Or they didn't like the guy," Faso suggested.

Taka shrugged and said nothing else.

"I didn't know all of this was happening, of course," Faso said. "And I wouldn't have approved of such a thing. Bassalhan, it turns out, had been keeping a lot of secrets from all of us. And I had absolutely no idea that she was about to kidnap Taka – without my permission I might add."

Taka glared daggers at Faso. "She didn't need your permission, Papo. This was a dragonseer matter. I thought you said you wouldn't say a bad word about her?"

"I didn't. And you already know what I feel about the ethics of the situation. Despite this, Taka, I'm your father and you were willing to go away without telling me. Have you any idea how that makes me feel?"

Taka shrugged, and Faso huffed, then turned back to me. "Anyway, back to my story. Alsie and her minions didn't stay to fight, fortunately, as I didn't think we'd fare well against them even with the dragon automaton in our arsenal. I've seen what those things can do. But they left pretty much as soon as I left the field, just about the same time as Yol, Castlonth, and the other four dragon queens arrived."

Faso explained how he'd steered the dragon automaton away from the conflict as soon as the dragon queens had entered the fray. He didn't take much time to question what was going on.

"The Gordoni Rays led me right to you, Pontopa," Faso said. "When you turned into a dragonwoman, you were emitting so many of them. But Alsie Fioreletta and her kind were filling the air with them as well, and I didn't think you'd be traceable. Fortunately, when they left, I was able to pick up your signal, even though it was faint. It was enough for me to follow you across the Southlands. Lieutenant Talato kept Velos augmented, and he seemed to want to come along for the ride. It wasn't long until we found you here on Gahl."

I knew Gahl well – it was one of the largest islands in the Southern Approach and also the closest in the archipelago to the Southlands.

"I guess you were the only ones fast enough to keep up with me," I asked.

"Yes... It's astounding really, I would love to study your physiology." Winda gasped and Faso glanced abashedly at her. "I mean, as a dragonwoman, of course. You are faster than the dragon automaton and the armour when they're unaugmented."

"But you didn't reach me fast enough to stop me," I said. It was then that I realised Alsie had only been there to prompt me into action. All this had been a part of Finesia's grand scheme.

"We weren't far behind you," Faso said. "We saw Bassalhan's corpse, and we saw the Grey dragons flocking around it like confused bats."

I shook my head as my mouth soured. My stomach heaved in revulsion. I retched, and spewed the contents of my stomach onto the ground.

After I'd rinsed my mouth and had regained my composure, Winda, Faso, Taka, and I continued to eat in silence. Over the crackling of the fire, the only voices to be heard were those of the two lieutenants – Talato and Candiorno – speaking in soft tones.

Talato, I noticed, was smiling and I wondered for a moment if she'd found a kindred soul. Candiorno's cheeks also glowed red on his round face, and he chuckled as he told his stories. Behind them, Velos' snores rumbled across the landscape, harmoniously complementing the swishing of the wind.

This relative silence was to be short lived. Suddenly, a great roar filled the air coming in from the south. Half expecting Alsie to have returned, I craned my head up towards the sky. Thousands of V-shaped silhouettes danced in a twisting formation over the setting sun. Normally, I'd be able to feel their approach, but both the cyagora and the helmet were doing their job well.

Taka turned around to look at them. "It's Yol... Castlonth sent her out with a search party for me, and I've called her in."

Faso glanced over at me. "Pontopa, you better hide... She can't find you here."

Taka reached out for his spear. "Papo?"

"Taka, we've talked about this. Give the woman a chance. Those dragons will want blood as soon as they see her. But if she can hide herself out of sight, no Gordoni Rays can escape from that helmet and reveal her location."

Taka clenched his jaw. "Fine," he said. "Go... But if I sense that you've removed the helmet, I'll reveal all."

I stood up, my head spinning. I lowered the visor and I clambered off into the trees.

15

YOL TINASH and what must have been a good hundred dragons descended towards the clearing, their menacing shadows stretching over the land, just as the sun's final rays began to sink beneath the horizon. The rest of the dragons circled around in the air, keeping watch for any signs of danger.

Red clouds streaked across the sky, and a sudden chill had enveloped the island. I kept myself hidden in a thick bush of *calianai*, the large serrated red leaves shading me in darkness. The pollen from the voluminous pink flowers made my nose feel stuffy beneath my helmet. Thorns scratched through my shirt, and I shivered in the cold of the encroaching night, making me wish I was by the fire pit.

But if I emerged and Yol or any of the dragons other than Velos saw me, I was almost certain I wouldn't live to see another sunset. I kept my breaths shallow, even though I knew that I would be too far away for the dragons to hear them. So long as they hadn't seen me scurry into the underbrush, I should be safe for now, assuming the helmet masked my presence as Faso had promised, and no one let on to Yol about my hiding place.

A good ten Greys came down first, landing not far from where

Velos had been previously sleeping. Velos roared to greet them, and I wondered if he'd reveal my position. I couldn't get a reading on his emotions in the collective unconscious anymore, and I honestly wasn't sure what he'd do in this situation. Faso might have convinced Taka to stay silent, but no one save Taka could tell Velos what to do.

But there was no sign of any alarm as Yol landed in the circle that the Greys had made for her. Velos might have been angry with me, but despite that, he remained a loyal friend, and for that I was grateful.

More Greys came down to land around Yol in a neat concentric circular arrangement. They sent up a thick cloud of dust that concealed them from view for a moment. It soon settled, and the sky once again looked like it was on fire.

Yol wasn't as big as Bassalhan, and I think she was just a little shorter than Gerhaun. Still, she towered over the Greys, and Velos, who craned their heads up at her as she strolled towards the fire pit on her two thick hind legs. She stopped and looked down upon the party before her.

"I'll speak out loud, so all of you can hear me. Now, could you please explain how you all came to be here? Because Bassalhan is dead – killed by the woman Pontopa Wells, who has become a servant of Finesia."

Taka stepped forwards. "She carried me here. I witnessed her kill Bassalhan Cagari with my own eyes."

My heart jumped in my chest. Taka was about to reveal all... Faso watched the boy with wide eyes, but he didn't dare say anything. I readied myself to scarper, though I wasn't sure I could outrun the Greys if they came after me. I could, of course, take off my helmet and turn back into a dragonwoman. Right then, though, I would rather die than let Finesia back into my head.

"I see," Yol said. "Where did she go?"

"She flew off in that direction," Taka pointed to the sky slightly to my right.

I let go of a breath that I hadn't even realised I had been holding. "Thank you, Taka," I muttered under my breath.

"And why would she do that?" Yol asked. "What good would you do for her or Finesia here?"

"I don't know…" Taka said. "Dragonseer Wells was meant to take me to join the migration, and then she seemed to change her mind. I think there's still some aspect of my Auntie Pontopa in her, Yol Tinash. There's still some light in her, I think."

Yol sniffed the air, and looked from one side of the horizon to the other, as if searching for me. For a while I thought her yellow eyes must have locked on to me, and she paused and sniffed the air again. She snorted out some grey smoke and then turned back to Taka.

"Even if there is a trace of her former self," she chimed, "we still need to find her and bring her to justice. Which begs the question, how did the rest of you end up here?"

"I developed technology to track her," Faso said. "The trail led here, but I lost it shortly afterwards."

Yol studied Faso discerningly. "And Bassalhan had told me that your dragon automaton was faster than one of Finesia's creations. I would have thought you'd easily catch up."

"Velos and the dragon automaton are only faster when using secicao fuel," Faso said. "It wasn't enough to catch her. Maybe Pontopa Wells is different when in dragon form. I don't know. I still find it hard to come to terms with the fact that people can turn into dragons in the first place. Do you know how unscientific that is? I can't work out where all the atoms come from to change their constitutions like that, not to mention the fact that their clothes just seem to disappear."

While Faso was prattling away, I was crouched here, my heart thumping in my chest. I shifted, and leaves rustled and crunched underfoot. A twig snapped, and Yol snapped her head towards me. She edged a little closer inquisitively, and I sank back as quietly as I could into the bush, thorns pricking my back through my shirt. Fortunately, the dragon queen seemed to think nothing of the noise, and she turned back to look at Taka again.

"Dragonseer Sako, I've also been instructed to act as your new escort to Slaro. Castlonth has ordered that we should execute Bassalhan's orders as originally planned. Which I trust —" Yol looked at each of the party in turn – "you are now all aware of."

Faso stepped forwards. "Look, Yol. I understand tactically why you have to take Taka to the city. But I wish to come too, so I can at least spend time with my son."

Yol let out a deep, rumbling growl. "Faso Gordoni, you don't belong in the palace. People will start to question your sudden appearance there."

Faso placed his hands on his hips. "I'll have you know that I used to work in the palace as King Cini's most trusted inventor. No one will care if I resume my role. In fact, I was such a phenomenon at the time, I'm sure they'll think it quite natural. Cini held no grudges against me, at least until I joined Gerhaun's forces in the Southlands. But none of that was made public. I saw nothing mentioned about it in the magazines, anyway."

All of a sudden, I heard some rustling from behind me. I glanced over my shoulder to see something rushing through the bushes in the distance. It was large enough to be human, or perhaps some kind of feral animal. Dragonheats, whatever it was, I didn't want it blowing my cover.

Instinctively, I felt for my hipflask at my hip, but of course it wasn't there. So, defenceless, I crawled out on all fours away from Yol and her landing party, to get a better view of whatever it was that had been spying on them.

I emerged from the bush on all fours and scoured the terrain for my quarry. I'd purposely hidden myself at the top of a rise, so I could get away quickly if I had to. This allowed me to descend, completely concealed from view from anyone by the fire.

It was difficult to see through the glass of my helmet as I stared right into the deep shadows of early night. I was close to the equator, and so the sky would be dark very soon. Fortunately, the helmet still had the heat sensor vision that Faso had installed before the Ginlast Massacre. I flicked the switch to turn this on.

Ahead, I saw shades of blue, with the *calianai* flowers coloured green, the pink outlines of some rabbits scurrying through the underbrush and, in bright red, a well-built male human looking straight at me, perhaps one hundred metres away. I couldn't see his face, and he seemed to notice that I'd spotted him, so he broke out into a run.

"Dragonheats," I said under my breath again, and I bit my tongue to stop myself calling out for him to stop. I crawled a little further down the hill and checked over my shoulder to make sure I was completely concealed from view. Then, I took off at a sprint after the figure.

He wasn't as fast as runner as I thought he might be, given his athletic frame. The heat signature vision made it impossible to see any details, but I knew I had no chance of tracking him otherwise. He led me down a narrow path through the *calianai* which scratched at my calves as I went. We descended even further, and I stopped myself just in time from stepping off a cliff.

The man, who stood next to me, had also stopped himself dead in his tracks.

"Who are you?" I asked. "Why were you watching us..."

His voice came out, ever so familiar. "Darling, don't you remember that Finesia knows exactly where you travel?"

I couldn't believe my ears, even though I'd known I had to eventually face him again. I flipped the switch on the side of my helmet to make sure. The light from the heat signatures faded away, and I saw the man I once knew... His hard-edged features... His slicked-back hair, looking exactly as he had that time at the lava lake...

"Rastano Wiggea," I said. "What the dragonheats do you want?"

THE CONVERSATION I had left behind had become distant now. I could still hear the voices, but I could not hear what they were saying. Yol's voice was louder than rest, with a deep sonorous boom to it that seemed to fill the night and drown out the rushing of the wind and the hoots of the owls. With Wiggea's arrival, the air had become even thicker with that bitter pollen smell. Now, the sun had set, everything around me felt cold.

Night had completely descended, but the moon had also emerged from the clouds to the south. This allowed me Wiggea in his human form. He looked just as he had been at the lava lake when I had kissed him... Before Colas had killed him, and he'd risen as one of Finesia's servants.

If I could fight Finesia, and Charth could once fight Finesia, maybe he could too. If I stuffed a pill of cyagora down his throat, what would happen? It didn't matter though, because I didn't have cyagora with me, and I wasn't going to go crawling back to Lieutenant Talato to get it. Not while Yol and her Greys were stationed there, ready to tear my life out through my throat.

"Darling, what's this thing you have on your head? Is this

what is keeping Finesia out?" Wiggea reached out with both his hands towards the helmet.

I pushed his hands away. "Don't touch."

Wiggea had a smirk on his face. "And what will you do to stop me if I decided to force the thing off you?"

I checked my garters first for my knives, but Taka had removed them. So, I scanned the ground looking for a weapon, but there was nothing nearby. Wiggea watched me passively with wide eyes and a sorrowful look on his face.

"Would you really try to hurt me after everything we've been through? You loved me once, and I still love you..."

"Stop saying that," I said, with my teeth clenched. "While you are Finesia's servant, you are incapable of love."

"Oh, but it was you who made me this way," Wiggea said. "Thrown into the lava lake and reborn from your blood. Wasn't it because of you that I fell? Because Finesia tells me that you chose Faso Gordoni's life over my own."

"I didn't make that choice..."

"But you did, through indecision. You couldn't kill either of us, so instead Colas did it for you. Now, you choose to block Finesia out through similar indecision. Even without her in your head, you cannot deny your attraction to me. Embrace it, my darling, and you can have everything that you want."

"The last thing I want is you, right now, Rastano."

Wiggea narrowed his eyes. "You lie. You have that drug in your body, and that helmet blocking Finesia out of your head, and all this is clouding your vision. When you get rid of both, you will remember what you truly want."

"This isn't about want," I said. "And it's not Rastano Wiggea I'm talking to anymore. I lost that man a long time ago, and I will never see him again."

Wiggea took a step forwards, so that I could smell his sweat and the musky light cologne that he used to wear. He looked at me with a sultry gaze, and for a while I wondered if there was a trace of the old soldier left in him.

He used to be a loyal man who would never make the first move, since that would get in the way of his duty. He took hold of my hand. His skin was dry, and for a moment I thought I could feel rough dragon scales pushing out of his skin.

I stood looking at him, breathing heavily. Then I took my hand away.

"What do you want, Rastano?" A slight breeze picked up from the sea and whistled around the helmet. Bats flitted nearby, looking for rodents on the shore.

He cocked his head. "I want to make sure you stay safe. I care, you know…"

"Then why are you here?"

"Because there is a dragon queen and a good several score of grey dragons to the south who will kill you if they see you. But under the cloak of night, I can carry you away to safety. Finesia has been waiting for you…"

"I don't want to be carried anywhere."

"Darling, if you sink into the pits of despair, I won't abandon you there. I am yours forever, and you know that."

"How many times do I have to repeat it? You are nothing to me. If I had the means to kill you now, I would."

Wiggea's lips curled upwards into a sly smile. "As you wish, m'lady," he said, and he reached down once again for his hip. I lurched backwards as he drew a dagger from it.

I readied myself in a defensive stance, but he seemed to pay no mind to that. Rather, he spun the dagger around in his hand so he was holding the blade between his thumb and forefinger.

He stepped into my stance, and he placed the dagger in my right hand and closed my fingers around it, the blade pointing towards him. With the other hand, he raised the dagger to his throat, and he rested his head against the glass of my helmet as he gazed at me with puppy dog eyes.

"If this is what it takes for me to prove my loyalty to you, then I place my life in your hands. Choose to take it if you must. But know then, it is the real Rastano Wiggea that you kill. I will love you from beyond the grave, Pontopa, if you choose this path, and I will remain yours eternally."

I stood still, my chest heaving with heavy breaths, not daring to shift an inch. This was my chance to avenge Wiggea's spirit and stop this terrible monster inhabiting his body. He would thank me for it. Hastina, I was sure, would thank me for it, if she knew. And I would gain a slight sense of peace knowing that Rastano Wiggea had finally been put to rest.

I clenched my fist around the hilt, and I readied myself to pierce his throat, to end it now. Finesia could send someone else after me if she had to. Or I could just go out and announce my presence to Yol and suffer the consequences.

But as I studied his eyes, an image flashed back to my mind of Wiggea dangling tied to a wooden pole above the lava pit. He'd looked defenceless then, and he was defenceless now. He had displayed fear then, and right now his bottom lip trembled, and his eyes looked ever so slightly wet.

Was this a trick? Did Finesia want me to see this because she could no longer get inside my mind?

Part of me wanted to believe that there was still a trace of Rastano Wiggea left in him. Not just Wiggea, but all the dragon-men. Maybe, as Winda had suggested, there was a way of bringing them back to the light. I just hadn't a clue where to start.

My hand was also trembling, and so Wiggea put both his hands around mine and fastened his grip.

"Don't be afraid," he said.

"I'm not..."

"You are."

"So are you," I said. "Or at least a part of you..."

"Isn't that because we love each other?"

"No," I said. "I don't love this version of you, Wiggea. But I cannot kill you either."

I lowered the dagger, careful not to nick Wiggea's throat. When it was a safe distance away, I dropped it to the ground. It landed in the ground with a clink, blade down. Wiggea looked down at it, then he lifted his hand and placed it on the glass of the helmet so I could see his palm.

"Why don't you take this off?" he said.

"Because the dragons might sense me here. Particularly when I'm so weak."

"But you learned long ago how to keep them out. Gerhaun Forsi trained you to mask your mind, didn't she? And if she didn't, you know that I can carry you away from them fast enough. You are safe with me, Pontopa Wells."

I shook my head. "Faso has developed technology. He can detect me, and he should be able to detect you here as well."

"He might, if he was looking. But I also eavesdropped on the conversation, and I don't think Faso will want to show Yol the technology that he can use to find you."

"He might... He knows that if I keep the helmet on then his equipment can't detect me. But what if I took the equipment off?"

Wiggea cackled so loudly, that I knew I wasn't speaking to the old soldier, but the Finesia controlled version of him. "Darling, Finesia has seen that man look at you many times. He claims that he cares about Asinal Winda, but really, he cares more about you... But he knows that he can't get you. He knows you don't have the same kind of feelings for him as you have for me..."

"If Faso cares about me, he has a funny way of showing it..."

"Don't most men? But with me, you can trust me to tell you what I think. You can trust me to tell you how I truly feel."

I turned back towards the ocean. I couldn't see the bats there anymore, but I could hear them squeaking through the night. Suddenly, I had an idea for how I could set things right. I did a one-eighty and I strolled off towards the fire pit, though I could no longer hear it roaring into the darkness or see any signs of it at the top of the rise.

"Where are you going?" Wiggea asked.

"Back to turn myself in," I said. "It's about time I faced up to any justice I'm due for killing Bassalhan Cagari, even if it means my death."

"But don't you see? You're already too late." He pointed up to the top of the rise. "Finesia sees and hears many things. Watch, just about now…"

First came a mighty roar from above, which was so loud it forced me into a crouch. Then came the flapping sound of hundreds of wings, and another squeal of the dragons communicating with each other.

A rush of air came from above, parting the *calianai* around me. I quickly switched on the night vision, to see hundreds of dragons pass overhead.

Yol led the way, with two brightly lit dragons on her flank. One of them was Velos, an intense brightness in my vision coming from the armour wrapped around him, with three humans sitting on top, one much smaller than the other two. It must have been Candiorno, Talato, and Taka. On Yol's right, the other dragon emitted a massive heat signature, that I knew it must be the dragon automaton, with Faso and Winda on the saddle, as before. The rest of the Greys followed behind.

Dragonheats, they'd deserted me, leaving me alone on this island with Wiggea – the dragonman who wouldn't give up until I had gone back over to Finesia's side.

17

As I watched the dragons leave, my heart sank to the pit of my stomach, which was churning and growling, and I felt as if I wanted to throw up.

They continued north for a little while, then they veered to the northeast in the direction of Slaro. Yol, Velos, and the dragon automaton slowed down to allow the Greys to catch up and enter a defensive formation.

If they encountered any enemies over the Costondi Sea before they reached the Southern Barrier – an archipelago that separated the Northern Continent from the rest of the world – then the Greys would protect the more vital members of the team – namely the dragon queen, Velos, and the dragon automaton.

Wiggea approached me from the bottom of the rise, and I scowled at him. I certainly didn't want to be left alone with this ghost of an imagined past. I sprinted down the rise and took a sharp right to avoid him. I watched the ground carefully, pushing as close as I possibly could to the cliff edge. The dragons had travelled some distance away, but not that far. Still close enough, I hoped, to hear me as there was only sea and bats between us.

"Stop!" I called out. "I'm over here!" Not one dragon looked back, so I tried even louder. "Over here! Come and get me! I'm ready to turn myself in!"

But the only creature it sent stumbling towards me was Wiggea. "What do you think you're doing?" he asked, not sounding even remotely out of breath.

"I'm not going to be trapped here, alone with you. Who knows what you might do..."

"Really, is that how you feel?" Wiggea asked with his hands on his hips. But I knew it was all for show.

I ignored him. "Over here!" I called again, waving my hands in the air. "I have Wiggea here too!"

"They can't hear you," Wiggea muttered. "They're too far away."

"Then I'll just have to reach out to them in the collective unconscious." I clutched both my hands around the helmet. "I'm sure I can do so before I let Finesia in..."

I started to pull the helmet off.

"No!" Wiggea called out, and the next thing I knew he was launching towards me. He hit me from an angle, so he didn't send me flying off the cliff's edge. He knocked me over, and flattened me to the ground, taking the wind right out of me.

Wiggea sat on top of me, straddling my hips. He reached out and flicked the night-vision switch, so I could see the features on his face again, and what looked like innocent eyes. Then he held his hands over my helmet and pushed it firmly down on my head.

I pushed up my hands again and tried to claw the helmet off me, but Wiggea's grip was too strong. He was a dragonman after all, and I – without a trace of Finesia in my head – was nothing.

"I thought Finesia wanted me to take the helmet off?" I asked. "I thought she wanted to get back inside my head..."

"Not if you're going to use it commit suicide," Wiggea replied. "I told you that I wouldn't let you topple over the abyss."

This time, it was my turn to bark out a laugh. "What's the matter? Are you telling me you can't take on Yol and her dragons? Are you telling me that you're no match for them? Didn't you bring allies?"

Wiggea leaned in towards me. "It's just me. I didn't come with anyone else... And I came on my own will, because I wanted to be close to you."

"Will you just shut up, Rastano? It's not you, but Finesia talking inside your head, and I'm not going to believe you when you keep parroting her words."

Wiggea looked out into the darkness. I couldn't see anything there without the heat vision, but perhaps he could, or at least sense Yol in the collective unconscious. "Once they're far enough away, you can take it off."

"Then I will leave it on. I'll find another way to turn myself in."

"That's your choice..." Wiggea said, and he leaned in a little closer. His gaze was set on mine. The moon shone brightly in the sky now, and the light from it bathed his eyes in silver.

He reached out and flipped the switch to open the visor of my helmet. He pushed it all the way up so that glass was pointing away from the top of my skull. "You know, it's clear it's not me that you want. So, I'll bring back the one who you truly want to spend time with."

All of a sudden, something changed within him. He didn't look upon me lustfully anymore. Rather his eyes were human again – full of compassion.

"Wiggea, what are you doing?" I asked.

"Dragonseer Wells, it's me... Please, I just want to take one look at you... I just want to remember."

"Wiggea? Rastano?" He did seem different.

He put his hand to my cheek. It felt dry and cracked, but warm. "Finesia lets me back sometimes. I've missed you, Pontopa... But I'm sorry. I need to be free of this form... All the things I've done. I can never forgive myself."

"No... This has to be another trick."

Wiggea lowered his head, and said nothing. The way he moved; the way he looked at me. Somehow, I just knew...

"So, you are in there somewhere... There is a light in you. Wiggea, we must find a way to bring you back. Just hold on..."

He lifted himself off me, and then he offered me his hand. I took it, and he pulled me up in his strong grip. He looked away out into the darkness, just as if he was staring out into the lava lake, pretending I wasn't there.

"I can end this," he said stepping closer to the edge. "I don't have to face her anymore." He bent his knees.

"Wiggea, no!" I called out, and I rushed forwards and took hold of his hand.

He stopped and turned back to me. "Pontopa, the things that I've done... I can't let myself hurt anyone anymore."

"And do you think Finesia will let you jump? You dive off this cliff, and she'll take control of your mind again. Then, she'll turn you into a dragon again before you hit the bottom."

Wiggea turned back slowly towards me. "How do you do it, Pontopa? How do you keep her out?"

I grunted. "I've failed at that abysmally lately."

"Why? What happened?" Wiggea asked, his eyes wide with concern.

"I—" I wanted to explain to him. But I could see the silver moonlight glinting off his lips, and I'd longed for that kiss again for so long. Besides, I was starting to develop an idea. If I could just distract him for long enough...

I took hold of his hand again, and this time I leant in.

"Pontopa..."

"Shh," I put my finger to his lips, then I replaced this finger with my own lips. His felt dry and cracked, but they seemed to soften on touch. I reached out for the small of his back, and I drew him in towards me.

Wiggea pulled back. "You know this is an illusion. You know that Finesia will never let this last."

"That's why I want to keep her from your mind..."

"Pontopa, what do you—"

I kissed him again, both to shut him up, and because I wanted to. Then, I reached up to my head with both hands and clutched the helmet. It was tighter than I expected, but with a solid yank I managed to pull it away. I ignored the pain that emerged at my temples, completely focused on the helmet and what I was about to do.

Wiggea's face twisted, and a black cloud started to rise around him, swallowing the light from the moon. But he didn't transform fast enough, before I took a step back from him, turned the helmet around, and placed it on his head. It didn't fit at first, but it seemed to stop the smoke rising.

I found the appropriate dial at the side of the helmet, and I turned it anticlockwise, until the helmet fell down on Wiggea's head. Then I turned the dial the other way to secure it in place. Wiggea was looking at me, his eyes wide in astonishment.

"Rastano Wiggea, are you still there?"

"Pontopa, what is this?"

"It worked for me, and I thought it would work for you as well. I think, Rastano, I've found a way to save these dragonmen. If we could get Faso to manufacture enough of these helmets... We can stop this..." I still had a while before the effects of the cyagora wore off, and if I could acquire some more in time, I could save us both.

Wiggea furrowed his brows. Then he looked down at his arms. I looked down as well, and my heart skipped a beat. I'd been so focused on his face that I hadn't noticed his arms had black dragon scales on them. "I'm still one of them..."

"No," I replied. "You can pull them back in, surely. Then there will be no trace of Finesia left in you."

"Maybe if I take off the helmet..." It was as if something within him was still fighting to gain control.

"Wiggea, focus. Turn back into a human again. You can do this..."

"I—"

I squeezed his hand. "I believe in you."

He nodded and then looked down once again at his arms. He closed his fists, and his face twisted in pain. For a moment, nothing happened. But then, the scales sank into the skin of his arms, creating thousands of grooves. The skin there billowed out, and it folded in on itself, as it transformed into the suede olive-coloured cloth of Wiggea's old uniform. He looked astonished, and admittedly I was too.

"I did it," he said, and he smiled, showing his teeth, which was a rare sight with this man. "I thought I'd be forever lost to the void with that mad empress raging inside my head. But this helmet... It's remarkable."

Finesia's voice came in my head. Her voice was weak, but still comprehensible. Which meant the cyagora wasn't working as well as it used to.

"It's only a matter of time, you know. You might decide to gain your lover back, but once the cyagora fades, you will come back to me. Though I'm not sure I can promise you a place by my side anymore. You're constantly disappointing me, Acolyte Wells."

"No," I said. *"I can hold you out, Finesia. I've been doing so for years."* I'd let myself get angry. I'd let the situation with Hastina, and Bassalhan, and Alsie provoke me. But now I had my loyal dragonelite, Lieutenant Rastano Wiggea, back, and with him by my side I could be strong.

But then I remembered... Wiggea was the husband of Hastina. Each of them had been presumed dead, and each of them had returned from the dead. Did he know?

I took hold of his hands again, and I looked him in the eyes. "Rastano Wiggea.... Do you care for me?"

He shook his head. "I—This right now is a lot to process. I was your sentinel, and then I became a monster. I'm not sure I'm ready to take you as a lover, much as you seem to need me right now, ma'am. But I am loyal to you always."

I took a deep breath. There was no easy way to break the

news to him. Particularly after the way I felt about him. "Then for now, you can resume your place as my dragonelite, Lieutenant Wiggea. But I also have another dragonelite, Lieutenant Talato. When we find each other again, I shall treat you as equals."

Wiggea broke my grip and saluted. "I understand, ma'am," he said.

A rustling sound came from my left, but I ignored it, assuming it to be a rabbit or some kind of wild fowl. "There's one more thing, Rastano... Something you really need to know."

"What is it?"

"I don't know how to tell you this, because I suspect Finesia never told you, or if she did that you don't remember. But your wife, Hastina Wiggea, the dragonseer. You thought she died that day in Oahastin, mauled by wolves. But she survived. She's alive, Rastano..."

Wiggea's jaw dropped, and his eyes widened. But he wasn't the only one to be surprised, because suddenly two objects landed at my feet. I looked down to see two leather bound books highlighted in the moonlight. Then came Hastina's sharp staccato voice from the direction of where they'd been thrown.

"You can say that again," she said.

I turned to see her angry eyes. This time, she wasn't holding her spear, but a Pattersoni rifle, the sights of which were pointed straight at my throat.

18

COLD SWEAT CLUNG to my skin, making the night feel even colder. The air tasted of ozone, and a distant pounding of thunder punctuated the silence. I waited for the bullet to come, my stomach tight and the taste of sweat on my lips. It would be a fitting end to the story – the monster would die, and the former lovers would be reunited.

But it didn't seem that they were on the same side, because after a brief moment, Wiggea called out, "No, Hastina!", as he sprinted towards her, and it looked as if he was ready to take her down.

Hastina turned her rifle slightly, and cracked out a loud shot, freezing Wiggea in his tracks.

"Don't take another step," she said. "I don't know whose life I should end first... The murderer of dragon queens or the ghost of my former husband who became her dragonman lackey. The truth is though—" she spat on the ground and worked the action of her rifle, readying for another shot – "I guess you're both already dead."

I gritted my teeth, then I put up my hands. "Hastina, I can explain everything... Please give me a chance."

She turned the rifle back towards me. Her finger tensing

tight on the trigger, I guess she wouldn't mind if she slipped and ended my life right now. "What exactly do you want to explain? How you were in love with my former husband and never thought to tell me? Or do you want to try and convince me that you're not actually an agent of Finesia, and you killed my mentor to try to save the world? Remember, I've read your secrets now. I know your mind."

I glanced at Wiggea, who was turning his head between the two of us, confusion plastered across his eyebrows. "You hardly gave me a chance to explain anything, Hastina. Since you arrived at Fortress Gerhaun, you've had it in for me."

"So what? You're saying that my hostility towards you has governed your actions? How do you expect me to behave towards the woman who spawned secicao in the Northern Continent and started the chain reaction that will destroy this world?"

"Hastina..." Wiggea said.

"And don't you start," Hastina replied without even glancing at her former husband. "You died to me when you left me to defend myself against those wolves in South Cadigan. You were drunk that day, Wiggea, do you remember? Too drunk to get to the town fast enough to call for help. And I would have died if I hadn't sensed Bellroot nearby and called out for him to save me. If he hadn't then flown me to Bassalhan, where I began my training as a dragonseer..."

"Hastina, I'm..." Wiggea's lips were trembling, much as they had when he'd been sitting on top of me looking at me. "I'm sorry... I was just a kid."

"Better a kid than a dragonman," Hastina said. "How many have you murdered under Alsie's beck and call? And now you belong to this dragonwoman as another lackey of Finesia. The Rastano Wiggea I once knew wouldn't go anywhere near her after knowing the crimes she'd committed. But I guess all of us are no longer the people we were."

Another crack of thunder came from closer now, and static

pulled up on my arms as lightning flashed overhead. My mouth was dry, and I could feel my pulse throbbing in both temples. Wiggea stepped forwards, and Hastina transferred her weight to her metal leg and fired another shot from her rifle. Once again, it wasn't aimed at me, but Hastina didn't hesitate to return the sights to the person she deemed the highest threat.

"I warned you," she said to Wiggea. "As I said, you mean nothing to me now..."

"Hastina," I said. "We've found a way to bring back the old Wiggea. He isn't a dragonman anymore, not while he wears that helmet. Faso found a way to block anyone's connection to the collective unconscious."

Hastina narrowed her eyes. A heavy drop of rain fell from the sky and hit me on the forehead. "Don't think I will fall for Finesia's tricks. I've seen virtually all of the games she plays..."

I clenched my teeth. "If you truly think I'm an agent of Finesia, then why haven't you killed me yet?"

I'd had enough of playing with fate. Really, if she was going to kill me, then I'd rather she just got on with it.

Hastina's right eye twitched, a nervous tic that I'd never noticed in her before. But what did she have to be nervous about? That was when I realised. The reason she was so hostile towards me, is that I was a mirror of herself.

"It's not just me, is it, Hastina? Finesia's in your head too..."

Hastina clicked her rifle, as if wanting to scare me. "You don't know what you're talking about..."

"Don't I? All this hostility isn't about me, is it? It's about you. You're angry with yourself for letting Finesia in, when you can't even help it. Which means... You're a dragonwoman too."

"You must be some fool to assume—"

"I'm not assuming anything," I interrupted. I was finally getting to the bottom of this. "How did you say that you escaped getting mauled by wolves again, Hastina? A dragon found you, and he just managed to staunch the bleeding and get you out to the Southlands alive..."

Hastina said nothing, but her rifle had started to shake. A streak of lightning shot down from behind her, and a gust of cold wind tossed up her wavy hair.

"Your mother, Indira, later became Travast Indorm. When I met him, or should I say her, she seemed to know the ins-and-outs of how Exalmpora worked quite intricately."

"What are you suggesting?"

"How early were you fed Exalmpora, Hastina? What did Indira do to you when you were young... You're a part of this too, aren't you?"

"I—" she lowered her rifle slightly, but still kept it pointed at my chest.

"All this time, you've been holding it in. The wolves couldn't kill you because you became a dragonwoman instead of dying that day. Like I'd become a dragonwoman when Colas almost killed me. But once you realised who you were, you couldn't return to Wiggea. So where did you go? To the Southlands perhaps? To Bassalhan?"

"She..." Hastina's voice had softened. "She took me in, and you killed her..."

"No... Finesia killed her."

"But you let her in, and that's why you've become a monster. Meanwhile, Bassalhan still taught me how to keep Finesia out. She taught me how to stop becoming one of those monsters."

I shook my head. I wished she'd realise that the only difference between the two of us was that she'd been trained to keep Finesia out. But if I had any chance of surviving this, I had to stop her thinking about Bassalhan, and try appealing to Hastina's better self – if she in fact had one. It seemed prudent to take a leaf out of Asinal Winda's book. "Everyone has a light inside, Hastina. We have to believe that."

"No... There is only darkness once you let Finesia in. My mother is no different than Alsie Fioreletta and Charth, and you, and Wiggea – there is no redemption."

I took a step forward, and Hastina didn't stop me. "Hastina,

I'm sorry... But I want to learn. Teach me what Bassalhan taught you. Teach me how to keep her out."

"No..." Hastina said. "There is no way back. Gerhaun Forsi couldn't train you early enough. She lost Charth, and then she lost you. But Bassalhan always explained to me. She'd saved me and she'd saved Taka before it was too late."

She had her rifle ready, and her eyes tightened with a resolve that told me she was about to fire. But with the way that she spoke about Gerhaun, the way that she had dishonoured her death, I felt the rage building in me, and I couldn't stop it. The effects of the cyagora must have been wearing off much faster than I'd expected.

Black smoke rose around me, and I gnashed at the air as I charged forwards. The shot came, and I felt the pain of it glancing against my shoulder. But that pain became a pleasant tingling sensation as scales tore at my skin, and I roared, another boom of thunder joining my chorus.

I tackled Hastina to the ground, sending her rifle spinning away. She tried to writhe out of the way, but I had her pinned by the shoulders, beneath growing claws.

"That's it my acolyte..." Finesia said. *"She must now finally embrace her own destiny or die."*

The scales tore at my skin. I didn't want to fully transform, but I tasted blood and death on my tongue. Hastina screamed out, and then I saw the features on her face start to writhe. She bared canines far too sharp to be human, and her eyes became faceted gems. I lunged towards her throat, but she twisted out of the way. Then I felt her sharp claws against my back, and I roared with pain that soon fuelled even more rage. I came in for another bite, my maw now starting to lengthen.

"Stop!" Wiggea shouted, and I felt the coolness of raw rifle metal against the front of my neck.

Both Hastina and I froze. The scales pulled back into me, and Hastina's face also returned to normal as her fiery hair billowed out around her once more. She sat beneath me, her chest heaving, and Wiggea kept flicking his eyes between us, as if to try and determine which of us posed the greater threat.

Another rumble of thunder came, but this time it seemed more distant. The storm, it seemed, had passed us without unleashing the rain.

"Neither of you are going to kill each other," Wiggea said. "Not until we work this out." I snarled at him, and then I realised that it wasn't me that was snarling, but the servant of Finesia. I glanced once more at Hastina, but this time I guess my look had a hint of apology in it. I stood up and stepped away from her.

Wiggea now turned the rifle towards Hastina's throat, and she stood up slowly, watching him.

"So that's it?" Hastina said. "After all this time, you'll kill me now, and you'll do it because you want to be with her…"

Wiggea gulped. "I don't want to kill anyone… I just want to make amends for what I've done, and if that means stopping either of you from entering the darkness that I've lived with for so long, then I'll do what I have to do."

Hastina smirked. "Such a hero, Rastano Wiggea. Always the man to put duty first."

"Aren't you the same?" Wiggea said.

Hastina said nothing. Instead, her head snapped around and her ears pricked up. "Shh," she said, putting a finger to her lips. "Can you hear that?"

"What?" Wiggea said, but he wouldn't be able to sense it with his helmet on. Because I also felt a disturbance in the collective unconscious. Black dragons… Hastina and I had been so immersed in our combat that we'd not noticed them passing through the night. The beating of their wings cut through the darkness, and I could sense them in the collective unconscious…

"Dragonmen," I said. "Is it Alsie?"

But it wasn't Alsie. Instead, there was another voice in the collective unconscious. *"How fitting I should discover the two of you here. Finesia informed me you might be close."*

The voice was deeper than Alsie's, and it also sounded terribly familiar. "*Travast Indorm...*" I said. "*Or should I say Indira?*"

"*Oh, so you remember,*" Indira said, and I saw a shape pass over the moon. "*I see that you've found my daughter here too. And, what's this? A love that you both share. For now you might think you've stolen him away from Finesia, but she will claim him back.*"

Hastina was looking up at the sky, searching for Indira. "*I am not your daughter,*" she said.

"*Yes, you are. After all, you were born of my blood. You also look like me. And now, you share Finesia's gift. So then, if you're not my daughter, what else could you be?*"

"*I am the woman who will kill you,*" Hastina said. "*I've waited for this moment a long time...*"

Indira laughed out in the collective unconscious. "*You know, you were feisty like that when Colas plucked you out of the womb...*"

I shuddered. Colas? It was the same mad scientist who fed Exalmpora to Taka from a very young age.

"*Why are you here, Indira?*" I asked.

"*Well, where should I start? Should I tell you how pleased that Finesia is in your reunion, because she has hope that we'll finally recruit both of you to our cause. Or should I tell you about the imminent attack on your dragon queen Yol. You know, Dragonseer – or should I call you Acolyte? – Wells, you should join us on another massacre. We will take no prisoners in our mission to retrieve the boy..*"

I gasped out. "*No!*"

"*We're not doing it on purpose, mind. But you are all so obstinate in stealing the boy away from us. If you just let us take him so we can execute Finesia's plans, then none of this would have to happen.*"

"*You'd kill them eventually,*" Hastina said. "*You'll kill us all if we let you have your way.*"

"And how do you plan to stop us?" Indira said. *"Both of you have been chosen by Finesia to join us, and still you fight, and in doing so you're only making it worse for yourselves. Meanwhile, Alsie, I, and all the other dragonmen and dragonwomen only want to show you a better life."*

I looked at Hastina, and she looked back at me. She no longer seemed to want to murder me. Rather, it seemed I'd found a temporary ally, despite what I'd done.

"Dearie me," Indira said. *"Is that the time? I must be taking my leave. I've got a massacre to be getting on with, and Finesia will be angry if I leave it too late. Feel free to join the party. It will be a ball, I promise you."*

A gust came from right above us, and then I saw shapes move through the darkness. Finesia was shouting something loudly in my mind, but I'd made a promise to Wiggea now that I'd keep her out.

Wiggea had lowered the rifle and was scanning the sky as if wondering what we were looking at. Hastina was also looking up and northwards, with narrowed eyes.

"So, what do we do now?" I asked her out loud.

She looked at me, and the anger hadn't left her face. "Do you promise me, Dragonseer, that you'll do your best to keep Finesia out, even if it might mean losing your own life?"

"I do..."

A trace of smile stretched across her lips, then a cloud of black dust started to rise around her feet. "Wiggea," she said. "Get on Bellroot and follow us. I stationed him to the south."

He raised the rifle and it clicked. "Hastina?" he said, looking at the rising darkness around her.

"This isn't the first time I've done this. I know how to stay in control..."

Wiggea lowered the rifle to his hip, then he saluted, and started to climb the rise. I made to go after him.

"Not you, Dragonseer Wells. I need you here. Now turn into

a dragonwoman, and do so without letting Finesia in. I trust you can do that much?"

"I can..." I said. I transformed into a dragonwoman, and I took no pleasure in doing so.

"Good," Hastina said. "Now be warned, you must do exactly as I say, and if you deviate from the path, you will forfeit your life."

PART IV

"When given a chance to emerge from perpetual shadow, how can you tell if you're stepping out into the darkness or the light?"

— *RASTANO WIGGEA*

19

THE OUTLINES of the waves below stretched into the cool night. To my right, the secicao clouds over the Southlands glowed green slightly, and beneath me, even the *calianai* had some luminescence. In the distance, ahead of me, I could just make out the distant forms of Indira and the black dragons. Still, Yol, the Greys, Velos, and the dragon automatons were nowhere to be seen.

I flew alongside Hastina, wondering why she was letting me accompany her. Just moments ago, she'd wanted to kill me for being a traitor. And I was a traitor. I'd killed Bassalhan, and I didn't doubt that after Hastina had juiced the information she needed out of me, then she'd make sure I saw justice for my crimes. We'd left Wiggea far behind us, and Hastina had tasked him with looking after Bellroot. A standard dragon like him had no chance of keeping up unaugmented, even if he was one of the two remaining coloured dragons left in this world.

"*Now,*" Hastina said in the collective unconscious. "*Do you hear Finesia inside your head?*"

I considered what to say to her. But really, there was no point lying about it. "*Of course, I do... She's always there, nattering away. Don't you?*"

"Then that's the first step you need to take. Stop hearing her..."

"What? That's impossible! Or do you mean don't listen to her? Because that's what I've been doing, not listening to her."

Hastina let out a deafening roar. *"Didn't you say that you'd do exactly what I'd say? Then don't argue back if you want to survive this day. Good. Then, right now do you hear the swishing of the sea, the gentle breeze, the distant call of the bats, the even fainter sound of gulls calling dangers from afar?"*

"Come to think of it I do..."

"Probably only because I drew your attention to them. That is the key. It's not enough not to listen. You've got to focus on not hearing her. Then, she won't have a chance of getting in your head."

This was one of those kinds of frustrating conversations I'd had with Sukina many years ago, when she'd started to train me as a dragonseer. She'd told me to let my worries drift by and focus only on what I could control. She'd urged me to do this when I was in an airless and pitch-dark room, all the while having the spindly legs of a spider automaton crawl over me.

"It's not easy," she'd told me, "yet it's the easiest thing in the world." But now, it seemed, Hastina was talking about a whole new level.

"How can I not hear her?" I asked Hastina. *"She's always going to be there nattering away."*

"I practise this every day. Didn't Gerhaun teach you to do the same?"

"Gerhaun and Sukina taught me to silence my mind..."

"If you're hearing Finesia there, then your mind is not silent."

"What do you mean?"

"Focus on the rhythm of your breath, the beating of your heart. Hear everything that surrounds you and put your full attention into that act. If you do this well, you will hear nothing in your mind."

"But what if I need to think? What if I need to solve a problem?"

"That's what the collective unconscious is there for. All the wisdom of the past and the future is there to guide you. It takes faith to let it be your beacon, and without that faith you are truly lost. Dragonheats, no wonder we've had such problems with you. It doesn't sound like you've ever believed."

I guess I knew this, and I guess I'd experienced these states of super relaxation that she referred to. But I'd not practised getting into one for a while. It really was so easy – but also incredibly easy to forget how to get there.

"I know what to do," I said.

"Do you?"

"Yes..."

It was incredibly simple when it came down to it... I had to focus on being. It wasn't just about clearing my mind. Nor was it about ignoring whatever thoughts I'd had in my head. These cumbersome methods weren't the most effective.

I'd feared the dragon form so much, that I had never even thought to experience actually being a dragon. As I focused, I felt the rolling air brushing the tips of my wings, the burning sensation in my stomach of fire ready to be breathed, the way that the wind howled past me when I entered a soar, and the way it battered my wings when I flapped to keep myself aloft. I could feel the stretch in every single muscle of my wings, hundreds of them designed to keep me aloft. I could feel my sharp teeth rubbing against my rubbery gums and the heaviness of my thick eyelids each time I blinked.

Out here, I could hear so much for miles around me. The cries of distant gulls that Hastina had drawn my attention to, not to mention the call of a foghorn from even further away. The air tasted rich with ozone from after the storm, and the saltiness of the water below whisked through my nostrils as I flew.

"Did you do it?" Hastina asked.

"Yes, I did... But if it's so easy to do, why didn't someone just teach me how to do this in the first place?" I could feel myself getting a little irate. *"So much of this could have been avoided."*

"Calm yourself, Dragonseer Wells... It's one thing to do it once, it's another to practice it day after day, without letting yourself slip. I'm still not convinced you can sustain this, but at least I know you are safe for now."

I took a breath of cool fresh air, and calmed myself as she'd requested.

We kept the same distance from Indira's dragons, as we were in the same form as them and so we could only just match their speed. I soon heard the swishing of wings coming closer in the distance, and I could sense Velos ahead of the black dragons.

With my mind finally empty of Finesia, my bond felt stronger to him, and so I sang a song in the collective unconscious to alert him that he was in danger. None of them knew, it seemed, that Indira was sneaking up on them from behind.

Hastina roared to gain the black dragons' attention, and to also alert the allied dragons of the dangers. I joined in the roar, and then, I heard the Greys start to call out to each other in warning.

"Ah, so you came to join the battle after all," Indira said. *"I'm so proud of the both of you. Now, allow Finesia in, and she can show you the right path."*

"We're doing no such thing," I said. *"We're going to control this form without Finesia's intervention. Aren't we, Hastina?"*

"Don't reveal anything," Hastina snapped back. *"You are meant to be doing exactly what I say."*

"Ah, so now I understand the balance of control," Indira said. *"You were always a strong one, Hastina. Always the one to take charge."*

"You know nothing of my childhood," Hastina said. *"You sent me right into the arms of Colas, and he wasn't a loving guardian."*

"Oh, Colas... Yes, your protector. You know, he couldn't come today, but he's also out there now in a much more perfect form. Finesia chose to reward him, you see. Don't you also want to claim Finesia's rewards?"

I could see the dragons in the distance now. Yol carried on flying straight ahead with the dragon egg in its harness dangling from her claws, while Velos and the dragon automaton guarded her flanks. Velos' armour and the dragon automaton faintly glowed green. Taka, I could see, was safe upon Velos' back, right between Candiorno and Talato.

The rest of the formation had begun to wheel around, the riders with their Pattersoni rifles poised and tracking the enemy. Indira's dragonmen had slowed down. They had their claws raised and their teeth bared. This battle was going to get bloody, and the allied dragons needed our help.

"Hastina, will the Greys still listen to us?" I asked.

"Why not? The songs are the same."

"Good, because they're heading right into a slaughter, and it's better for them not to fight head on. But what will stop the black dragons from latching on to our strategy?"

"Dragonseer Wells, remember what I said about letting the collective unconscious guide you? There's no way to keep these dragonmen out from the channel. If we discuss strategy, then they will hear too."

"Don't listen to her," Finesia said in my mind. *"Now, my acolyte, it's time to join your brothers and sisters in the—"*

That was as far as she got before I heeded Hastina's advice and once again focused on whatever sounds surrounded me, which strengthened my connection to the collective unconscious.

Hastina had already started to sing a song there, causing some of the dragons to flank to the left. I only needed to take the other half to the right to minimise the effects of the onslaught. I could also sense another force looming nearby. I couldn't quite put a finger – or should I say talon – on what this was yet, but I knew it was here to help.

I started to sing as well, and the Greys latched on to my dragonsong in the collective unconscious, not seeming to mind that it was I who sang it. The two flocks hit the dragonmen from the sides, slowing them and allowing Yol to gain distance away from the threat.

The sky became filled with roars and squeals, and one by one I felt my dragon friends – the Greys, not the dragonmen – slip out of the collective unconscious, before they fell towards the pitch-black sea below.

"Such a futile battle," Indira said in our minds. *"How in the world do you plan to win this one?"*

I didn't yet know, and I doubted Hastina did either. I just knew that we needed to buy more time. Because down there, somewhere on or over the Costondi Sea, another presence loomed. It was growing stronger, but I still had no idea what it was.

Several black dragons broke off from the flock, and they started speeding towards Yol, Velos, and the dragon automaton. Some rifle cracks came from the riders on the Greys, but there was no way that bullets from behind would pierce the black dragon's throats.

"Dragonseer Wiggea, we need to go after the breakaways."

"Lead the way..."

I clenched my jaw, not only because of my resolve to win this battle, but because a closed snout would act like a javelin tip, keeping me as aerodynamic as possible. As I had when I had killed Bassalhan, I tucked my wings close to my body and I entered a dive as the cool wind brushed past the narrow slits on the side of my head that formed my ears.

The moon painted silver glow on the crests of the waves as I accelerated towards them. I got as close as I could, before I could hear the rushing of the water, still turbulent from the storm that had raged over here while we were on Gahl.

I waited until I could taste the salt of the sea on my tongue, then I spread my wings. My underbelly brushed against the cool water. I used the momentum to pull myself back into the air and hurtled up towards the black dragons that were still flapping to keep up.

Hastina levelled up beside me, and together – as if sisters of the sky – we filled the scene with our roars. The black dragons didn't deviate from their paths, and so the only way to stop them was to cut in front of them using the extra momentum we'd gained from our dive.

We used our claws and wings as brakes, as we twisted around in the air to face the black dragons. There were four of them in total, still carrying on in a straight line.

"*You have become our enemy,*" one of them said in my mind.

"*We may have been born of your own blood, but Finesia is our true master,*" another said.

"*You are a disappointment to her,*" the third said.

"*No longer her Acolyte Wells, but now her Fallen,*" said the fourth.

They divided into two groups of two, slowing themselves down by bracing their claws and buffeting their wings. At first, I considered letting out a scream in the collective unconscious, but then I remembered it wouldn't disorient any servant of Finesia – this ability was, after all, one of her gifts.

Two of the dragons charged at me. One headed beneath me, while the second had its claws pointed straight at my throat. My muscles tensed, and I braced my wings to take the brunt of the charge.

The dragon I faced tried to snap at my neck with its jaws, but I batted its head away with my cheek. Then, I twisted my neck around and clamped my teeth around the black dragon's throat.

The dragonman crumpled in the air like paper in a rainstorm, and fell into the darkness. A dying rasp came from its open maw.

The remaining dragonman beneath me had caught hold of my leg and was pulling me down with its mouth, while it used its claws to try to pull me towards it. I roared, and then twisted myself upside down, and we entered a tumble towards the water.

It slashed at my face, and I slashed back at it, and then it lunged in with its mouth. I twisted my torso, so it bit into my shoulder instead of my throat, and this opened up its neck for me to sink my teeth into. I ripped out its gullet, and spat it out, sending it plummeting, with the defeated dragon tumbling down behind it.

Hastina had made short work of her assailants, so I turned back to face the battle. Many more Greys had fallen, and the dragonmen now outnumbered them. Claws flew, teeth gnashed, and dragons kept falling from the sky.

I searched around for Indira and spotted her right at the centre, flying towards the back of a Grey. She straddled the dragon from above, digging her claws into its sides. The allied beast tried to fight back and twist his head towards Indira's throat. But his struggles were futile. I soon felt the life pass out of it, as he shuddered, before Indira dropped his limp body into the sea.

"*We sent them on a suicide mission,*" I said to Hastina. "*We can't win this...*"

"*No, you can't,*" Finesia said. "*And I have decided I've had enough of you, my Fallen. Once she has killed—*" It was the doubt, it seemed, that opened my mind to let her in, and so I focused again on what was happening around me.

"*Just hold one more minute,*" Hastina said, and she was hovering in place, watching the battle, seemingly unwilling to help.

"*What? Why?*"

It wasn't Hastina that answered my question, but a shrill electrical pitch that hurt my ears and seemed to make the air shimmer.

It had come from behind me, and I glanced over my wing to see the moonlight glinting off the hundreds of flying brass automatons. They looked like massive crows, except their sharp long beaks looked more like those of sandpipers.

"*Rocs,*" I said. "*These were Cini's machines...*"

"And now they belong to the Masked Regent," Hastina said.

"Great," I said. *"Another enemy to wipe us out."*

"No, you don't understand. The Masked Regent is our ally, and after this is over, I must take you to her so she can decide your fate."

"The Masked Regent?" I asked... *"So we were working with her all along."*

"We are," Hastina said.

"It doesn't matter I guess. We still don't have a chance. These Rocs don't stand a chance against the dragonmen."

"The technology has evolved, I believe, since you last encountered them," Hastina said. *"Now get out of their way."*

The Rocs had missile launchers on their wings. Several years ago, I had had to flee from those missiles on Velos' back, and it was only due to the dragon armour that I managed to escape them. When I saw the missiles scream out of their wings, I was paralysed in shock as one of the missiles headed straight towards me.

"I said to get out of the way!" Hastina snapped, and she launched at me from the side and sent me underneath the missile, missing me by inches.

She let go, the momentum sending me spinning for a moment. I recovered myself in the air, then I turned to watch the missiles heading towards the battle. Dozens of massive explosions lashed out from the missiles, that segued into what must have been thousands of smaller explosions – affecting friend and foe alike.

"This is one thing that Faso Gordoni has been working of as of late," Hastina said. *"The missiles have central intelligences in them, he tells me, that can work out where the throats of any beasts are around them and then target them directly."*

Come to think of it, Faso did mention something by the campfire on Gahl. *"Does it distinguish between the Greys and the dragonmen?"* I asked.

"It doesn't..." Hastina said, and my heart lurched in my chest as I realised what that meant.

"It truly is a massacre..."

"We have no choice..." Hastina said. *"Each of the dragons was prepared to sacrifice their lives to their queen. Their bravery won't be forgotten."*

The billowing clouds of fire subsided, and dragons fell from the sky. A handful of black dragons remained aloft, but no Greys.

Indira hovered in the centre of her much smaller flock. Somehow the other dragonmen had protected her. She roared again, and with it came a terrible scream in the collective unconscious, sending my head spinning.

"You forget, my daughter," she said to Hastina. *"We can make many more of us, while you will only have a limited amount of your precious dragons. This is a victory for Finesia, because for you there is so much more at stake."*

"So long as you don't have any of us dragonseers, you can't use our blood to create them," Hastina said. *"Now, the Masked Regent has enough power in her arsenal to defeat you."*

"The Masked Regent is a fool, just like you, to think she can resist Finesia. The more you draw upon her gifts, the sooner you'll become one of us."

Hastina said nothing, and above us I saw the gatling cannons on the wingtips of the Rocs getting ready to fire. They started to whirr slowly, and Indira roared again, then turned around and left us behind.

Hastina started to lower herself towards the sea. *"Come, Dragonseer Wells,"* she said.

"Okay," I replied. *"But before we go, I just want to ask you one thing. Why did you never tell me that the Masked Regent was our ally? I've been kept in the dark about so much."* I hated to think about the implications of this – about the conspiracy that Hastina and Bassalhan had woven around me. They would have

hidden this information from anyone who might tell me, including Doctor Forsolano, Faso, and my parents.

"*Because,*" Hastina replied, "*Whatever you learned, we suspected Finesia would learn from you soon after. But it seems, from what my mother said, that Finesia knows a lot more about us than we thought.*"

20

I'D NEVER SEEN a dragon carrier so large in my entire life.

The carriers we'd known in Fortress Gerhaun had space enough to carry fifty dragons, in stables below deck with winch-controlled access hatches that could deploy Greys rapidly into battle. But the ship I was looking at had four steam funnels that towered up into the sky and drove the eight massive propellors visible on its stern.

It must have had space for four hundred dragons at least, with a stable large enough to hold a dragon queen just in front of the rearmost funnel. The funnels spewed out green smoke with an eggy tang that, in my dragon form, drew me towards it. But I didn't let the sensation overrule me, as I feared this might allow Finesia slip back into my mind.

The ship glowed slightly green along its outline. Whoever had engineered this juggernaut of a machine had taken a leaf out of Faso's book and used secicao to power the entire thing.

As I approached, I could see Yol's enormous head rising out of the hatch, and I marvelled at the fact that the hull was deep enough to contain her. She had wrapped her body around Gerhaun's and Velos' egg – I was happy to see that it had survived the onslaughts of the previous day and night in one piece. The dragon queen was fast asleep, and I could hear the faint murmurs of her dreams in the collective unconscious.

Other hatches were open as well, and some – but not many – of them contained Greys. I saw Velos in a compartment, looking up at me with anger and disdain for me still boiling inside his belly.

We had entered Yol's protective bubble of the collective unconscious. Now the effects of the cyagora had worn off a little, I could feel what Velos felt once again, and I didn't like it. The dragon automaton was in the stable next to Velos, but I couldn't see any sign of Taka, Faso, Winda, or the two lieutenants. They must have been on board at least one of the ships in this fleet though, because we were right in the centre of the Costondi Sea, with no land around for miles.

Hastina came in to land first, focusing on a landing platform stationed between the two central funnels. She scuffed down against the metal, sending up sparks. I followed her down. I landed just as the black smoke started to rise around Hastina, and she had soon taken her human form.

A guard in a pale-blue coat and neck scarf approached Hastina, carrying her spear. She took this from him, raised it, and pointed it at me with that same angry glare in her eyes. Dragonheats, I was half tempted to lurch forwards and snap the spear in two with my jaws.

"Do it," Finesia said in my mind, then I remembered—

"Dragonseer Wells, what are you waiting for?" Hastina said in my mind. *"Turn human."*

I didn't hesitate. I willed the scales back into me, cringing in pain as I felt my face contort. The black smoke faded around me, and I emerged fully clothed, wearing the same torn shirt and leather trousers I'd been wearing before.

I turned around to talk to Hastina. She looked just as unfriendly as she had been at Fortress Gerhaun. Her glare passed right down the shaft of the spear towards me, and she looked ready to force the spear into my throat if I took one false step. This time, she spoke out loud.

"I told you once, Dragonseer Wells, that you need to pay for your crimes. Now, it is time for you to do that."

I nodded. At least she was still calling me 'Dragonseer', and not 'Servant of Finesia' or anything like that.

Hastina glanced over her shoulder and nodded at the guard. "Did you get the cyagora off Lieutenant Talato?"

"Yes, ma'am," the guard replied, and he reached into the pocket of his coat. He produced that same jar that Talato had had on her person before.

"Thank you... Now hand it over." She held out her hand to the side, while her other kept her spear in place. She wasn't pricking my neck this time, but her stare made me shudder. She'd gone completely cold on me again, but then I didn't blame her. "Hopefully, I won't have to use this, although if I do it will signal the beginning of your death sentence. Now, throw her in the brig."

My heart jumped in my chest. "Dragonseer Wiggea, is this really necessary?"

She scowled at me. "Yol used to sing praises about you. Now she's already considering your execution. Dragonheats, if the Masked Regent wasn't asking for you personally, probably we'd end up doing exactly that. Besides, I'm still not sure what I feel about you. How could I forgive you for killing Bassalhan?"

Her threats were one thing, but what she'd said about the Masked Regent had really taken me aback. I'd only just learned that the Masked Regent was on our side, and now it seemed that there was much more to it than that... "Wait, so you're saying that you're taking orders from the Masked Regent? I thought a human could never call the shots over a dragon queen."

"She isn't exactly 'calling the shots'... And once again, you're asking too many questions. Take this time to prove that you can keep in control and keep Finesia out, and then you might have a chance of surviving this ordeal."

I sighed. "Then please, just answer one more question. My parents... General Sako... Doctor Forsolano... Are they safe?"

Hastina nodded. "They are safe for now, and if you can prove yourself, then there is a chance that you may get to see them again."

"Thank you," I said, and I gave her a slight bow before I let the guards escort me away below deck.

We descended the small staircase leading down from the landing platform, and I heard the familiar cry of a dragon, coming from the south. I peered against the glow of pre-dawn to see Bellroot with Rastano Wiggea on his back. My old dragonelite was still wearing his helmet. He saluted as he came in to land, but I didn't know if his gesture was intended for Hastina or me.

THE SHIP'S brig was one of those rooms you always heard about in stories – particularly if your travels involved sailors, as mine used to. Most of those who heard the stories, and many who told them, would have never even been in one. Details were often glossed over about furnishings and whatnot. Still, every time, the stories said that the brig was the worst room on the ship, located deep in the recesses of its underbelly. This couldn't have been closer to the truth.

The dragonelite took me down a spiral stairwell that wrapped around one of the central funnels. It was already hot at the top of the staircase, and the bottom of it was a furnace – and I say that almost literally.

A brass boiler stood at the bottom of the staircase, propped up against the wall of the funnel. The heat coming out of the sealed glass window at the front of the boiler, seared my skin as I walked past.

It didn't have a hatch on it, and so wasn't one of those old-fashioned boilers that you threw coal into. Rather, a pipe led away from the bottom of this into a raised sealed section beneath a door. The section, I guessed, contained secicao oil, and some more stairs led over this section up to the door which had a valve to seal it airtight.

The guard turned the hatch's wheel, and I wondered for a moment if there would be any ventilation in the room above the steel secicao container. The hatch opened outwards, and the guard pushed me gently inside.

He didn't seem to hate me, as many of Bassalhan's guards had at Fortress Gerhaun. Come to think of it, I'd never seen this man around the fortress, with his long nose, cleft chin, and eyes a little too close to each other. That was when I realised that these guards hadn't just belonged to Bassalhan but had instead been part of a larger organisation.

But if the Masked Regent wasn't heading the organisation, as Hastina had suggested, then who was? I had a feeling I'd find out soon enough.

The room had two metal beds, against opposite walls, with no mattresses on them and a hard pillow for support. The smell in there wasn't too dissimilar from General Sako's breath. Clearly the textured steel plates on the floor and the sealant spread between them, weren't enough to keep the secicao fumes out.

The walls were also made of metal, which conducted the heat from the burner around the room. A bulb swung without a lampshade on the ceiling, flickering together in harmony with the undulation from the sea. There was a tiny shaft in the ceiling for ventilation, but it was nowhere near large enough to provide any means of escape.

"I'll leave it on," the guard said nodding to the bulb. "I can't imagine the nightmares you'll have here without it." He smiled at me, almost apologetically, and then he closed the hatch and sealed it shut from the outside.

I was already sweating profusely. But at the same time, I'd reached the pinnacle of exhaustion. I lay down on the bed –

which was so well heated I had no need for a blanket – and I quickly fell asleep.

I DON'T KNOW how long I'd been passed out before a scratching sound at the hatch woke me. The hatch swung open, and light and heat blasted in from the furnace. I opened my eyes, squinting to make out the two figures standing in the hatch.

The first was the guard, and the second Wiggea in his helmet. The guard wasn't so gentle with my former dragonelite as he had been with me. He threw Wiggea onto the bed opposite me, and then slammed the door shut behind him, without even offering me a glance.

As the guard sealed the hatch, Wiggea looked up at me for a moment, then shyly turned his head away.

"So, they didn't reinstate your duties?" I asked, casually. "I would have thought Hastina would welcome you by her side as a dragonelite."

Wiggea shrugged but didn't turn his head. It seemed that he didn't want to look at me. But then, he had just seen me try to kill his former wife. "I'm a criminal now, just like you... They know what I did at Szuztko Port. I razed a whole town, and the worst part is that I don't remember any of it..."

"But that wasn't you..."

He shook his head. "Where do we draw the line between light and darkness? There must have been part of me in there, just like there must have been a part of you in your head when you did what you did."

I wondered if he was referring to the murder of Bassalhan or my attempted murder of Hastina. I decided that it was better to change the subject. "So, why would they bring you here, anyway? Surely, it's better to keep us apart... Given our former situation..." I almost said, 'relationship', but that word didn't sit right on the tongue anymore.

"There's only one brig on the ship..."

I laughed. "So, they're punishing you by sending you to me. Rastano, you're certainly not the last person I'd want to spend time with right now." I leaned towards him, and I considered taking hold of his hands.

He looked away once again. "You were sleeping. Before I came in."

"I was..."

"Do you need more rest? Because I feel I might need some."

"We can sleep at the same time."

Wiggea reached up to the helmet. "It's just this thing..."

"It's more comfortable than it looks, you know. Because of the padding inside, it feels like a natural pillow."

Wiggea shrugged. "I just thought... Maybe you'll need it."

"Rastano, if you take that thing off, you'll be lost to Finesia again. Then who knows what they'll do to you. Don't worry, I can look after myself. Hastina taught me a few things"

"As you wish," Wiggea said, and he lay down on the bed and turned away from me. In a matter of seconds, I could hear his soft snores.

I sat there, wondering why Hastina would send Wiggea down to the same room. She wanted to punish him, and she wanted to punish me. But really, there was more to this. What she'd said before had sounded like she wanted me to prove that I could keep Finesia out of my head. Perhaps sending Wiggea here was a test.

Without lifting myself from the bed – I didn't want to wake Wiggea – I started scanning the room for peepholes, or any way that the guards could be monitoring us. I found nothing. I knocked quietly on the wall, but it seemed solid. I cupped my hand to the wall and put my ear next to it, but I couldn't hear anyone outside.

I seemed to be getting anxious again, which gave Finesia a perfect cue to get into my mind.

"That dragonman has failed me," she said. *"You can end his life now and make it better for all of us."*

"If I do such a thing," I said. *"Then I will surely be executed on the spot."*

"Do you truly think they'll be able to kill you, my Fallen? You have such little faith in your superior form. Maybe if you trusted me a little more, then you wouldn't have got into this mess in the first place."

"It was you who made me kill Bassalhan, and now you want me to kill the man whom I love. You can give me nothing of value, Finesia. Even your promise of taking a place by your side was a complete ruse."

"I gave you the choice, and you chose not to accept it. You had potential, but it looks like Alsie was meant to be my aide after all. Charth also chose not to accept what I offered him, and so I took matters into my own hands and destroyed his mind. I might do the same with you, my Fallen, unless you can find a way to redeem yourself."

"I would rather redeem myself with the dragon queens and those who have nurtured me over the years, than the mad empress who wishes to destroy the world."

"You know full well that in that way lies death."

"Then I shall not die a traitor at least."

"Whichever way you turn, you will die a traitor… That, it seems, is what you've been destined to become all along."

Every time, I found myself returning to this place. Having conversations with my enemy in my own head, inching me ever closer to becoming a complete monster. Hastina had shown me exactly what to do to keep her out and I was failing at it abysmally. As Finesia said, if I continued this way, then I would end up exactly like Charth – an empty husk lacking mind and soul.

I lay back on the bed, and I focused on what surrounded me. Wiggea's soft snores. The lightbulb that wouldn't stop swinging, creaking and flickering as it did; the ever so slight drafts created by the convection currents; the rocking motion of the ship. The intense heat that seemed to blast out from every wall, as well as the floor and the ceiling. The dry and sour taste of regret in my mouth. The guilt that had nested deep inside my chest, making my lungs feel heavy and my breathing shallow.

I stared up at a point on the ceiling, unable to sleep, given the hardness of this bed. That's when I realised exactly what Hastina was up to. She had sent me to the place she knew that I'd be most uncomfortable, and she'd put Wiggea here to make it even more awkward. It was her version of the spider automaton in the dark room.

Now, I had two options. Either I found a way to accept the discomfort and the circumstances I'd landed myself in, or I broke.

I took a deep breath. I'd come this far, and I wasn't going to make any more mistakes. I closed my eyes and the last thing I focused on was an image of Sukina that had emerged in my head. She wore the same floral dress that she'd worn on the first day that I'd met her at my hometown's – The Five Hamlet's – town hall. She looked at me with soft eyes, and she proffered her hand to me.

"*Come, Pontopa,*" she said in the collective unconscious.

Completely mesmerised and fully immersed in the land of dreams, I took hold of her hand and let her lift me out of the darkness and into the astral world.

Six years ago, on an airship buoyed above the smouldering Pinnatu Crater, an old man named Colas had shot me in the stomach, and I'd almost died. I'd been in so much pain that I'd blacked out, and then I'd encountered Sukina in my mind. She lifted me out of my body then, and she took me across the astral pathways of the collective unconscious to bond with Velos, so he could rescue Faso and provide transport for my rescue.

I guess Sukina appeared when I needed her the most.

Now, thousands of threads of light pierced the darkness in front of me, and I travelled along them, floating through the sky with my hand in Sukina's. She took me along a thread that lifted us above the clouds. We launched ever higher, before the threads underneath me dissipated. The sun had painted a golden glow over the top of the clouds, and I realised I was falling – tumbling through the sky.

"*Sukina!*" I called out, and I searched around for her as the gravity pulled against me. I couldn't find her amidst the panic, and rushing air, but I could still hear her voice in the collective unconscious.

"*Open your arms, Dragonseer Wells. For you are an Ambas-*

sador for the Gods Themselves, remember. A descendant of the great Candida, which makes you part dragon and able to fly."

I had no better options, and after all this was the dream world. Who said that I couldn't fly here? I opened my arms, and great wings buffeted out from between the outstretched pinions that were once my fingers.

My wings weren't black and oily like those of a black dragon, but blue – like Velos' – except they seemed inlaid with sapphire-coloured gemstones. They carried me upwards, and I soared alongside Sukina – who looked exactly like I remembered, except for the fact that she had shiny red wings – inlaid with what looked like ruby and garnet – in place of her arms. We carried on over a fluffy layer of candy floss clouds, before Sukina led us back down again.

"*Where are you taking me, Sukina?*" I asked.

"*To the land of hope and resolution,*" she replied. "*To the place where you know nothing but what you stand for. We shall enter another dream where the light replaces the darkness, and your true self once again begins to shine.*"

The way she spoke about it, I expected to enter a grotto with a glade surrounded by glowing crystals and a ceiling of brilliant blue sky. But instead, we dived beneath the regular cloud layer to find ourselves soaring over roiling brown secicao clouds, stretching out as far as the eye could see in every direction. While the clouds above had had definition with evident shadows, the secicao clouds just looked like a layer of thick brown mist.

"*You brought me to the Southlands? I thought you were taking me somewhere special.*"

"*The beauty you seek is within,*" Sukina said, and she dived down beneath the second layer of clouds.

I followed her, afraid that she would pass out of sight. As soon as I hit the secicao clouds, I gasped for air. I was a human in this dream, not a servant of Finesia. I felt for a moment like these clouds would eat me from the inside out.

"*Do not be afraid,*" Sukina said in my mind. "*You are bodiless here, and you can endure so much more than you can in the real world."*

I looked back at my legs and saw that my skin was shimmering and slightly transparent. It glowed, casting a faint aura through the clouds. It took me a moment to notice that this glow was in fact pushing the secicao clouds away.

Sukina landed in the thick tangled secicao shrub. As her feet hit the ground, a wave of energy pulsed out from her. It looked like a bubble expanding outwards, with all the colours of the rainbow stretched lightly across its surface. The secicao wilted beneath her bare feet, leaving only coarse soil.

I landed next to her, but I didn't produce the same bubble as she did. Still, I had enough power within me for the secicao to wilt around me as well, any branches that touched me crumbling into ash. Both mine and Sukina's wings folded away, to be replaced by our natural arms.

Now that we had landed, it made more sense to speak out loud. "Sukina... Why did you bring me here? What are you trying to prove?"

"I wanted to show you something important..." Her aura cut a path through the secicao as she traipsed through it. I followed her, breathing the fresh air that circled inside the bubble that I'd created.

The path led us to a tree towering high above the secicao. It had an incredibly wide trunk, and the branches of it looked just like tangled shrubs of secicao growing from the ground. It had no leaves, but the secicao clouds seemed to gather even thicker around it – so much, in fact, that I couldn't see the top of it through the murk.

"The Tree Immortal..." I said. "But why?"

"Because all your roads lead to this one point, where you will battle Alsie Fioreletta, either killing her forever or allowing secicao to thrive under Finesia's reign. If you give up your quest now, the world is lost... You must understand that, Pontopa."

"But why me? Why not Hastina? Or even this Masked Regent I'm hearing so much about?"

Sukina looked at me with her kind almond eyes, the brownness of them seeming to reflect the secicao around her. "You still don't get it, do you?"

"Get what?"

"The Tree Immortal... Have you not worked it out yet? Do you even realise what the Tree Immortal is? Do you realise what it can do?"

I shook my head slowly, wondering for a moment if this was just one of those silly dreams that never went anywhere. If so, at least I was finally dreaming something normal again, rather than the stuff that Finesia had been injecting into my head for the last two years.

"Look closer... Examine the bark..."

Sukina twisted to the side so I could see what the dragonheats she was talking about. As I edged past her, the secicao seemed to curl back towards me slightly, but then I took a deep breath and it retreated once again. My chest felt heavier as I approached the tree, and my heart started pounding in my chest. Something awaited me that I didn't want to discover. But at the same time, a part of me had known all along...

I heard his voice in my head. *"Auntie Pontopa,"* he said.

"Taka?"

"Sukina brought you, didn't she? Is she with you now? Can you get me out of here, Auntie Pontopa?"

"I—" I was breathless... Speechless. *"Taka, where are you?"*

He didn't answer. I ran my hands around the rough bark of the tree, feeling my way around the whorls and knots. It had that same sticky feel of secicao resin to it that made my skin itch upon the touch.

My gaze was drawn to a large section of the bark in front of me. At first it didn't look any different to any other part of the trunk, until I noticed it twisting slowly, as if floating on a pool of oil. I squinted my eyes as I tried to make out the patterns. There was something familiar about them... Something I couldn't quite—

Taka's face looked out at me from the tree. It had no colour to it, taking on the same greyness as the rest of the tree. But still I noticed the small nose, the round cheeks, the wide almond eyes just like Sukina's. He blinked at me.

"I'm in the tree, Auntie Pontopa... Finesia told me I had to stay here. She told me this is my destiny. But I don't want to. I tried to escape... Please, get me out Auntie Pontopa. I want to—"

All of a sudden the earth shook, and the next thing I knew, the tree was dashing away from me as if it was being pulled by an invisible steam train. The secicao grew back in its place, and I spun around to see it growing behind me as well. It twisted and writhed until it had formed a circle around me and Sukina. But still her protective bubble kept it out.

"Taka... He gets trapped in the tree?" I asked Sukina. "Is that what you want to tell me? Is that why Alsie wants to lead him away to the Saye Archipelago? How will she do this?"

Sukina took a deep breath and lowered her head. She turned to look at where the Tree Immortal had just been. "My daughter, stolen away from me when I was young. Both her parents of dragonseer blood for the first time in history. Fed Exalmpora to turn him male – causing the cocktail of his blood of the Ambassadors and human blood to mix with dragon blood and secicao, a product of everything that was immortal from the original myths. Thus, the world comes full circle and history repeats, except in much darker shades."

My breath caught in my throat. I had a sense of where this was going, but I didn't like it one bit. "Are you telling me Taka is essential for Finesia's rebirth?"

Sukina tightened her lips. "If his blood was to feed Finesia, then eventually he would become consumed by the device she will use for her rebirth, namely The Tree Immortal."

The words hit me like a steamroller... This didn't make sense. How could a god be born from a boy? This was surely one of those dreams. A vision like all the others I'd been subject to under Finesia's command. She wanted to trick me, but why?

Yet, at the same time I knew this couldn't be one of Finesia's dreams. It was the real Sukina I'd been talking to. It had to be – or at least her spirit in the collective unconscious. The dream just felt too different. Too close to goodness and too distant from Finesia's lust for power.

I gazed at Sukina, and I opened my mouth to ask another question. I still didn't understand the role I played in this.

But no words came out, because she also opened her mouth and as she did, a bright yellow light filled around her. She didn't have her hands in mine anymore, but instead one at her hip and her other held a spear, and she was banging its shaft against the ground.

2 2

"D RAGONSEER W ELLS, WAKE UP!"

"Sukina?" I reached out and I leaned forward. A wave of heat blasted back at me from behind her.

"What did you say?"

I opened my eyes, to see Hastina standing in the hatch, her red hair seeming to blend into the light coming out from the window of the furnace behind.

"I..." I considered how much I should say. "I'm sorry, I was just having a dream."

"I know all about your dreams," she said, and she glanced at Wiggea who was lying over on the bed, now facing me. His eyes were fastened shut behind the glass of his helmet. He smiled as he breathed gently through his lips, as if he hadn't had a chance to sleep like this for years. "I hope they were of the favourable kind..."

I scowled at her. "Dragonseer Wiggea, I promised that I wouldn't let Finesia back into my head. I know what I need to do now to keep her out."

Hastina gave me a curt nod. "Good. Because Yol wants to see you. Trust me, she's going to be a lot harder to convince than me."

I had only met Yol once. This was just after Gerhaun had died, and she had been a lot more hospitable than the other dragon queens who had arrived with her. But still, if she thought I was a foe, I was sure she wouldn't hesitate to tear me to pieces with her sharp teeth.

"Are you going to follow, or are you going to just stand there dawdling all day?" Hastina asked, looking over her shoulder. She had already crossed the corridor and stood at the bottom of the staircase that wound around the funnel, not seeming to mind the heat. "I would have thought you'd be happy to get out of the brig for a while."

I gave her a meek look, then I traipsed out past the guard who had locked me in there. The hatch creaked shut behind me, and I heard him turning the wheel behind me. A cold draft rushed down the stairs at me as Hastina opened the hatch above, sending up goosebumps on my skin.

We emerged underneath a bright blue sky with a thin layer of clouds to the south, where the sun poked through. The warmth from it helped alleviate the cold northern wind, but still, by the time I got to Yol's stable, my teeth were chattering and my feet had gone all numb inside my boots. Hers was the only hatch open out of all the hatches to the stables. Only a few sailors were visible on deck.

A staircase led down one wall into Yol's compartment, and I hoped that she'd invite me inside so I could at least get some shelter from the wind. But she wanted to see me suffer, it seemed, and so she stood, peering over the rim to the trapdoor, a reptilian smile stretched across her golden lips. She had positioned herself to block the dragon egg from sight, as if she thought that I might try to damage it.

"Yol has instructed that this is for you and her privately," Hastina said. "However, stay facing in this exact direction, and know that I have the best sharpshooter in our detachment stationed above deck, with his rifle aimed straight at your throat."

I gulped, and I decided it was better to stay absolutely still. "Very well."

Hastina stepped out of view, and I didn't dare turn my head to watch her go. Rather, I listened to her footsteps against the steel deck plating – staying as aware as I could to every surrounding sound and sensation, so that Finesia couldn't find her way back in.

"*Dragonseer Wells,*" Yol said in the collective unconscious. "*We meet again.*"

I nodded as I bit my lip. "*I wish the circumstances were more favourable...*"

"*I do too...*" Yol lowered her head. "*Every single one of the dragon queens, but one, believes you should be executed...*"

I raised an eyebrow. "*Are you the one who doesn't?*"

"*Unfortunately, no... Believe me, I hold no grudges against you, Dragonseer Wells, and I never have. But as for the servant of Finesia, who I fortunately haven't met... Well, you must have even debated yourself whether extermination is the best option for her.*"

"*Many times... But—*"

"*I know about your dreams,*" Yol butted in. "*Bassalhan had hoped in Fortress Gerhaun that keeping you away from any of your active duties might eventually keep you away from Finesia. It is unfortunate, I admit, no one gave you the training to do so.*"

"*I tried... I really did.*"

"*You can't keep the demons out of your head through trying, Dragonseer Wells. You can only conquer them through belief and resolve.*"

I shuddered, and this time it wasn't just because of the cold. A wind whipped up, this time warmer and from the south, bringing a whiff of secicao with it. I took a deep breath and tried to spot the sniper using my peripheral vision. But I couldn't find him.

"*Well,*" Yol said. "*Is there anything that you might tell me in defense of your case? I never thought it possible, but Dragonseer Wiggea now seems to think you might be redeemable after all.*"

I shook my head, and clenched my fists. Then I remembered myself, and thought it better to control my anger. "*All this time, if someone had just taught me what to do to keep Finesia out. If I'd been given the same training that Hastina and Taka had, then this might not have happened. But no one seems to be taking this into account.*"

Yol exhaled sharply. "*If only it were that simple.*"

"*What do you mean?*"

"*Taka's mind is young and supple, and Bassalhan trained Hastina many years ago, before Finesia had a chance to gain a stronghold in her mind. But before we even had a chance to consider putting you through the same regimen, you had already passed too far over to the other side. We've been careful of who we reveal the techniques we use to, lest Finesia discovers them and finds a way around them. The danger is what could happen if she found a way into Taka's mind, and I fear I'm now revealing too much.*"

I took a deep breath. "*About Taka... I had another dream last night that involves him.*"

Yol moved her head backwards. "*You mean Finesia visited you again? Dragonseer Wiggea showed me your sketches...*"

"*No... It wasn't like that... I didn't see Finesia, but Sukina. I think she might have communicated to me via the collective unconscious. She does that sometimes, though admittedly I've been seeing less and less of her lately.*"

This time, Yol leaned forwards, the thick ridges that made up her eyebrows sloping down towards me. "*Tell me...*"

"*She took me down into the secicao forest, and I saw... She showed me the Tree Immortal with Taka in it.*"

"*But this sounds like it's just Finesia trying to trick you.*"

"*No!*" I said, and I think I might have uttered it out loud as well. "*This was different. Finesia's dreams always had a certain quality. I don't know how to describe it, but I always felt dirty when I woke up from them. It was as if I'd been drinking the night before and had hardly got any sleep at all.*"

"But what has Taka got to do with the Tree Immortal?"

I looked away. *"I don't know... I mean I do have an idea, I'm just not sure."*

"Enlighten me..."

"Yol Tinash, have any of you worked out why Alsie Fioreletta and Finesia want Taka so much? They wanted to take him on the migration, but even Taka couldn't understand why he was so important to them."

Yol leaned in again, her great neck looking stretched to its full extent. If she wanted to, she only needed to snap her jaws once like a jungle flytrap, and she could swallow me whole. Fortunately, she seemed too intrigued to want to do this. *"Go on..."*

"Sukina told me something in this dream. She told me that Taka was needed for Finesia's rebirth in the Tree Immortal, and that the Tree Immortal will eventually consume him. I just don't know what any of this means, if it means anything at all..."

"I see..." Yol Tinash said, then she turned her head so I was looking into her yellow faceted eye. She studied me for a moment with it, her gaze rolling from my left eye to my right, and then back again.

"Does it mean anything?" I asked. *"Or do you think it's another trick by Finesia? Because I'm sick of this, Yol... If I'm so damaged that I'm going to end up contributing to the destruction of the world, I give you permission to end my life now."*

My heart pounded in my chest as I said those words, and the last of them came out much slower in the collective unconscious than I intended. But I was ready to die if I had to. The monster inside me had done enough damage, and she had to be silenced one way or the other...

Yol pulled her head back, and she closed her eyes. On the furthest funnel from me, I saw something glinting in the light – the rifle. I took a deep breath, then I closed my eyes, ready to enter the next world.

"*I believe you,*" Yol said. "*Or at least I think this might mean something You know, there is someone who might be able to help.*"

Footsteps clanked along the deck, and Hastina soon emerged and stood next to me. "You called for me, ma'am," she said out loud.

Yol opened her eyes and looked up at her. The dragon queen also spoke out loud in a deep, bellowing voice. "Hastina, order the guards to open the hatches for Velos, Bellroot, the dragon automaton and an escort of twenty Greys. We need to leave in the next ten minutes."

My eyes went wide. "We're going somewhere?"

"We are," Yol said. "We're going to Slaro. Because what you just told me is going to be of great interest to the Masked Regent, indeed."

PART V

"In times of turmoil and times of strife, it's too easy to become so focused on what you have lost that you neglect to acknowledge what you have gained."

— PONTOPA WELLS

23

THE MAGAZINES HADN'T QUITE PAINTED an accurate picture of how much secicao had spread through the country of Tow. It grew in patches, suffocating the life out of the surrounding forests. Even though it was now spring, there were few leaves to be seen on any of the trees and, when viewed from above, the way the brown secicao clouds stretched across the land created a mottled, tortoiseshell facade.

I rode on Velos, with Candiorno behind me, and Talato in the seat at the back of the dragon armour, keeping guard with her rifle in case any dragonmen attacked from the east. Hastina was on Bellroot, flying him close to Velos. She kept glancing over her shoulder at Wiggea who rode on Bellroot's rear, probably to check that he hadn't removed his helmet.

Taka rode upon Yol, and a flock of ten Greys separated us from the dragon queen. The dragon automaton flew on Yol's right, Faso and Winda astride it as before. Yol held the harness with the dragon egg in her claws, and I wondered what it was about Slaro that would make it safer than anywhere else. I guess when we finally marched into the palace, the lookalike would step down and Taka would take command of Slaro's soldiers, to help us fight the war.

We carried on across Tow this way and, as I looked down in horror at how much the land had changed, I longed for my former home. I can't express how much I missed the taste of bacon and eggs lingering on my tongue as I sat at the kitchen table in my parent's farmhouse, while Mamo prepared the secicao and Papo sat with his feet up, reading the Tow Observer. Somehow, I doubted I'd ever see times like those again.

Eventually, the capital came into view. Slaro looked completely different to both what I had expected and how I remembered it. The first sign of the city always used to be the brown smog, created from burning too much secicao to supply the secicao houses that fuelled workers with the much-needed energy to get through the long workdays.

Now, strangely, there was no smog. Rather, some invisible force seemed to be pushing away the patches of secicao clouds closing in from the plains beneath the Caprio mountains. We were beneath the snow line now, and the air coming off those mountains tasted unusually fresh.

"Talato, have you ever been to Slaro before?" I asked.

"No, ma'am... Why?"

"It's just... It's not usually like this. Do you know if another dragon queen is stationed here?"

"From what I heard, all five remaining dragon queens, excluding Yol, are stationed in the Southlands. But maybe I've not been told everything."

"That's quite possible," I said, sucking the cold air coming down from the mountains through my teeth. This bubble of protection around Slaro was much larger than Gerhaun, or even Bassalhan, had managed to provide around Fortress Gerhaun. The factories scattered across the city had also stopped producing smoke, and I wondered from where the army must be getting its weapons.

"I have heard rumours that the dragon queens will move north soon," Talato said. "Really, I don't know the details of this, though."

That got me curious, but I didn't ruminate upon it for too long, as I needed to get ready to land.

The lack of smog allowed me to see Cini's former palace from further away than I would have normally been able to. The towers on it didn't point upwards, but rather in a fan-like arrangement. They were tapered at the tips to represent the hands of a clock. King Cini II had apparently designed it this way to symbolise the necessity for industry and working hard around the clock. Hundreds of Greys had taken nest around the palace. Designated stables had been built for them in open-ceiling stone stables scattered around the main complex.

The airships usually stationed here now hovered in the distance, keeping the courtyard free for our arrival. Those familiar pale-blue suited guards had replaced the redguards of King Cini's reign.

Yol flew another circle around them, watching the ground below as if searching for possible dangers. She still had the dragon egg dangling from her talons, and I wondered what she planned to do with it. A channel opened up from Yol for Hastina, Taka, and I in the collective unconscious. *"This is where I shall take my leave."*

"You're leaving us?" I asked. *"I thought we needed a dragon queen here to help support the Greys and keep the threat of secicao out."*

"It is not my place, but the Masked Regent's, to decide how much to reveal to you... for now, know that the city is safe."

"But what about the egg? What are you going to do with that?"

"It will stay here in a safe place. But I must go there now."

She circled around one last time, then headed towards the Caprio mountains. Velos landed and then craned his head up to watch Yol go. There was a certain longing in his expression, as if in Yol he saw part of Gerhaun. I reached out to stroke him on the neck, and now with Finesia out of my mind he didn't seem to have any problem displaying affection. He crooned gently, and then he lowered his back so Lieutenant Talato could crawl down the ladder on the dragon armour. I followed her down, and I put my hands on my hips and took in an immense breath of fresh air.

Hastina also dismounted, holding her spear but this time pointing it at no one. Neither she, nor Taka made eye contact with me. Talato stayed close to me, but even Faso, Winda, and Candiorno lingered in the distance by their dragon automaton, as if even they had finally decided I couldn't be trusted.

"Everyone must stay here," Hastina said, turning to look at all the soldiers, officers, and scientists in turn. "The Masked Regent wants to see the three of us dragonseers alone. For different purposes, I'm sure."

Only Talato seemed fazed by this, and her lips displayed a slight grimace. Hastina seemed to notice and snapped her head around to look at her. "Is that understood, Lieutenant Talato? You may remain loyal to Dragonseer Wells, but you are no longer her guard."

"Yes, ma'am," Talato said, and the expression vanished from her face.

Hastina nodded and turned towards the stone steps that led down from the airfield. She marched on, and it was more than obvious that she wanted me to follow.

THE PORTRAITS of King Cini's family, the taxidermies from their hunts, and the opulent golden statues had been stripped from the corridors of the palace. Rather, this place had gained a certain institutionalised look, with nothing on the grey stone walls at all except for patches of paint, in places.

When I had last walked these corridors, I had been entirely drunk on Exalmpora for the most part. So, I barely remembered the way to the throne room, yet Hastina and Taka seemed know it well.

We passed through the great mahogany double doors. Across the hall, in front of the throne, the Masked Regent stood holding her sceptre. Next to her stood Taka's lookalike, wearing the same clothes as Taka, except that the lookalike's hadn't been torn during his travels. The room smelled cleaner than I remembered it, as the palace and everything in Slaro had once stank of secicao smog. Now the fresh air from the hunting grounds outside the palace swept through the northern windows, redolent with the scent of pine.

The Masked Regent's appearance was even scarier than her pictures displayed in the magazines. Her dragon mask looked so much like the face of one of Alsie's dragonmen, that I wondered if she was actually one herself. It seemed to merge seamlessly into the loose black cape that hung off her shoulders down to the floor, trailing behind her as she walked toward us.

"I heard you had troubles along the way," she said. Despite her appearance, her voice came out pleasantly soft and had a strange air of familiarity to it, though I couldn't work out why. I also couldn't tell at first who she was addressing as I couldn't see her eyes through the mask.

"We did, ma'am," Hastina replied. "It seems your Rocs are in good working order. With enough of that technology, we might be able to hold off a siege here. Perhaps, if all goes according to plan, we may even be able to win this war."

The Masked Regent shook her head. "So long as secicao spreads across this land, then it will eventually choke our supply lines and the men who support our operations. Until today, I thought civilisation was on its last legs. But Yol brought news to Cralanein that has given us hope again."

"Cralanein?" I asked. "Who's Cralanein?"

Hastina and the Masked Regent both ignored me. Instead, the Masked Regent stepped up and put her hand on Taka's head, but she didn't rub it as if afraid that she'd mess up his neatly coiffured haircut. "It's good that you finally made it, Dragonseer Sako. But as you know, from this day you must resume your role as Prince Artua. We shall meet with the press, and we shall set a date for the coronation for next week."

Taka nodded, then he bowed by lowering one knee to the floor.

"Stop that at once," Hastina said to him, and she spat the words out sharply enough that Taka would hear them but quietly enough that the guards at the door wouldn't. Then her voice came in the collective unconscious, keeping me in the channel as well. *"Remember what we talked about? The guards must believe you are in charge now that you've come of age, even though the Masked Regent will still make the decisions around here."*

He was fourteen years old, which through tradition was old enough for a king to become a monarch, even if he had to wait two years until he could marry an accompanying queen. Taka lifted himself up promptly, and an embarrassed smile played across his lips... *"I'm sorry,"* he said.

I exhaled a slow breath. The Masked Regent turned her head towards me, and I tried to see her eyes through the black pools in the mask. "Dragonseer Wiggea, why don't you take the boy to his quarters. Quite a lot has changed, my young prince, since you lived at the palace. But I'm sure you'll still find your chambers suitable for our needs."

"I thank you graciously," Taka said, but it didn't come out naturally. He still had a lot of work to do on this king thing.

Hastina led him out through a door at the back of the room. It creaked as it shut. The Masked Regent then addressed the rest of the throne room in a louder voice. "If you will please excuse us, I have need for a private conversation with the young dragonseer."

Both guards by the door saluted in unison, and they also left the room. The doors closed behind us, and I was left alone with this unfamiliar, yet at the same time familiar, masked figure.

I scanned her body for any trace of weapons. A bulge underneath her robes that might clothe a sword. A flared hem of her dress that might indicate daggers hidden in her garters. A knot in the folds at her hip where a pistol or blunderbuss might be concealed. But the robes flowed naturally over her gentle curves as she moved even closer towards me.

She put her hands on my shoulders, and this time when she bent her head, I knew she was looking at me. "I've been so long in hiding that I thought I'd never get to see you. Particularly when the news came about Bassalhan, I thought you'd been lost to the void."

I frowned at her and wanted to back away from her. This just didn't feel right. "Who are you?" I asked, "and what do you want?"

She sighed, then she put her hands to her mask and lifted it off. A mass of blonde curls sprang out of it, framing intense blue eyes and firm cheekbones. She looked just like me, except with a thinner nose and more wrinkles around the eyes.

I blinked in disbelief. This couldn't be true. It had to be some kind of trick...

"I say it again. Who are you?"

"What do your eyes tell you? What does your heart tell you?"

I looked away. "No," I said, my breath catching in my throat. "You're dead. Doctor Forsolano transferred me out of your womb into my birth mother's. Then my mother and father... They saw you die."

The woman narrowed her eyes. "All the while, a man called Colas loomed in the nearby woods, waiting. It was he who had shot me in the first place, but he'd fed me Exalmpora first... Cralanein's blood, it seems, sealed your fate."

I blinked in disbelief. Was I still dreaming? Another dragonwoman who had hidden herself from history. But could she be any different from Alsie or Indira? Could she have truly stayed all this time in the light?

"Mother?" I asked.

24

TEARS FLOODED TO MY EYES, and I let them flow, warming my face for a moment. Finesia tried once again to enter my mind, but she had no place here. I wouldn't allow anyone to interfere with this sacred moment, and especially not her.

As the tears intensified and a cold draft whipped through the throne room windows, sending a chill up around me, that emotion quickly became replaced with another. I couldn't describe it as anger, nor could I describe it as confusion. Rather, a deep-rooted part of me wanted to fight back against the chaos this development could cause in my life. I had parents, and I didn't need a new one.

"All this time, you've hidden in shadows," I said. "While two good people raised me, whom I'm proud to call my parents. Now you come here, claiming to be my mother. What right have you to that title?"

"I make no pretences. You can probably imagine in this world how my absence from your life was necessary. Most importantly, I needed to ensure you stayed safe from the regime that was hunting you down. I also needed to close off any attachments I had, to reduce the risk of letting Finesia in."

I took a deep breath. "You leave this world for dead, and then think you can just come back into my life? Now, it seems like you're orchestrating everything. I guess you also ordered Hastina and Bassalhan to take control of Fortress Gerhaun. Do you know how they imprisoned me there? They took everything I had away from me, and Hastina was ready to kill me, no doubt at your command...."

"No one could have predicted what you would do to Bassalhan," she said shaking her head slowly. "I'd hoped that Finesia hadn't grown too strong in your mind. I wanted to find a way back for you, believe me. But then I feared I'd let you travel too far into the abyss."

I clenched my teeth. "Then it was you who's been manipulating me behind closed doors. Let me guess... It was also you who tutored Hastina Wiggea and taught her how to keep Finesia out. Why didn't you give me the same training? All this could have been avoided..."

Her eyes were studying me, but there was no sign of compassion behind them. There was no sign of tears. This was what you had to do to keep Finesia out, it seemed – become an empty shell.

A cawing sound came from one of the windows, and I turned to see a crow perched on the low stone sill. It bent down to pick up a centipede in its grey beak, and it lifted itself back into a flock that had gathered outside.

"Tell me once again about your dream," my mother said. "Because it sounds like you have discovered a key that we've been searching for all along. All this time, who'd have thought that it was nestled inside of you... But who put it there, I wonder... Finesia or the Gods Themselves?"

I looked back at her, my eyes now a little dryer. Whoever this woman was, she wasn't my mother. She might have been it by blood, but not in heart. Her history, it seemed, had taken any trace of what she was out of her.

"*So, the plot thickens,*" Finesia said in my head. "*Here I am, still nestled in your emotions. You cannot escape me. None of you can. Even the lady that you see before you – the one you know to be your mother – she will eventually bend to my cause. You will see soon enough...*"

Dragonheats, I'd let her in. I blinked, and then I focused on the window again. The crows had left the courtyard outside, and a beam of sunlight filtered through, the dust dancing and glistening within its radiance.

"Dragonseer Wells," my mother said. I looked back at her. I wasn't going to let my concentration slip. I wasn't going to tell her now that Finesia had found her way into my head again. She could never discover how imperfect I was.

"You can call me by my first name, at least..."

"Your birth name might be Pontopa, but doesn't your position as a dragonseer fill you with pride? You can find your way back to being one... I wish I'd had a chance to have taught you how all along."

"Why didn't you?" I asked, and I folded my arms under my chest.

She ignored my question. "The dream," she said.

"At least tell me your name, because don't think for a moment I'm going to start calling you mother."

"Others simply call me the Masked Regent," she said.

"Your name..."

She paused. "My name by birth is Valpeonia. You may call me that if you wish. Now... The dream?"

I inhaled a thin breath. "I saw Sukina," I said through tightened lips. "It wasn't like the other dreams."

"I know..." She was staring deeply into my eyes. But it wasn't a look of love. It was one of focus. One that wanted to study me as if I was a specimen in a lab.

"How do you know?"

"Because there is no trace of any darkness when you recall it.

You can tell if you look close enough. There's always a slight green glow in the irises before a transformation or whenever Finesia speaks inside one's mind... It comes from accessing the part of your brain where Finesia resides, or at least that's what our scientists' studies have shown. Hastina reported she saw that in you the first time she met you. But then, she wasn't completely sure."

"Really?" I asked, raising my eyebrows.

"Really. Now, skip the details, and tell me exactly what Sukina said, and if you can recall it word by word, that would help immensely."

I shook my head. How could I forget... A sigh filled my chest as I centred myself once again. If Valpeonia could help me, I had to tell her all. I recollected everything I remembered about the dream, without missing a single detail. The images from it flashed through my mind so vividly that I felt as if I was reliving it once again.

Once I had finished, my mother looked towards the doorway with her hand on her chin. She lowered her head as if in thought. I waited, frustration brimming in my chest.

All these years apart spent wondering who my mother had been. Had she been a good person like Sukina, or a monster like Alsie? I'd always assumed the former, but now with the way she lacked emotion, I wasn't sure she was either. More, she behaved like a non-entity. Like a cog in a machine.

She turned back to me. "Pontopa Wells... There's something I wish to share with you. All these years I had a mentor. In the palace, we protected each other, while I hid in the shadows, and she endured the tortures of the years. Then, after Cini's death, we were both free to throw off our veils. Mine was of camouflage, hers of thorns. Now come, she wants to meet you..."

"Who?"

My mother had already turned and was walking towards the windows, and her hands worked their way around the wall. She touched something that was loose there and ended up pulling out a loose stone. Behind it lay a small circular wooden board with four indents in it that looked like sabres arranged in a propellor arrangement. I recognised the symbol immediately. This used to be King Cini III's insignia.

"A secret passage?" I asked, and this time I said it out loud. "I thought these things only existed in novels?"

My mother reached out underneath the robes at her neck and pulled out a talisman. It had the same design except this time the sabres were embossed rather than carved into the hardwood.

"It's an intricate mechanism," she said. "Apparently one of Faso Gordoni's inventions when he used to work for the king." She put the talisman to what I realised was the lock, and I noticed it had a tiny handle on the back. Holding the talisman in place with a delicate finger, she turned the handle with two fingernails.

"What? So, Faso knew about this passageway all along?"

My mother shook her head. "He only designed the lock, I believe, and the blueprints for the door. He didn't install any of it. But then, the king's inventor rarely did the grunt work in those days."

There came a click, then a shrill whistle coming from the window, and I jumped before I saw some steam rushing past it. Cogs started to grind from behind the walls, and the stonework slid to the side, blocking out the light coming from the windows. In place, it revealed a passageway leading to what looked like a cavern below. She removed the amulet from the lock, and a couple of oil lanterns flickered to life by the entrance. A line of lanterns then followed suit, turning on one after the other and pushing away the purple shadows with a warm orange light.

"Before I go anywhere," I said. "I want you to tell me where you're taking me."

My mother looked back to me, and a faint smile traced her

lips. "I've mentioned her twice now, can you not remember who it was?"

I put my hands on my hips. "I'm guessing Cralanein. But you didn't answer me earlier when I asked who she is."

Valpeonia cocked her head like a crow. "Cralanein," she said. "Is the oldest of all the dragon queens."

25

As we traversed the cavern, with the air getting colder the deeper we went and the air pressure pushing against my eardrums until they ached, the puzzle pieces started to fit into place.

We soon entered a chamber with vats of silver liquid bolted onto the cavern walls. The torchlight passing through them, made the silver blood glow from within like moonlight. I could feel my blood coursing through my veins as I stared at one vat, entranced by what bubbled within.

"It was under the palace all along," I said. "The Exalmpora…"

Valpeonia looked up at the vat I was looking at. Then she shuddered and looked away. There must have been around four gallons of liquid in that one container. I counted thirty vats in this room, all containing around the same capacity of Exalmpora.

"Cini never knew of this place," she said. "These vats filled up with the blood that Colas extracted from Cralanein. And with her blood kept constantly drained, Cralanein's strength became limited. She could create a weak protective bubble of the collective unconscious that extended to the inner courtyards of the palace, but nothing more... I've wanted to get rid of it, but we've not worked out a way to dispose of it safely yet."

I reached out to touch the vat, and I started to salivate. I wanted the Exalmpora. I wanted it more than anything in my world. It was, after all, my lifeblood. It fuelled who I was – an all-powerful dragonwoman, destined to inherit the world...

"That's it my darling," Finesia said. *"Smash the glass and drink it up. Think of the power you could hold. Think of what you could become."*

I felt the scales pushing through my skin. Growing teeth pushed into my gums. My muscles started expanding, and the skin around my shoulder blades started to tear.

But Valpeonia yanked me back with strong arms. Her voice rasped in my ear, much more gravelly than before.

"Don't make it a mistake for me to have brought you here, Dragonseer Wells. This place is a work of monsters. You mustn't turn into a monster yourself."

She pulled me further down the corridors, through an open iron door. She closed this with a bang, and bolted it behind me. With her arms fastened around my waist, she waited for me to stop struggling.

"Kill her..." Finesia said in my head. *"You don't need a mother if you choose to spend your rest of your life by my side. If you can prove yourself, I might consider reinstating your future position by my side."*

But there was something about the coolness of the cavern, and the faint clicking of the bats within this lair. Those sensations reminded me what I was meant to be doing. I wasn't a dragonwoman. I was Pontopa Wells, a dragonseer and a good person.

There was still light within me, and I had to battle to stop that light going out.

Once I had pushed Finesia out of my head, I felt a source of the collective unconscious drawing me closer. It pulled me deeper into the cavern, much like the Exalmpora had pulled me before. Except this time, the emotions attached to the sensation weren't ones of craving, but rather of belonging, as if what loomed further behind the shadows would complete me.

The cavern passageway narrowed into a ledge that hugged the wall on our left-hand side. On the right, a sheer drop suddenly plunged into the darkness.

I soon saw Cralanein sitting on a larger ledge that cantilevered off from our one. An orb-like shape in front of her belly glistened in the torchlight. As I got closer, I saw this to be the golden egg that Gerhaun had laid. I could sense the baby dragon queen inside, waiting patiently for her time to emerge into this cruel and bitter world.

The torches ended at the edge of Cralanein's ledge. Beyond this, the cavern seemed to curl around back into open darkness, and I could hear the wind howling from beyond it.

"The passageway leads out underneath the foothills of the Caprio Mountains," Valpeonia said. "King Cini completely closed this off to the public so nobody would discover his secret. Upon his death, one of the first things I did was open it up again."

I nodded. That must have been the route Yol took to deliver this dragon queen egg. I just hoped she was right that this would be the safest possible place for it. Because the last thing I wanted was for the baby dragon queen perish due to decisions made beyond her control.

My attention returned to the dragon queen, who looked very different to the other dragon queens. Cralanein lacked muscles around her chest, arms, and legs and it seemed as if she was almost supporting herself on sticks. Her wings had been severed down to the base, making her look like one of those dinosaurs that got reconstructed in museums. The sockets where her eyes should be looked sealed with some kind of metal wire. Her scales also didn't shine like the other dragon queens I knew, but were tainted with a green patina.

"It's horrible," I said. "This was the work of Cini?"

"No." Valpeonia shook her head, looking into the darkness. "This was always Finesia's work. Say what you want about Cini, but he was always a puppet working for Finesia without ever knowing. Her puppeteer – namely Alsie Fioreletta – made sure that he never really knew what went on beneath his palace. He might have known about the existence of the Exalmpora, but if he had realised a dragon queen lived behind the iron door, he would surely have ordered her executed."

"So how did you manage to stay under cover?" I asked.

"Through an awful lot of stealth... Alsie Fioreletta never knew of my existence, and without Bassalhan's training, this would never have been possible."

"You mean to say you worked for Bassalhan first?"

"I worked for Bassalhan for a while," Valpeonia said. "Then I worked in the palace as the king's personal seamstress. I had to straighten my hair every day, so no one had any idea that I was here under ulterior motives. Because if they saw that I shared your natural curls, then I'm sure at least Alsie would have worked out the connection pretty fast."

She reached out to brush her fingers through my curls.

"There were so many spies working on Cini's staff," she continued, "that I knew I could trust no one. I took a holiday when I heard that you and Sukina visited the palace, because I didn't want to risk anyone recognising the similarity between us. It was torture knowing you were so close, but it would have endangered so much to have made myself known."

Tears were pushing at the corners of my eyes, and I wiped them away because I didn't want to be sobbing before I introduced myself to this dragon queen. I wondered why she hadn't reached out in the collective unconscious yet. I could sense her, and I guessed she could sense me. But this connection to her was different. I just couldn't find a voice to latch on to.

Valpeonia walked up to Cralanein and touched her palm to her shoulder. "Only through touch can you talk to her. She uses most of her focus now to create the bubble that helps keep Slaro safe."

I touched Cralanein lightly on the chest, and then a jolt of energy surged through me—

I saw the horrors she'd endured over the years. The pain as the electric saw bit into her wings. The whirr of the steam powered pump that extracted gallons and gallons of dragon blood from her, making her feel constantly faint.

The heavy beating of her heart as Alsie taunted her, calling her worthless, a dying breed, saying how all the dragons Cralanein had spawned were blights upon the planet, and how Alsie's lover, Cini, was exterminating them all.

Her roars and the headache when Colas Lamford gouged out her eyes, and then sewed up her eyelids with steel wire and a diamond tipped pin. All she wanted was to wither away into the earth, until she remembered that she had another purpose.

"*Dragonseer Wells,*" she said in the collective unconscious. "*Bassalhan was wrong and Gerhaun was right. You are truly noble...*"

I frowned at her. "*You've only just met me...*"

"*But you've just seen the horrors of my life flash before your eyes, and you reacted with pure empathy. The truth about you is evident. I can see that you have struggled within.*"

My throat tightened and I swallowed a pocket of air that had got trapped there. There was something about this dragon queen which made me want to reveal all. It had been the same with Gerhaun when I'd first met her. "*I never wanted to become a monster... I never wanted to let Finesia do what she did...*"

"*Most monsters are only skin deep,*" Cralanein replied. "*And though that skin might thicken and harden over many years, rarely won't there still exist a person underneath it all... Hold on to that person, and you can never become a true monster. As long as you're redeemable, there still is light.*"

"*But everything I've done? I've massacred. I've killed a dragon queen... Yet you're not angry... You're not afraid...*"

Cralanein let out a chuckle in the collective unconscious. "*There's little left in this world that can scare me, believe me...*"

I smiled, faintly. Then I realised that it was the first time I'd smiled in an awfully long time. "*What must I do?*" I asked. "*How can I stop Finesia winning this battle inside my mind?*"

Cralanein leaned into me. It seemed to take an awful lot of effort, and I felt a slight shimmer in the collective unconscious.

She got so close that I could feel her hot breath against the skin of my face. I wrinkled my nose, at first, because I thought I smelled death and decay. But then I noticed that there was something else underneath it all. A warm, familiar smell of the sulphurous fire burning within her – the one that kept dragons like her alive.

I knew I couldn't spend much longer with her. As Valpeonia had said, she must have been using an awful lot of concentration to create this bubble that protected the city.

"*Never forget who you are,*" she said. "*I can teach you mind tricks on how to keep focused on other things. Your mother and Hastina can do the same. But it comes down to knowing your very centre of being. Whenever you are solely aware of that, nothing else inside your mind can touch you.*"

"*My centre?*" I shook my head. "*I don't know who I am. I mean I thought I did when I was young, then I met Velos, then Gerhaun, and then so many more people... I changed so much...*"

"*You may have taken on many personalities; you may have worn many masks,*" Cralanein said. "*Haven't we all? But who are you underneath it all? Negate thought. Negate emotion. Negate any illusions you have of your identity. What remains is the place inside you from where you sing your dragonsongs. It's the only link you have to the collective unconscious. Guard that centre because, at the end of the day, it's the only thing you own. It's your essence – who you truly are.*"

"*I know what you mean. I think...*"

"*You think?*"

"*No, it's more than that. I know...*"

"Of course you do…"

"But still, I need to ask. This dream I saw with Sukina. What could it all mean?"

"It reveals another identity, I suppose," Cralanein said. *"Another façade; another puzzle for a busy mind. It may be another mask that you will need to wear, another shift in the substance that houses your being as you traverse the collective unconscious."*

"My destiny?"

"Oh, all this talk of destiny is such nonsense. There is never an end to the journey. There are only a series of steps to take to the next station along the line. Even after death, you will still travel – both in the collective unconscious and in other people's minds."

Suddenly, Cralanein raised her head and sniffed at the air. She turned towards the other end of the ledge where we'd entered through the iron door. *"Now, it seems trouble approaches. Return to the real world, Dragonseer Wells. You will discover your task soon enough."*

I had been so immersed in this conversation, that I'd forgotten my own body, my own existence… But that, I guess, is what Bassalhan had wanted to teach me. All this was transient. I felt something cold upon my shoulder, and I looked to see that Valpeonia had placed her hand there.

Someone was scurrying along the ledge towards us. On closer examination, I saw it to be Hastina, with her red hair whipping behind her, glowing amber at the tips. Using her spear as a walking pole. She reached us quickly, then she bowed down on one knee in front of Cralanein.

"Dragonseer Wiggea, what is it?" Valpeonia said. "You know not to disturb the dragon queen unless absolutely necessary."

Hastina's face was plastered in sweat and her hair looked dishevelled. Her hand was shaking as she held the spear, the shaft now pointing upwards. "I'm sorry, ma'am. I wouldn't have come if this wasn't urgent… But it's Rastano… He…"

"Spit it out, for dragonheats sake. I thought we had him under control?"

"So did I... But Charth Lamford was here too. He attacked the guards, bashed open Wiggea's cell, took off his helmet. I rushed down to attack him, and I battled him. But he was too strong, ma'am. Then Alsie Fioreletta herself marched through the throne room, killing every single guard on the way."

My heart lurched in my chest. "Taka..."

Hastina's head snapped towards me. She frowned and squinted her eyes in accusation. But then, she seemed to remember herself, and her face showed a hint of apology instead. "Yes... Taka... They took the boy, Dragonseer Wells."

Valpeonia glanced back at Cralanein, then she took two steps forward. "Then our next action is clear... We need to go after them at once."

26

THE STENCH of blood and death in the air hit me first, before I even had a chance to register the sight of the throne room. I took a moment to look around.

The two royal guards lay slumped by the door, trails of blood scratched across their chests, and another trail leading from each of them towards the throne. Other guards lay out in the corridor behind them, and a serving maid lay spread eagled on the red carpet which stretched across the centre of the room.

The throne itself had been toppled, and one pillar had been completely obliterated – the bas-reliefs that used to adorn it smashed to dust and debris. The door that led to Taka's chambers had been torn off its hinges.

My stomach heaved, and I keeled over, almost throwing up. I felt Finesia starting to surface in my mind, but I remembered what Cralanein had said. To find my centre...

I located that part of me deep inside, and I remembered who I was underneath it all. That was enough to ignore her, at least for now. I needed an anchor, so I summoned an image of a blue flame burning at the back of my head where I imagined my centre to be. This turned out to be an excellent way of keeping Finesia out.

I turned back and studied the clawed trail of blood that led from one of the guards at the door towards the throne itself, before disappearing. A draft whipped up from above, and I looked up to see the chimney up there. Alsie Fioreletta had used that as an escape during my last sojourn at this palace, and so I made a mental note of it, thinking it might prove useful. It was curved slightly, so as to protect against the rain, and so I couldn't see the open air from here.

Faso was standing by the doorway together with Lieutenant Candiorno, Lieutenant Talato, and several of the pale-blue suited guards. Winda, surprisingly wasn't with him.

Faso, seemed to notice exactly who was in charge. He strode forwards and addressed Valpeonia directly. "Who the dragonheats are you, and what can you tell me about what's happened to my son?"

Valpeonia lowered her head, and she pointed to her mask that now lay shredded by the throne. "I am the Masked Regent... I'm sure you know who that is. Given I'm in charge of the palace and the operations here in Slaro, that also makes me your employer, Faso Gordoni."

Faso turned up his nose. "Well, you don't seem to be doing a good job of that." He turned his gaze from her to me, and his eyes went wide. "Wait a minute..."

I shook my head. "Faso, we don't have time for this. The Masked Regent is my biological mother, and she's on our side."

"Your biological mother..." He said the words agonisingly slowly, then he seemed to remember himself. "Wellies, you're right. We don't have time for this. That woman, Alsie Fioreletta, I saw her rush down the stairs here, taking Taka with her. I almost stopped her, but then I realised I would be dead if I tried. So, I hid, and I saw her take down three guards. Taka, his eyes were glazed, and he looked like... Dragonheats, she gave him that stuff, didn't she? What do you call it? Exalmpora..."

"Faso Gordoni," Hastina said. "We will get them back. But we may need your help. Is your dragon automaton ready to fly?"

"Yes, of course it is. Winda's already on the platform getting it ready. I was just hoping to gather some backup. Maybe you and Pontopa can come on Velos... Winda's also making sure his dragon armour gets refuelled."

"And how do you plan to follow them?" Valpeonia asked. "We have no means of tracking them."

Faso guffawed. "I'll have you know, while you were busy doing whatever you were doing in the throne room, I was in the king's laboratory looking through his equipment. I found exactly what I needed to amplify the Gordoni Rays in my sensors, and I attached the device to the dragon automaton. Now, we can detect sources of the collective unconscious for miles."

Valpeonia started to walk forward, towards the double doors of the courtyard. "We need to move now. Are you sure this will work, Mr Gordoni?"

"There's a strong source of the collective unconscious under this palace, though I haven't the faintest what that belongs to. Then there's those three dragonmen. If we wait any longer than twenty minutes, my readings tell me that they'll fly out of reach."

"But you'll be able to continue to track them if we take off now," I said.

"Of course," Faso said with a shrug. "There's not much interference in Tow, and so I can sense emitted Gordoni Rays within in a good five-hundred-mile radius. That's an estimate, by the way."

Hastina had her jaw set, and I could see in her eyes that she understood the urgency of the situation. She shook her head hard, then looked at my mother for a long moment. She spun around and addressed Lieutenant Talato and Candiorno who were standing awfully close. "We really don't have much time... Lieutenant Talato and Candiorno, take Velos out and fly with the dragon automaton. Fully augmented... Nothing else will be able to keep up."

The two lieutenants looked at each other, and two faint smiles crossed their lips, before they turned back and saluted.

"What about Bellroot, ma'am?" Lieutenant Candiorno asked.

"Though it pains me to leave him behind," Hastina said, "I doubt he'll be able to keep up with the dragon automaton and Velos with his armour."

"I'll sing a dragonsong to command the other dragons in the palace including Bellroot to follow us," Valpeonia said. "They'll catch up when they can."

"And what are the three of you going to do?" Faso asked.

But he didn't need to ask, because a cloud of black smoke had already started to rise around Hastina.

"You've to be kidding," Faso said, and Ratter poked out of his flared sleeve and sat on his shoulder. "She's a dragonwoman?"

"One you can trust, Faso," I said. I turned to look at Valpeonia, who also had black smoke starting to billow up from her feet.

"Dragonseer Wells, can I trust you to do this and keep hold of yourself?" she asked. "Did Cralanein teach you enough?"

I focused on that part of me nestled at the back of my mind, imagining that blue flame once again. "I can do this," I said, and I bit my lip.

"Good," my mother said, in that same gravelly voice I'd heard her use when she'd pulled me away from the vats of Exalmpora before. The cloud of smoke rose even higher around her, and it soon faded to show a black dragon the same size as Alsie Fioreletta.

I looked up at her, marvelling, wondering if it should be my mother fighting her in the final battle and not me. Hastina had also turned into a black dragon at this point, and both of them had their heads craned, watching me.

Faso was turning between the two of them, and Ratter's eyes were glowing red, the automaton's back arched. As versatile as

Ratter was, I doubted he'd be any threat to either of these black dragons. I closed my eyes, and I also willed the black smoke to rise around me.

The scales tore at my skin, and the features on my face twisted and writhed. But this time, despite the excruciating pain, I kept my focus on that blue flame, never forgetting who I was...

I looked up at the chimney. "This way, I guess..." I said, nodding to it.

My mother looked at the chimney and nodded an affirmative. She tucked her wings into her and launched herself up it with her powerful legs, gracefully turning herself at the curve at the top to launch herself into the outer world.

I turned to Hastina, who had her scaly head cocked and her eyes were glowing yellow. "After you," she said.

I guess she still wanted to keep an eye on me. I crouched down on my heavy legs, and I used the power in them to launch myself upwards. There wasn't nearly as much space in the chimney as I'd thought, and I found myself scrabbling up the stonework with my claws, kicking down mortar and debris as I went.

I turned the corner into the opening. As soon as I emerged into the open air, I spread my wings and lifted myself as high as I could away from the central tower in the palace.

Hastina pirouetted out after me like a stone that had just been launched from a sling. She spread her wings as well, and the three of us hovered, facing the landing pad where Velos and the dragon automaton had already been set up.

The sun was low in the sky behind us, casting a fiery glow along the edges of the buildings below. Winda sat on top of the dragon automaton on the raised landing platform. She sat at the front, her back ramrod straight and her hands on the steering controls, ready to flee, or perhaps even attack, if the three dragonwomen she saw in the sky proved a threat.

She called out something, and I knew it was a cry of alarm to Faso and the two lieutenants who hurried out the palace doors and towards the landing pad. Faso hollered something back, which I didn't hear, and Winda relaxed, then clambered towards the back of the automaton and took her place on the mountable gatling turret. Faso also mounted, and he launched the great metal beast into the sky.

Meanwhile, Talato tight-roped up Velos' tail, then took the back at the back of his armour. I guess she was the more adept of the two lieutenants at controlling Velos' armour, even if she hadn't worked everything out. Candiorno took the safer route via the ladder, and at first, I felt Velos objecting to his new rider. But I reassured him through the link I had to my centre, and he calmed down.

As Velos lifted off and sped away from us in pursuit of the dragon automaton, spewing a trail of green exhaust in his wake, I took in a breath of the fresh air, and took a moment to appreciate the sounds of everything around me. Crows cawing in the vicinity. The bleat of horses below. The clinking of a hammer hitting iron, and a ferric burning smell coming from a local forge. I reached out with my forked tongue to taste how the different gases in the air changed as the currents swirled.

Once the dragon automaton and Velos had progressed a little further, they slowed down a little together. Valpeonia led the way towards them, and Hastina and I followed in her wake.

ONCE WE HAD CAUGHT up with Velos and the dragon automaton, I noticed Faso rummaging around for something in his seat. He produced something from the compartment underneath it, which I saw to be a megaphone. He placed this to his lips and called out through it.

"I am the only one who had the sense to pack such a device," he said. "And unfortunately, I haven't yet had the time to think of a contraption that will allow three dragonwomen to speak over the speaker circuits. But when all this is over, I will put my thoughts to such a device, I promise."

"Just get on with it, Faso," I roared, but I wasn't sure even as a dragon my voice was loud enough to combat the beating wind.

Faso clearly heard something though, because he raised his hand to his ear and shook his head. "I don't even know which one of you said that, but I didn't hear a word. Anyway, Winda has managed to latch on to the Gordoni Rays that those drag- onmen are emitting, using a second scanner that I've installed on her turret. We've done some calculations, and we estimate that if we fly full speed ahead within the next minute then we will catch them in half an hour. It seems that physics is on our side, because however strong they are, carrying Taka in their claws will inevitably produce drag, and give us a chance to gain on them.

"We must fly ahead, prepare our cannons, and no one is allowed to aim at whichever of those beasts is carrying Taka. Once there, we can reduce them down to that single dragon, and we block off its flight path, forcing it to land. Please, dragonseers and mysterious Mrs Masked Regent figure, I know you're the ones really in charge here. So, roar out it you agree."

It sounded good to me, so I opened my mouth and bellowed out to let Faso know that. The air shimmered around me as Hastina and Valpeonia joined in my chorus. Our roars seemed to meld into each other, as the sounds of instruments might in an orchestra, gaining in power.

"Good," Faso said. "Then Lieutenant Talato and Candiorno..." He must have had the speaker system activated so both soldiers could hear him from their positions. "Of course, I'm not General Sako or Admiral Sandao or any military leader like that. But you can probably take that as permission to augment. Winda, do the honours for me on this machine, will you?"

At the front of Velos, Lieutenant Candiorno saluted. Talato didn't salute Faso, but instead leaned down towards Velos' flank to turn the dial and augment Velos.

"Onwards!" Faso said, and Velos and the dragon charged forwards, leaving a slight green trail behind them. My mother and Hastina matched their speed, and I flapped hard to keep up.

"*Dragonseer Wiggea, about Admiral Sandao's fleet...*" Valpeonia said. "*We should have some dragons on the Cini-Sanito river by now, should we not?*"

"*If Yol relayed the orders as planned, then I hope so,*" Hastina said. "*I just hope that Alsie hasn't brought reinforcements.*"

"*Faso would know if they were nearby,*" I said. "*He has the device to measure them... But he told you this.*"

"*And do you trust him?*" Valpeonia asked.

"*Not on my father's wellies. But at least I know that he doesn't get his technology wrong often. The thing we should be worried about more is how are we going to take on Alsie and Charth? I mean, are we strong enough?*"

"*No one needs to die today,*" Valpeonia said. "*We only need to get Taka back, and make sure he's safe from whatever Finesia is planning.*"

While we were talking away in the collective unconscious, Faso was screaming something at Winda. Something was clearly wrong. I didn't have to wait long to find out what.

Faso raised his megaphone and pointed it in our direction. "I should probably tell you that there's been an error in our calculations. Nothing much to worry about, but there's another two dragonmen. They were flying in such a formation that they managed to hide behind the other three dragonmen. So now we have five to contend with.

"I guess, now you're going to be asking me how close they are... Well, this is where it gets tricky. Because three of them much closer than the other two. It appears that these three turned around. They're heading straight towards us, I'm afraid. You probably need to brace yourselves for a fight."

"*Dragonheats,*" I said in the collective unconscious to Hastina and my mother. "*What do we do now?*"

"*We take them down as quickly as possible,*" Valpeonia said.

"Then hopefully, we'll be able to make up the distance and snatch the boy out of what I guess will be Alsie Fioreletta's claws."

"She will destroy us..." I said. *"We can't take Alsie Fioreletta. Believe me, I've tried, and she's too strong."*

"You've tried in your dreams, but have you tried in the real world?" Hastina asked.

I shook my head, which felt rather odd in dragon form, particularly when flying. But it wasn't easy to discard human instincts. *"It's not just Alsie. She has Charth with her as an escort. Both of them are strong."*

"And when we reach them," Valpeonia said, *"there's two of them and five of us, not to mention the dragons' riders. Believe, for dragonheats sake, my daughter. We can do this."*

I gritted my teeth, and the fire raged hot in my stomach. A feeling of anxiety started to emerge there, and with it, Finesia's voice started to call from a distant part of my head. My centre... I found it again. I wasn't going to let her in so easily. Not anymore.

"You're right," I said to my biological mother. *"There's always a way..."*

A thin mist had started to rise from a lake and the Caprio Mountains framed behind it. Snow glazed the peaks of these granite rocks, and the mist seemed to be rolling down the hills like an avalanche. It made the three black dragons hovering there easy to see, and as soon as I saw them, I also felt their presence in the collective unconscious.

It was Wiggea's voice I heard, and he kept the channel open for all three of us dragonwomen to hear.

"Well," he said. *"It seems that my two lovers have finally arrived."*

27

SUNLIGHT SHONE out from behind the three black dragons, sending a fiery shimmer through the mist and imbuing the black dragons with an oily opalescent look. We edged a little closer to them. Behind them, very faintly through the mist, I made out the other two black dragons. One of them carried Taka, still in human form, in its claws. There was no getting to them until we got through these three. We had to take them down as quickly as possible.

Out of the three, only Wiggea spoke in the collective unconscious, while the two other black dragons remained silent.

"*Wiggea, this has to end now,*" I said. "*I hoped I could restore you. But I guess we've lost you now, just as we lost Charth...*"

"*Oh, don't be so melodramatic,*" Wiggea replied.

"*There's no need for drama at all,*" Hastina said. "*The outcome of this battle will be simple. You will die.*"

"*You know, I think I prefer my former wife in human form.*"

"*Either way, I will kill you. Don't think I'll show any remorse because you decided to take control of my husband's body.*"

"*You've got so cold in your old age. Sometimes I wonder if this is because Finesia is stronger in your mind than anyone else's.*"

Maybe it is you, Hastina, who's destined to become her aide after all."

There wasn't any time for further conversation because the dragon automaton and Velos' gatling cannons had already started to whirr.

They let out a volley of bullets at the two black dragons on the outside of Wiggea, who roared underneath the onslaught. All three dragons wrapped their wings around their bodies, diving through the sky to avoid the stream of fire coming out of the cannons.

If a single one of those bullets hit their throats, then they would die instantaneously. But their wings seemed to deflect the bullets well, sparks flying at the points of impact.

Winda also used her central turret to aim directly at Wiggea. But his moves seemed more graceful than the other two. Somehow, he managed to dive and pirouette underneath Winda's stream of bullets, and she didn't hit him once.

The cannons guttered out of ammo, and both Winda and Talato worked on reloading them.

The two black dragons on the outside took this opportunity to charge at Velos and the dragon automaton. Velos roared and darted away from his assailant. Candiorno pulled Velos upwards into a loop-the-loop. His eyes were tracking the black dragon coming towards him.

My heart lurched in my chest, and I readied myself to defend Velos, but Wiggea blocked my path.

"*I'll cover Velos... Kill Wiggea, Dragonseer Wells,*" Hastina said, and she went straight after Velos. Meanwhile, my mother pursued the dragonman chasing the dragon automaton.

I turned to face Wiggea.

"*My darling. You know, I still care about you immensely,*" he said.

This time, I couldn't let myself get sucked in by his games. I summoned that image of the blue flame of the back of my mind again, reminding me of my centre. Then, I charged at Wiggea.

He closed his wings, protecting his throat. I took him within my claws, wrapped my wings around him. Together we tumbled towards the ground.

We hit it moments later, sending both a wave of pain up my spine and a plume of dirt. I tasted some in my mouth, and some got caught inside my nostrils. I puffed it away, then let the pain wash over me. After all, I was nearly invulnerable in this form.

The impact had opened up Wiggea's wings, and I got ready to lunge in towards his throat. But I hesitated too long, and he roared and rolled out of the way.

He'd grown stronger since I'd last fought against him, as if Finesia had granted him even more power. His momentum sent me rolling across the ground. I used my wings as brakes to stop me going too far.

I took a moment to glance upwards, concerned about my friends. The mist had now enveloped us, and I couldn't see the battle through it. But I could hear the gatling guns firing above, and roars cut through the clouds, though I don't know who they belonged to.

Wiggea's claws scuffed into the dirt, and he charged at me with a grunt, kicking up rocks and a trail of dust in his wake.

I pirouetted out of the way, ducking halfway through the turn, as I lowered my wing to trip Wiggea up.

Then I was on top of him, straddling him. Wiggea tried to wrap his wings around himself again, but I ripped them apart using the strength in my forearms. This opened up a space at my chest, and he slashed out with his claws, all the while gnashing with his teeth.

I turned my neck to the side, and I brought one foreclaw across to knock his head aside. I bared my teeth and I readied myself to lunge in—

"Pontopa stop!" Wiggea's voice came in my head, stopping me in my tracks. Then... *"No, Pontopa, don't listen to me. Do it! You need to end my life now. This monster can never return..."*

"Rastano," I said. *"Finesia let you back in."*

"Don't worry about me. My life ended long ago."

But hearing him again had stolen the fight out me. *"Rastano... I can't."*

"You know you must. This is the right thing to do. I'll make it easier for you. I won't let you see my face again. You won't have killed me; you'll have killed a dragonman..."

I lifted myself off him... *"But if Faso has the helmet, maybe he can bring you back. We won't let them do this to you again. I can teach you how to keep Finesia out."*

"I don't want to risk this. Please, Pontopa... I ask you only one thing..."

But I couldn't... I really couldn't.

I stepped back, paralysed, as I watched him, clueless what to do next.

There came a swishing sound from above, and one of the enemy black dragons fell limply through the sky and crashed into the ground. Hastina came after it, her wings tucked into an elegant dive, and I could see her target. She was headed straight towards Wiggea.

Wiggea closed his eyes, and I heard his voice in the collective unconscious. *"Until death do us part... Thank you, Hastina..."*

I turned my head, unable to watch. My breath had caught in my throat, and I heard Finesia in my head. *"That one is a pure traitor to my cause. If one day you kill her, then I may reconsider your destiny as my right-hand aide."*

I remembered myself immediately, centred that blue flame, and turned back to see Wiggea's throat drop from Hastina's sharp-toothed maw to the ground.

He was gone... Finally put at peace, and I hadn't been able to do that one thing for him.

I hadn't had the strength... But Hastina had...

Another roar came from the sky, and the third black dragon came plummeting through the mist, its wings and limbs flailing as it fell. It hit the ground, this time making a small crater in the soil. It was over... We'd won the battle, but we needed a moment of respite. We needed time to collect our thoughts and regroup.

I willed the scales back into me. I felt dirty in this form, and I felt I deserved the intense pain that shot through every muscle in my body as I became human again.

Hastina stayed in her dragon form for a moment, looking down upon Wiggea. She said nothing – not aloud, not in the collective unconscious. I felt I should give her that moment, so I turned away.

Valpeonia broke through the fog next, diving rapidly, but she broke into a soar just before she touched the ground. Wiggea hadn't turned human again, as if Finesia wanted to memorialise his dragon form.

Hastina turned to my mother. "*We should go and rescue Taka,*" she said. "*This can't have been for naught...*"

Valpeonia shook her head and grunted. She lifted her head to the sky, and I saw the dragon automaton soaring, green smoke rising up from its flank. On it, Faso had the loudspeaker by his side. He spotted us, pointed at us. He lifted the megaphone to his lips.

"Mayday! Mayday! Requesting crash landing."

Faso seemed to have it under control. He landed the dragon automaton just by a lake a good hundred yards from us. Instead of coming over to check on us, he vaulted off his automaton and got straight to work repairing the damage.

Soon after, Candiorno brought Velos in to land, and I considered it a blessing that my dragon had at least got through all this unscathed.

PART VI

"In the war against magic and technology, technology will ultimately prevail."

— FASO GORDONI

THE MIST LIFTED after around an hour, stealing away the heat of the day as it did. A thick grey cloud loomed, that let little light through, occluding the snow-laden peaks of the mountains. We crouched around an open fire, a boar that Valpeonia had slain in the nearby forest roasting on a spit, mashed potatoes hissing away in their pot beneath this. The cooking stirred up a smoky scent around us that did nothing to sweeten our sour moods.

Alas, before we'd set up this fire and Valpeonia had gone out hunting, Faso had announced to us that his Gordoni Rays could actually detect lifeforms for up to one thousand miles, as opposed to the five hundred he'd announced before. He'd already admitted that he'd neglected to tell us that using this extra capability, he'd discovered that the dragonmen we'd been pursuing were about to meet up with a much larger force.

"Faso Gordoni... Never withhold information from me again," Valpeonia said to him. "I can't act strategically without knowing the entire situation at hand. If we are to employ you, I need to know that I can trust you."

Faso shook his head, while Winda put her hand on his knee. "You wouldn't have gone after Taka otherwise," he said. "We had a chance to reach them before they reached the larger force.

We could have rescued Taka, whisked him away, and got him back to Slaro, where you no doubt have enough munitions to shoot them down. I saw that you finally made those modifications to the Rocs from the blueprints I provided. Against these automatons, Alsie Fioreletta and her dragonmen don't stand a chance."

Valpeonia shook her head. "We only have a limited number of those Rocs, who are currently stationed with the Third Regent Fleet at Sandstone Bluff. If I'd have known that Alsie Fioreletta had brought her forces here, then we could have regrouped with Admiral Sandao at the Cini-Sanito river and planned a large-scale assault."

"Perhaps if I knew all that, then I might have suggested something different."

"Mr Gordoni, if we gave men like you all the information about our military strategies, then you wouldn't have time to focus on the work you do best. Respect the chain of command, for dragonheats sake, and don't be so arrogant to think you can handle everything yourself."

"But what about Taka? I've only heard bits and pieces of rumours so far, but from what I know it sounds like he's in danger, and we might never get him back. What was this migration that the men are talking about? The dragonmen are moving to the Saye Archipelago, I've heard, and who knows what fortifications they have there. Meanwhile, I had the ability to track them using my Gordoni Rays, and so I decided to take advantage of my quick thinking. Isn't that what you want to employ me for, anyway? My mental acuity... The brilliance of my mind?"

I didn't even feel like scowling at Faso right now. He was so incredibly smart with many things, but at others he was incredibly stupid. All I could think about was Wiggea's voice, telling me to end his life... His last request, and I'd failed to respect it. Because I'd been too much of a coward... Unlike Hastina.

My mind whirled back again to the time I'd stood with

Wiggea by the lava lake, as we watched the sulphurous black plumes rage over the magma from below. Then, I'd held his hand, and I'd leaned in to kiss his warm lips, and the harshness of the world around me had seemed to soften, and everything had been perfect...

But it wasn't meant to last...

Hastina didn't say much either. Instead, she reached out to slice off a piece of boar with her pocketknife. She noticed me looking at her. "What? I need to eat to stay strong, and you should too."

I took a shallow breath. My stomach really didn't feel like it could hold down anything right now, and I had no idea how Hastina didn't feel the same.

I stood up, slowly. "I'm going for a walk," I said, and I left Faso and Valpeonia to argue.

Hastina shrugged, then sliced off another piece of meat.

I passed Talato and Candiorno on the way, who were busy setting up some tents for the night. Faso would need an extra half a day to make sure that the automaton was in working order again, and the plan after that was to liaise with Admiral Sandao and the fleet that he was bringing up the Cini-Sanito river.

Given how important Taka was to us, it looked like they might have to change their plans – particularly if what Sukina told me in my dream was true. Taka, right now, was in grave danger.

I took a few steps towards the forest underneath the mountains, and the cold, still lake that stretched into the distance. Thick boots scuffled over the forest floor from behind me. I didn't turn to see Talato approach, but I knew it was her.

She put a hand on my shoulder, and I took a deep breath. "Ma'am, I wanted to let you know that I'm still on your side, despite everything..."

I turned to her, and I saw her loyalty in her eyes. But then Wiggea had also been loyal and look what had happened to him.

"Thank you," I said. "But you'll probably be pleased to hear that I'm no longer public enemy number one around here. The Masked Regent... She's my biological mother, you know?"

Talato gave me a faint smile. "I heard... The moment I saw her, I thought I could see the resemblance. After she took the mask off, I mean, not before..."

I'm not sure Talato quite got the irony of her words. I put my hand over hers on my shoulder. It was warm to the touch, despite the chill coming down from mountains.

"Thank you, Talato. I appreciate you..."

"You're more than welcome, ma'am. If you need the cyagora, by the way, at any time – I've kept it secure."

I gave her a curt nod. "Not yet... By the way, Valpeonia told me something... If at any point, you see a faint green glow in the irises, that's when Finesia's at risk of closing in."

"I'll bear that in mind, ma'am. Anyway, I better get back to helping Lieutenant Candiorno with those tents. The Masked Regent told us you're going to need an early night."

I looked over at Candiorno, who was watching us from the corner of his eye. He seemed to notice me looking at him and pretended to busy himself hammering in the tent pegs. "Yeah," I said. "Looks like he could do with some help over there."

"Yes, ma'am," Talato said, and she started to walk away. Then she stopped, as if considering something. She turned back to me. "I was thinking. Are you going to need me in your tent tonight? I remember what happened at Ginlast, and I don't want to desert you if need me. But I just wondered if..."

She looked abashedly at Candiorno, and I got immediately what she seemed too shy to tell me.

"I'll be okay..." I said, and she nodded with a sympathetic smile and sauntered back to the tents.

I joined Hastina, Valpeonia, Faso, and Winda by the campfire, now feeling cold down to my bones. I sat next to Hastina on the log, and I grazed on a portion of meat and mashed potatoes.

It tasted blander than it smelled, though I didn't have much of an appetite admittedly, with the stone-like ball of despair sitting in my stomach. The food warmed me slightly, but still the chill lingered in my hands and feet. From behind, a roar broke the silence. I turned to see hundreds of Greys with pale-blue suited guards astride them coming in from the north. Bellroot was amongst them.

Faso and Winda had stepped away from the fire and were working on setting up their tent – or rather I should say that Ratter and Winda were doing all the work and Faso was supervising. Candiorno and Talato by this point had also set up tents for me, Hastina and Valpeonia.

"Dragonseer Wells, you really should eat a little more than that," Hastina said, and she proffered me another bit of meat hanging off her fork. I took it, then I leaned forwards and scooped out another serving of potatoes.

"Thank you. Have you had time to work out the plans?"

"So far what I know," Valpeonia said, "is that we'll have to send out a force to the Saye Archipelago. I'm still working out the exact logistics of this operation."

"And Taka?" I asked.

Valpeonia took a deep breath. "Let's hope that we can get to him in time to stop whatever Alsie Fioreletta and Finesia have planned."

I nodded, and I gazed back over my shoulder at the lake. But all I could see within was the reflection of the grey clouds that darkened the sky overhead.

I SLEPT in the same tent as Hastina that night, then we buried Rastano Wiggea at dawn.

Reinforcements of dragons – including Bellroot – and dragon riders had arrived while we slept, which made the task a lot easier than it would have been for the seven of us who had camped overnight. The sky remained grey, though the fog had left us now. Still, the air retained its bitter chill as if it wanted to mourn for Wiggea alongside us.

Six dragons worked to churn up enough soil and create a big enough hole to house Wiggea's massive form. The same six dragons lifted him into the soil, hovering above the ground slightly to do so. Wiggea had ridden all these dragons at Fortress Gerhaun before he'd become Sukina's dragonelite, so they seemed the most appropriate for the task.

After Wiggea had been lowered into his resting bed, and both Hastina and I had shed a tear, Hastina picked up a shovel and she threw the first spade of dirt on Wiggea's dragon form.

I closed my eyes, and turned my head, because I didn't want to remember him this way. He would always remain human in my mind. I had hoped that Finesia would honour him by somehow returning him to his original form, but it wasn't meant to be.

More tears flooded to my eyes as the dragons approached and kicked the dirt up over him in a flurry. Once he was covered enough that his aquiline head was no longer visible, I closed my eyes and imagined Wiggea staring back from underneath the soil.

That's how I wanted to remember him. A good man, and not a monster. A loyal soldier who fought until the very end. Full of love, full of compassion, and always true to his purpose.

The other two dragons also got a burial, but we never uncovered who they'd been in their previous human incarnations. A tribe member, perhaps – one of the East Cadigan Island natives who had helped me climb the Pinnatu Crater before Colas had caused the volcano to erupt and turn their home to pyroclastic ash, ready to birth secicao anew. Or one of the slaves at the factory who I had converted to a black dragon using fire from my own stomach.

I'd never understood why it was my blood that they needed. There must have been something about my makeup that made me unique, and it wasn't just about being a dragonseer. Perhaps it had something to do with my unique bloodline, or having grown from two wombs.

Valpeonia approached Hastina and I at the end of the funeral, and she put a hand on each of our shoulders. "I've received news from the scouts, and the Saye Explorer is now a hundred miles from here," she said.

Hastina blinked away her tears, and when she looked at me, it was as if she hadn't been crying at all. I gave her a sympathetic nod, because the one thing I acknowledged was that Hastina had invested a lot more time with Rastano Wiggea than I had. She might have known a much younger version of him, but he was her husband all the same.

"I guess we should ride on our dragons," I said.

"That would be wise," Valpeonia replied. "I hope you understand that I won't be coming with you on this mission."

My heart skipped a beat. "I thought—"

Valpeonia put up a hand to silence me. Whoever she was in my life, she'd been trained to act as a responsible leader in this position, not as a mother. "Cralanein needs me in the palace to help with her affairs. Also, my absence from the palace could spark riots if the press latches onto it. Once they learn no one is there overseeing the running of the country and the Sovereign States, then with such a threat emerging on the horizon, what would stop the land devolving into anarchy?"

"Plus," Hastina added. "If anything happens to us, your mother might be the only one left who has a chance of defeating Alsie Fioreletta."

I shrugged. I knew from Hastina's tone of voice what she was implying. If we became lost to either death or Finesia, then Valpeonia would stand behind the battlements at Slaro and fight to her last until secicao took over the world. But I sincerely doubted Valpeonia would stand a chance against the threat. Dragonheats, without knowing exactly what Finesia was up to, I wasn't sure anyone stood a chance.

I opened my arms to Valpeonia and wrapped her in an embrace. She still felt a little cold to me, not just in the fact that she didn't really meld into my hug like Versalina Wells – the mother who'd nurtured me all these years – did, but also less warmth came off her than felt natural.

Valpeonia broke the hug, and she placed the palm of her hand on my cheek. "Make sure you come back to us, Dragonseer Wells," she said. She looked at me as if she wanted to love me, but didn't know how, and then she looked at Hastina in exactly the same way. "And you Dragonseer Wiggea…"

She stepped back, and a black cloud rose from around her ankles. It whipped up like a dark cloak around her, and I was soon looking upon her oily dragon form, her massive head looking back down at me, her yellow eyes not blinking.

"*Good luck, dragonseers,*" she said to both of us in the collective unconscious, and she lifted off the ground, sending up brown dirt behind her. I gave her a little wave, even though I doubt she saw it.

Hastina gestured to Velos and Bellroot who were standing beside each other, both ready to launch. Talato sat at the back of Velos' dragon armour, and Candiorno was in front of her in the middle, leaving the rider's seat free for me. Given Bellroot didn't have any armour, it would have been impractical for him to take a second rider, not to mention the fact that I doubt any soldier dared to steal Hastina's mount.

Hastina turned to me, and she took hold of my hand and squeezed it – the first sign of affection I'd received from her. "I hear that Admiral Sandao has some intel. Let's go and find out what they've discovered."

She let go of my hand and strolled over to Bellroot. She mounted him by scrambling quickly up his tail. I took a deep breath and walked over to Velos.

Talato and Candiorno watched me from their perches. Something was developing between them and, though I was happy for them, seeing them like this made me feel even more empty about what I had lost.

THE CINI-SANITO RIVER was wild near its source, or at least it was this time of year during snowmelt season. We flew just south of the King's Canal that connected Slaro to the river proper. From up here, I could hear the roars of its rapids tossing white foam over the brown water.

Despite its ugly colour, the rushing water had an intrinsic beauty to it. I imagined how it would have been before the world discovered industry, when you could wade through the river, and fish trout and minnows from the waters.

Part of me wanted to be down at ground level, washing my feet in the water. But that brown came from both the secicao pollution of the city and, more recently, the secicao that sucked up the nutrients from the soil surrounding it. It carried on like this all the way down to Sandstone Bluff, eventually rendering the land non-arable to anything but secicao.

Now, mottled patches of secicao diseased the land, choking the forests of life from their edges. This wasn't the world Wiggea or any of us had wanted to inherit. It wasn't the world we wanted to pass down to our children. Dragonheats, it wasn't the world Wiggea had fought for, and I would do my utmost to return it to a better state, whatever it took.

We flew on in formation – Bellroot, Velos, and the dragon automaton forming the tip of the V of our flock, whilst the other dragons followed in our wake. The sky was clear, and the sun beat down from overhead, though a strong breeze stopped me from overheating. The ground around the river looked windswept. Much of the land in the centre of Tow used to be verdant forest, and even the farms that should have displayed vivid greens and yellows, were now shaded in an unsaturated brown.

As we traversed the dying landscape, I kept the image of that flame burning at the back of my mind. It had been the one constant that I'd managed to gain through the trials and tribulations of the last several days. I'd got much better at this, and now I didn't even feel Finesia pressing at the recesses of my mind.

She didn't seem to enter my dreams either. So long as the last image I had in my head when I slept was of that blue flame, then it also seemed to be there when I awoke.

With my mind in this esoteric state, and sadness in my heart through losing both Wiggea and Taka, we eventually saw the first glints of ships on the river. The banks were much further apart by this point, and the waters a lot less turbulent. In fact, there was enough room for four cruisers side by side. In the centre of the formation, aging Saye Explorer frigate floated on the river, with its two funnels towering up into the sky, green smoke trailing towards the Sandstone Bluff cliffs to the south.

Behind the Saye Explorer was a line of smaller dragon carriers – the kind that could only carry fifty dragons each. There were so many of these that it looked like they were bringing the entire population of the Southlands up north. A row of four transport ships, followed by a couple of rows of cruisers formed the fleet's tail.

What's happening?" I asked over the speaker system. "Do any of you know about this?" I looked back at Candiorno and Talato, who both shrugged.

"I heard that they were ordering the dragon queens up

north," Faso said. "The six largest cities in the Northern Continent that aren't overrun by dragonmen each get a dragon queen. But I've not found any confirmation of this fact. In this new world order that your mother has set up, Pontopa, it seems that information doesn't flow as freely as I'd hoped."

"Do you know anything about this, Hastina?" I asked, my teeth clenched.

She was a little slow replying, as if lost in thought... "I knew something," she said. "Castlonth and the other dragon queens were planning a migration, but I didn't know which locations they chose to inhabit. Let's wait until we land, then we can talk strategy and fill you in on everything."

The Saye Explorer had once again been modified. It only used to have room on the quarterdeck to land only a single dragon. More recently, much of the equipment had been stripped away at the top of the ship to create a landing deck long enough for three dragons, one in front of the other. An interior deck lay below this, housing the bridge and the briefing room.

Now that we were close enough, I could see Admiral Sandao, General Sako, and my parents sitting at a table on the landing deck with a cafetière and four cups of secicao. I can't express how happy I was to see them all alive and well, particularly my parents.

General Sako stood up and waved to us. His ruddy face was even redder than normal, I noticed. It looked like the old man had caught the sun, a little.

Admiral Sandao, on the other hand, looked healthily tanned – as you would expect of a sailor. He must have been stationed at sea for a while. Papo also had a reasonably healthy tan on him. He would appreciate this, I was sure, after being stuck for so long on a continent that never saw sunshine. Mamo's skin on the other hand seemed to glisten in the light, no doubt an effect of slathering on layer upon layer of sunscreen oil.

There were two empty seats at the table, and Faso seemed to take issue at that.

"I hope that invitation is extended to me and Winda also," Faso said in a haughty voice. "Because it doesn't look like they've created enough space for all of us."

"Oh, stop moaning, Faso," I snapped. "I'm sure there are more seats, and if not, some of us can stand."

"The military can stand, I trust... Civilians, not to mention essential scientists, like me and Winda should be treated with the respect we deserve." Faso looked back at Winda, who was shaking her head.

"Very well," Hastina said. "We'll send you straight to the laboratory where you can work on the necessary augments the Masked Regent has ordered for the automaton sharks that we acquired from Cini."

"Oh goodie," Faso said, "that beats drinking secicao with you military types any day."

Three yellow circles designated landing zones, each with a D at the centre. Velos touched down on the front one. Hastina brought Bellroot in after behind Velos, and Faso brought the dragon automaton down last.

Velos immediately put his head down and fell asleep. Honestly, I didn't blame him for being so exhausted, and I kind of envied him for being able to sleep through anything.

I dismounted first, this time via the ladder, as I didn't want to wake Velos by scrambling over his head. Mamo stood at the bottom to greet me, and she embraced me in a warm hug that I just seemed to mould into – it felt completely different from hugging Valpeonia.

"Pontopa," she said. "You had us so worried... The guards at Fortress Gerhaun, the new ones, they told us you were to be executed, and then they wouldn't tell us anything after that. We didn't know what the dragonheats was going on..."

I shook my head and clenched my fists. Hastina hadn't dismounted from Bellroot yet. Instead, she sat on his back, staring at the sun setting over the riverbanks as if it couldn't hurt her eyes.

"Tell me exactly what happened, Mamo," I said, without breaking the hug. "After I left the fortress, I heard that General Sako got tied to a chair and I know Bassalhan left…" Actually, I had *seen* General Sako tied to that chair, but telling Mamo that would raise far too many questions. I wasn't ready to tell her that her daughter was a dragon queen murderer. Not yet…

Mamo stepped back from me, and hesitated, probably thinking where to start. She steepled her hands and rested her chin on her fingertips as she spoke. "We thought for a while that Bassalhan had left us for dead. Without her, we thought that the secicao would close in and suffocate us all. We wanted to leave, but the guards said they'd shoot anyone who even tried to put on their wellies and jungle suit.

"Then, that new dragon queen Castlonth arrived, and she ordered the fortress on lockdown. General Sako was already in prison by that time – he'd apparently failed to respect the chain of command or something, while Admiral Sandao had been stationed out here for a long time and no one knew why. It was an awkward situation and created, well, a stiff environment all around the fortress. We had to queue up to get tokens from an office they'd set up in the infirmary, so we could go to the canteen and get food. If we didn't go to the canteen at our allotted times, we wouldn't get anything to eat at all.

"This went on for three days. Then, all of a sudden, a guard knocked on the door of our tearoom and told us that we were to go to the docks. It was one of the nicer guards, you know that young man – not much younger than you – with the button nose and the crew cut. We asked him what had just happened, and he told us that a flotilla of dragon carriers and transports was ready to sail up the Balmano river, and that everyone was moving north. He told us that Castlonth would be leaving very soon to the city of Cargorst in Clam, and so everyone needed to evacuate Fortress Gerhaun before the secicao clouds closed in.

"As he escorted us to our ship, that nice young man filled us in on all the information we'd been missing. The dragons were leaving the Southlands so they could help protect the humans using the collective unconscious, so that people could still breathe in the cities when the secicao swallows them whole. He asked us where we wanted to move. Apparently, the dragon queen Yol was moving to Spezzio, and we thought given it's close to home that we'd rather go there. Have you met Yol?"

I smiled. Out of all the dragon queens I'd known since Gerhaun, she was the one I appreciated the most – excepting Cralanein, of course. "I have, and she's much more, let's say, palatable than some of the other dragon queens."

"That's nice, darling. Anyway, the young man also explained why they had taken Taka. He said it was because the population of Tow thought he was rightfully king, and so they would take orders from him. The boy they'd been masquerading could only convince the population for so long. Particularly when it came time for the boy to make a speech. Someone would know. A member of the press would see that this wasn't quite Taka..."

I sighed. "Things have changed now Mamo... So much has changed."

Tears welled in my eyes again, and Mamo pulled me back into a hug. Her breathing became slow and careful. "Is it true what they say, darling? Did you kill Bassalhan? There seems to be so many rumours floating around, but this is the one I really can't believe."

"I didn't kill her, Finesia did. But things have changed, and I've learned so much since then... Mamo, there's so much to explain, but right now we've so little time."

Mamo pulled back and lowered her head as if considering what to say next. "Are you on the cyagora again, darling?"

"No... Not cyagora. I've found a better and more natural way."

Surprisingly, Papo had managed to steal himself away from the Tow Observer, and he now stood behind Mamo. He gave me a fatherly hug, and I sank into the warmth of it.

These were my real parents... My biological mother, the

Masked Regent, I may have had her genes, but she didn't raise me. Papo held me for a while, rubbing my hair and saying nothing. His arms shook as he held me. Eventually he broke his embrace.

"I hope that this will end soon... Your mother and I, we want it to all be over, and the world to return to normal. But we understand what you have to do."

I thought about telling them about my biological mother, but I realised it could wait. They'd clearly had enough stress and worry for a while, and I didn't want to introduce another complication to them.

Faso had dismounted from the dragon automaton, and was loitering nearby, watching us, as if unsure what to do. Winda stood next to him and Hastina had just jumped off Bellroot and strode towards us. From the other side came General Sako's heavy footsteps. Admiral Sandao had also now stood up, and he had a clipboard tucked under his wiry arms.

The general approached, with his secicao pipe clenched between his teeth. He stopped, took it out, exhaled a breath of pungent eggy green smoke, then put his hands on his hips. "Blunders and dragonheats. Though I respect you need time for your family reunion, Dragonseer Wells, I heard some terrible news about Taka. I think we all need to get down to the briefing room pronto."

He turned to Papo and looked at him. "Military only this time, I'm afraid, Cipao, I hope you understand. Oh, and Gordoni, boy, you and Winda now count as military, given that you crew of one of our most powerful weapons. But don't think that gives you any special rank, or the ability to order my men around."

He turned back to me and glanced over at Hastina. "It doesn't matter who we're reporting to, so long as we're fighting on the right side. But now, for Taka's sake above everything else, we need to shift our plans."

THE OVAL STRATEGY table stood between the two funnels on the upper interior deck. The front funnel obscured the commander's chair and the operations of the officers used to navigate the ship, the rear one obscured the staircase that led down to the lower decks. Below deck, two massive boilers powered the propellers which ploughed the ship forward, and they had done for decades.

The steel table shone across every square inch of its surface without a speck of grime or dirt to be found. A rolled-up scroll lay upon it, wrapped in a ribbon, and sealed with a wax stamp. Beneath this was a manilla envelope with 'Top Secret' stamped in red bold lettering over the seal.

The air smelled as it always did in these warships. Rich in metal and oil, with the faint lingering eggy aroma of secicao. General Sako and Admiral Sandao took their places at both ends of the table. Talato and Candiorno sat down next to each other, and Hastina took a place in the centre, directly opposite them. She had her spear with her again. As she sat down on the chair, she placed this neatly across her thighs, one hand wrapped around the hemp bindings on the shaft as if afraid it might slip away.

Faso nudged past me next, and Winda passed more gently. Before they took their seats, Faso turned back to me. "Oh, by the way, Pontopa. I managed to procure that helmet if you ever need it again." He spoke quietly, as if afraid someone might hear.

"Hold on to it for now," I said. "I think I'm not going to need anything like it again, but you never know. The Masked Regent taught me how to keep my cool." I thought about mentioning the dragon queen underneath Cini's palace as well, but he would doubtless disbelieve me.

Faso raised an eyebrow. "Well, I was just thinking, in case you need to—" He leaned in conspiratorially – " you know. You might want to slip away again. I've got you covered."

He sat down next to Lieutenant Candiorno, leaving Hastina by herself on the other side of the table. For a moment, I also considered sitting on the same side as them, but this was my old self talking. I had no reason to fear Hastina anymore.

Once we were all seated, General Sako coughed into his hand, and plumes of green smoke seeped out from between his fingers. He stood up, broke the seal of the scroll, and unrolled it, revealing a map of the Saye Archipelago, which he flattened out on the table.

"Right," General Sako said. "Now that the seal has been broken, let this briefing commence. The issue at hand, is that Taka got kidnapped by Alsie Fioreletta during his sojourn at the palace, where he was meant to be coronated. I wasn't told any of these plans of course, and if I had we might have prevented this whole situation." He glared at Hastina, then coughed up some more green smoke.

Hastina stared back at him, unblinking. She said nothing.

"Anyway," General Sako said, and he took a blue felt-tip marker from his breast pocket. "We have managed to send some Hummingbird scouts ahead to gather some intel, and we've discovered that Alsie Fioreletta and her black dragons have set up a base on this crescent-shaped island here. For the uninitiated, or in other words, folks who haven't visited there such as myself, it's called.... Sorry, what was the name again, Admiral Sandao?"

"Crescent Island," Admiral Sandao said, giving the general a meek smile. "Also known as the most common habitat for the cyagora plant. Or I guess it used to be..."

"Yes, well... Of course, Crescent Island. How could I forget that one? And cyagora, really? I guess that there's not much of that left nowadays."

Admiral Sandao nodded, and I opened my mouth to correct General Sako and Admiral Sandao. But then, I thought there was no point delaying this briefing with unnecessary trivia. Better the general got on with it so we could get on with our mission as soon as possible.

"What was that? Did you want to say something, Dragonseer Wells?"

"No, go ahead," I said, shaking my head. "Nothing important at all."

I shot a glance at Lieutenant Talato, and she gave me a nod. Undoubtedly, the fewer people who knew about our secret stash of cyagora the better. Otherwise, people would start gossiping that I should go back on that stuff.

"So, do you have any intel on the island itself?" Hastina asked. Clearly, I wasn't the only one who wanted to get straight to the point. "How many are we facing? Possible breach points? Structures?"

"I was getting to that," General Sako said, and his moustache twitched again. "The Hummingbird scouts that managed to get close and get away, took some photographs..."

He produced a letter opener from his breast pocket, and he slid it underneath the seal of the envelope. From this, he removed a dozen photographs that he spread out on the table.

They weren't great photography by any means. In fact, the background was such a dark grey that it was hard to see anything, other than what looked like lightning strikes in the sky. But even from here I could see a central shape in the photographs. The Hummingbirds had been programmed to focus on the centrepiece that towered above Crescent Island into the sky, which in turn was easy to discern against the foam that graced the island's shore.

The island had some kind of massive tree on it, and my heart lurched when I recalled seeing the exact same shape in Sukina's dream. "The Tree Immortal... It can't be..."

General Sako nodded. "I don't know about that, but it's certainly a very large tree. It's a remarkable invention, photographic paper, don't you think? Thirty years ago, this wouldn't have even been possible."

Faso leaned in to study the photographs. "Remind me sometime, to get you an upgrade, Admiral. This 'remarkable photographic paper' you mention is outdated. You know, we can take photographs in colour now."

"It's enough to make out what we need," Hastina said, and she reached out and traced one of the photographs with her fingernail. "What's this thing around the tree, though?"

I leaned forward. "It looks like some kind of protective bubble... Like the dragon queens produce, except—"

"Except, this time it seems to be holding the secicao in," Admiral Sandao said. "That's as much as we could work out. But we have no idea what's producing it, or how it's holding up like that."

"So, it's like an anti collective unconscious barrier?" Faso said. "Once again, another phenomenon we've encountered that doesn't make any sense. Are you sure this isn't some kind of trick?"

"Did you manage to get any more photographs?" Hastina said, looking at Admiral Sandao.

Admiral Sandao gave a frown that expressed his disappointment. "Only five Hummingbirds came back. Each had time to take about ten photographs, but most of the shots came out overexposed."

"I see," Hastina said. "And how many Hummingbirds did you send out?"

"Over a thousand... They weren't programmed to stay for long, and we sent them under the cover of a storm. It must have been an intense force that took them down, but I have no idea what."

"Maybe the lightning?" I asked.

"Pontopa, Pontopa," Faso said, shaking his head. "Lightning wouldn't strike so many at once. It doesn't choose its targets."

"Unless Finesia is behind it," I said, with my jaw clenched. "We've seen her control a storm before."

"What baloney," Faso said. "I've never heard such idiocy in my life."

"Would you please stop this nonsense, Gordoni, boy?" General Sako said. "We've all seen things that we'd never have thought we'd believe."

I pulled a photograph in front of me, and I studied it with narrowed eyes. "He's right... It wasn't lightning that brought the Hummingbirds down..."

"What the dragonheats do you mean?" General Sako asked.

"Look closer," I passed General Sako the photograph. "If you squint hard enough, you can make out the shapes. There's a lot of black dragons inside this bubble, flying around the top of the tree, and you can see them resting on the branches. Then there's something on the branches too. Can you see the glows within the barrier?"

"Are you saying they're weapons?" Hastina asked with her head cocked.

"Blunders and dragonheats," General Sako said. "You're right, that tree is a veritable war machine."

He passed the photograph to Hastina, and she squinted at it and nodded.

Faso was laughing from the base of his stomach. "Oh, and so now I've heard it all. Are you telling me that there's a tree in there in the middle of the ocean that can lob projectiles of light at its enemies? Winda, are you hearing this?"

Winda gaped at him.

Hastina had tightened her grip on her spear. "Does that pompous idiot ever shut up?" she whispered to me.

I smiled. "Sometimes when he's sleeping... Between his snores."

"Really, I don't know how Winda puts up with him. I would have murdered him in his sleep by now."

"I'm sure she's been close to doing that, many times..."

General Sako was trying to stare Faso down, and the inventor crossed his arms and stared back at the old general.

"Look," I said. "We're all worried about Taka, and each of us have our reasons. But if we sit here talking about him all day, then who knows what might happen to him. I mean, do any of you know what they want with the boy?"

General Sako harrumphed. "Quite right," he said, turning away from Faso. "I really haven't the faintest. I thought that they had just held him hostage so that they can make further demands."

I shook my head. "There's more to it than that. I have good reason to believe that Alsie Fioreletta wants him for some kind of ritual that will involve the birth of Finesia. In other words, his life could be in danger. We need to find a way to go in there and get him out."

Hastina stood up, and she banged the butt of her spear against the floor. "I agree. Admiral Sandao, how long will it take to send the fleet to the Saye Archipelago?"

He shook his head. "We have civilians here, Hastina. Pontopa's parents and other merchants who took refuge in Fortress Gerhaun. We can't abandon them, surely..."

"They will have to either get off here and find their own way," Hastina said, "or stay on board as we sail across the Saye Ocean. We can't waste any more time here..."

I shrugged. I knew for a fact that Papo would be happy to see a battle. "We can't just abandon them here, surely?" Admiral Sandao said.

To which Hastina shook her head with a frown on her face. "Look, it's completely each civilian's choice. The truth is, if we fail at this mission, then secicao will kill them anyway. We need to get Taka back, not just for our own personal sake but for the sake of this world."

I nodded. I hated to admit it, but Hastina was right. Faso murmured under his breath, and General Sako shot him another angry glare.

Admiral Sandao stood up and leaned over the table. He studied the map for a moment, then straightened himself. "I'll give the orders to prepare a deployment party for anyone who wants to disembark here, then order us to leave for the Saye Archipelago as soon as possible...."

"But how long will it take?" I asked, as I tapped my feet against the deck plating.

"At full secicao power, we should be able to do it in three days, but we may overheat the engines and arrive with our fleet at reduced capacity. Best bet is for us to do it in three and a half. That way, we'll also arrive under cover of night."

I took a deep breath, and I looked at Hastina. Both of us knew that we could turn to our dragon forms and take Velos and the dragon automaton with us to get there quicker. But we would stand a much better chance in numbers against these dragonmen.

Footsteps resounded from the bridge behind the fore-funnel. Commander Pulan of the Saye Explorer emerged, wearing a sharp indigo suit with a star on his breast pocket. "Sir, I have word from a Commodore Garanidi of the Third Regent Fleet. They ordered us to meet with them just south of Sandstone Bluff so that we can launch an assault on the Saye Archipelago."

I raised an eyebrow, and turned to Hastina. "Is that the same fleet where we met up with Yol after we'd flown out from Gahl?"

Hastina nodded a confirmation but said nothing, as she kept her eyes focused on the commander.

Admiral Sandao also looked at the commander. "Who gave them the orders?" he asked.

"They came from the Masked Regent in the palace, by Hummingbird courier." That was good news to me, that Valpeonia had made it back safe and sound.

Admiral Sandao looked back at General Sako. "Well, I guess that's our decision made for us." He turned back to the commander. "Very well, it looks like we should follow their orders."

"And what shall we do about the civilians who want to leave?" I asked.

"Send out a fleet-wide announcement that anyone who wishes to disembark here has fifteen minutes to do so, and make sure they understand it's not compulsory to do so. Presumably, The Masked Regent sent the coordinates?"

"Yes, sir," the commander said.

"Very well," Admiral Sandao said with a nod. "Then set course. We will leave in twenty minutes sharp. If you excuse me, fellows, I'll probably be needed on the bridge."

He walked off with the commander around the fore-funnel, from where I could hear the busy calls of the officers shouting commands to each other behind the whirr of machinery. I watched him go, then I took my leave and went back up the staircase to the quarterdeck to talk to my parents before they received the announcement.

I'd decided that I'd request for them stay on the Saye Explorer, because in all honesty I wasn't sure whether they'd be safer with the fleet or on land.

PART VII

"Honour lives on when all else has crumbled to dust."

— *LIEUTENANT TALATO*

WE ONLY HAD AROUND fifty civilians working across the whole fleet, and half of those thought it best to dice with the fate that awaited us at the Saye Archipelago. The other half chose to disembark join the overland convoy. Sandao sent this group out to the riverbank on two tugboats, with a light escort of twenty marines. He didn't bother to call the tugboats back before we set off.

The subsequent journey down the Cini-Sanito river involved no further delays. I spent the time drinking tea and secicao up on deck with my parents. We agreed not to mention anything about the war, or the difficulties that had assailed me over the recent years. That might lead to discussing what had happened to Wiggea, and I was in no mood for talking about this yet.

We instead kept our conversation light, discussing various cheeses and wines we used to enjoy once, stories of my long-gone childhood, and the holidays we used to spend in the countryside cottages in forests across Tow. Admittedly, we were dreaming of a past we all knew we'd never live again. But this felt better than fearing what lay ahead.

We eventually emerged into a much rougher Costondi Sea

than I'd expected. In fact, it was choppier than I'd ever experienced it in all my years of travel. The Saye Explorer wasn't a small ship, and it heaved from side to side as if suspended from its centre by an enormous wire, then tossed every which way by the wind.

By this point, my parents had gone down to their cabin because they found it easier on their stomachs to lie down. I was the only one up here on the deck, and I sat watching the dark waves that looked like massive hills, rising and falling out of the water.

It helped for me to watch the sea, as I could predict to some extent the motion of the boat before it moved. Fortunately, the regular sailors didn't seem as affected as those who hadn't quite achieved their sea legs, and they handled the necessary manoeuvres with ease.

The Third Regent Fleet had reached the target location long before us. It was the same fleet that had carried Yol and the egg across the Costondi sea. Though the hatches were closed on the four dragon supercarriers, I could sense that they were manned at full capacity with Greys. As dragonseers, Hastina and I would have thousands of dragons at our disposal – many more than I'd led into any battle before.

The dragon queens must have donated many more of their roosts to this operation, which told me it wasn't just being orchestrated by the Masked Regent, but every single dragon of power in this world, including Cralanein. But there were no dragon queens on any of the carriers here, and by now I guessed they would have reached their destination cities in the Northern Continent.

Once we had liaised with the allied fleet just south of Sandstone Bluff, it took another half an hour for us to set off again, and we did so over the increasingly turbulent waves. Though we met no rain, the sky seemed to get increasingly grey and gloomy.

The journey continued like this, and everyone on board

found it hard to keep the food down that we'd need to give us strength for the battle. The staff at the galley were smart enough to feed us smaller portions, involving plenty of non-acidic foods that wouldn't unsettle our stomachs. I slept a lot, and I spent the rest of the time on deck, watching the patterns of weather. Occasionally, when I needed a break, I would take Velos out for a flight.

It didn't take Sandao long to cotton on to this idea, and he also started sending the troops and dragons out in squadrons for flying practice, to give them a break from this terrible sea more than anything else. Commodore Garanidi, who was in charge of the Third Regent Fleet, also took on this practice, sending out his Greys at the same time. After a couple of drills, Hastina thought it a good idea that we should turn into dragonwomen and join them.

We were on the quarterdeck of the Saye Explorer at the time, and according to our expert navigators, we'd left the Costondi Sea and were now well into the Saye Ocean. The boat was pitching so much that Sandao had ordered anyone up here to wear a harness and clip themselves to lifelines using karabiners.

The waves formed strong breakers when they smashed against the ship's hull. The spray hit us so hard that I could taste salt on my tongue. By this point, the ocean was covered by a thick fog, and we couldn't see the waves coming.

A squealing sound came from above, and a Grey emerged from the murk, then disappeared again. The rider on it also wore a harness, connected to a rope around the dragon so he didn't get blown off his mount by the wind. Together, they disappeared back into the fog.

"I'm afraid," I said. "What if Finesia manages to take control again?"

"We're all afraid," Hastina said, and her expression both seemed to glower and have a hint of compassion in it. "Everyone in this war is afraid, and we have to do horrible things. But we need to believe we can defeat Finesia, or we might as well give up now."

A plume of black smoke rose by her feet. She transformed quicker than I'd seen her transform before, and she darted up into the air, leaving the karabiner swaying on the lifeline as it clinked against the railing. I gritted my teeth, and then I did the same.

The next thing I knew, I was cutting through the fog, wearing a skin of oily black scales. I didn't need to be grounded on a smelly deck and feeling seasick. There was a taste of something in this murk, something that seemed to fill me with power and that pulled me towards a massive object looming far to the southeast. I could almost drink it, and it tasted just as fresh as the secicao gas did in those dreams that used to involve Finesia.

"*The Tree Immortal*," I said to Hastina in the collective unconscious. "*I can feel it out there. It's as if it's pulling me towards it.*"

"*I can feel it too,*" she said. "*But we must focus on the dragonsongs.*"

"*But this gas... This is secicao I can taste... How have the clouds spread so far over the ocean?*"

"*I said don't worry about it... Though it's good to know the nature of our enemy, it's not good to let anxiety about it paralyse you.*"

She was right, because I noticed that when I became more conscious of that tree's presence, I lost my connection to the Greys. Not only that, but I could feel an aura of hostility emerging from them in the collective unconscious, and at the same time I could feel Finesia trying to crawl out from the recesses of my mind.

I focused on that blue flame in the back of my mind, and then I sang the song I could hear coming out from Hastina in the collective unconscious. I mirrored her notes perfectly, and slowly I felt the antipathy from the Greys fade. I could also sense

Velos out there, and he levelled up beside me, then roared in appreciation before getting blown away by the wind.

Hastina and I continued to orchestrate the dragons through various manoeuvres, using the wind to our advantage. We knew we couldn't keep the dragons up there for too long, so we eventually brought them down towards one of the supercarriers – namely the Gileas One of the Third Regent Fleet.

All this time, we had left Velos and Bellroot on this supercarrier, where they shared a compartment. The two dragons had recently become a lot friendlier with each other, perhaps due to the fading enmity between Hastina and myself. Faso and Winda also stayed on the carrier, while they did some work on the dragon automaton – though I don't know how they managed in these conditions. Faso had left me the helmet that Rastano Wiggea had last worn, which currently lay beside my bunk in my cabin on the Saye Explorer.

After three days of travel, I went to bed after a small meal of bread, still feeling incredibly queasy. I was lucky to have one of the cabins above deck, but because of the fog there wasn't much of a view through the window.

Talato and Candiorno were sleeping in the adjacent cabin. Talato was looking after the cyagora again. In all honesty, I'd not seen either of them at all for the entire trip. I was so tired, despite my stomach, and as soon as I collapsed on the hard mattress, I entered a deep sleep.

There came a banging on the door. I jerked up in bunk, reminding me of the state of my stomach and the incredibly convenient bucket beneath me that lay just next to the helmet on the deck floor.

"What is it?" I managed to say, though speaking was hard.

"Dragonseer Wells…" It was Hastina, and she didn't sound too good for the wear either.

The door swung open to the outside, and I saw her framed by the darkness, except there was a green glow coming from somewhere in the distance.

"What is it?" I said again.

"You need to get up now," she said. "We've arrived, and we're under attack."

That was when I noticed that the green glow was getting brighter, as the projectile it was attached to streamed through the sky towards us.

33

A HOT HOWLING wind whipped over the boat, tossing up the waves around us. I couldn't see the water, it was so dark, but the flecks at the head of each wave glowed with a haunting green luminance.

Hastina made her way across the reeling ship first, keeping one hand on the railing and the other on her spear as she moved with careful sidesteps. Her metal leg clanked along the deck-plating as she went, and she kept steady by keeping her weight on her good leg.

The Greys were already aloft. Not only could I feel their presence in the collective unconscious, but I could also hear their roars as they streaked through the sky, fighting to be heard over the cry of the wind.

The Tree Immortal stood tall in the distance, or rather its outline did, secicao sprawling along its trunk in a motion that started at the ground and pushed upwards and then out towards its branches. From these branches, tiny green specks of light started as little pinpricks. They hurtled towards our fleet and the surrounding ships, growing into massive green fireballs when they got close.

A faint green glow surrounded the Tree Immortal. It seemed

to wrap around it like a ring balanced on its side. I thought I noticed other shapes flying around inside the glowing area. Silent and bat-like, they flittered around but never emerged from their protective barrier.

Closer to us, a projectile hit a nearby dragon carrier – one of the smaller ones – and erupted. Fire lashed out across the ship as if from an ignited oil bomb. A sailor on board screamed out, and dived into the ocean, sending up a faint trail of green gas behind him. The water opened up to embrace him.

My heart lurched in my chest, as there came a crashing sound and a dragonman spiralled out from the waves into the sky, emerging from the exact same point where the sailor had entered. It didn't head towards the Greys. Rather, it cut a straight line through the night towards the Tree Immortal. I traced it for as long as I could, until it was swallowed up by the night.

Our dragons – and there must have been a good twenty of them – moved in to attack the glowing barrier. Flames streaked across the sky in the distance, but they didn't break through.

Together, Hastina and I made our way to the spiral staircase that led up from the rear funnel to the bridge. Before Hastina ascended, she put her hand to her head and stopped in her tracks. My head started to reel.

"*Come to me...*" the voice said in my head. Dragonheats, how had Finesia found her way in? "*Come to me and prove your worth. Your destiny lies within the Tree Immortal.*"

I swallowed hard. "Hastina?"

She turned to me, and a trace of green flashed in her eyes. "Yes?"

"I—You hear her too? Finesia..."

She nodded, her jaw set. "The battle has begun, and we must use all the tools we have available to keep ourselves together."

"But I've been doing everything I can to keep her out."

"So have I, for wellies' sake."

Her gaze roved over to the tree in the distance, then focused on another green fireball sailing through the darkness. This went wide of the ships, and a roar of pain boomed out from the distance. Glowing green, a Grey keeled over in the sky. Both dragon and rider screamed out as they fell, both bathed in a fire that stuck to their forms.

The sea opened up a valley to accept them, and a behemoth of a wave washed over them. My heart pounded in my chest, as I waited for a repeat of what I saw before. A black dragon shot out from the crest of this bigger wave. Its roar turned into a piercing shriek that cut the battlefield apart.

"What is this?" I asked. "They can't create these dragonmen without dragonseer blood..." Then the realisation washed over me. "Taka..."

Hastina looked back at me, her eyebrows furrowed. The ship veered in the other direction, and I found a railing to cling to before the motion sent me towards the prow. Hastina took hold of my free hand, and she pulled me back towards the staircase.

"Come on," she said.

Again, came the voice of Finesia, on repeat like the same song playing over and over. *"Come to me... Come and embrace your destiny. Alsie Fioreletta is waiting."*

Hastina was already halfway up the stairs. I focused on the screams, the cry of dragons, the crashing sounds of the waves, in an attempt to push Finesia away.

Salt and ozone hung in the air. The pungent smell of secicao seemed to burn at my nostrils. I did whatever I could to keep Finesia out, while at the same time trying not to slip down the stairs as the ship pitched once again.

Hastina and I struggled past the oval table that had been pushed and secured against one of the bridge's bulkheads. Around the front of the fore-funnel, General Sako, Admiral Sandao, and the officers on deck were busy taking paper readouts from the equipment, shouting out commands and information across each other. Sandao turned and noticed us approach.

"Dragonseer Wells and Dragonseer Wiggea on the bridge!"

he shouted with a volume that belied his smaller frame. "Clip yourselves onto a lifeline. This is going to be a rough one."

Both he and General Sako had placed themselves against the railing around the forwards funnel, and they had karabiners that connected them from the back of their harnesses to the railing.

"Where's Velos and the dragon automaton?" I asked Admiral Sandao after I'd taken position and clipped myself in. I glanced at Hastina. "Where's Bellroot for that matter?"

"They're all on the Gileas One supercarrier," Admiral Sandao said. "Talato, Candiorno, Faso, and Winda are waiting with them and more tech. We were just waiting for you to go out and lead that battle."

"Blunders and dragonheats," General Sako shouted, as he watched a fireball surge downwards and hit a nearby ship – this time a cruiser. It exploded on impact, bathing the cruiser in that weird green fire. "We need to break through that barrier. We've got to get those dragons and the automatons in the air."

"We need the dragonseers," Admiral Sandao said. "A coordinated attack. We've discussed this."

"Then why aren't you two dragonseers bloody up there already?" General Sako asked. "It took you long enough to wake up, Dragonseer Wells."

I shook my head. "I thought you meant to wake me long before we reached our destination."

"I don't know what happened," Admiral Sandao said. "All of a sudden, the ocean opened up, creating a rift in it with two waves surging on each side. We thought we'd hit an intense undercurrent that would swallow us whole – a sudden shift in the tectonic plates or something like that. But instead, this rift sped us here at over two-hundred-miles per hour. I'm sorry, we hardly had time to react. Now, here we are."

General Sako harrumphed. "And then that bloody tree started firing at us. Blunders and dragonheats, get out there. Really, those dragons need some control."

Hastina didn't need to be told thrice. She unclipped herself from the railing. "Follow me, Dragonseer Wells," she said. "Admiral Sandao, send the orders to launch Velos, Bellroot and the dragon automaton."

"Affirmative, ma'am," he said, and Hastina went to the second staircase that led up to the quarterdeck. At the top, the ship keened in the aft direction, sending Hastina and I reeling down the deck, our arms windmilling around us.

Hastina waited until we were just about to hit the aft funnel, then clipped herself onto the railing there with her karabiner. She grabbed hold of my wrist with her free hand, pulled me back towards the funnel, and clipped me onto the railing.

Three more explosions pierced the darkness; three more Greys with riders fell from the sky.

From further away came the cranking sound of the supercarrier opening the hatches. I heard Velos roar into the wind, though I couldn't see him.

"*It's about to happen...*" Finesia said in my mind. "*Our union will be beautiful. Now, take the form that I gifted to you, and all will be well.*"

I pushed Finesia away because that's all I could do. Even focusing on that blue flame couldn't stop her nattering away in my mind. Instead, I reverted to the my old strategy of completely ignoring her.

Hastina had that green glow again in her irises, only faintly detectable. Her jaw set, she stared out into the darkness, probably battling with the same demon. The wind whipped her hair out in multiple directions. A shudder went down my spine.

"Hastina, it's too risky to fly out there," I shouted. "Not with Finesia in our minds like this."

She looked at me, her eyes narrowed. The green glow intensified in her eyes. She blinked it away, and a pocket of air travelled down her throat.

"You're right, Dragonseer Wells." She looked out at the Tree Immortal. "We need to find another way."

"The helmet. I can use it to protect myself from her... But I can't control the dragons that way."

"It will at least buy you some time to think without her nattering in your mind." She unclipped herself and took hold of my hand. "Come, we'll return to the bridge."

I unclipped and let her pull me along the careening deck. She used her spear for support, clanking it along the deck plating as she went. As soon as we reached the front section of the bridge and clipped ourselves back in, I turned to one of the junior officers standing guard. "You there. I left my helmet in the cabin. Go grab it, and move fast!"

The junior saluted. "Yes, ma'am," he said. He rushed across the bridge and disappeared behind the fore-funnel. He'd be much faster navigating the ship in this storm than I would.

Hastina looked at me. "Good thinking."

I frowned, deciding to get straight to the point. "The helmet won't just keep Finesia out, but I can also use it to pilot Velos. But what about you, will you be okay?"

Hastina gave me a curt nod. "I can handle myself."

I nodded. "Good... I'll at least be able to see where Velos is heading through the interface that Faso installed in the helmet. We used it to defeat a whole shiver of automaton sharks, before Faso installed any of that Gordoni Ray technology. But I won't be able to give any commands, not without the dragonsongs."

"That will help us plan strategically," Admiral Sandao said, looking at me over his shoulder. A flash of lightning came from outside, reflecting off his bald pate which was slicked with sweat. "Faso has connected us to his speaker system, but he's not responding right now."

But it appeared that Faso was actually listening, because his voice came out of a metal box by the front windows. It had a single metal speaker at the bottom of it and a studio microphone sticking out of the front.

"I'm making the final adjustments," Faso said, sounding irritated. "Give me two minutes, okay?"

"Then, you can launch?" Admiral Sandao asked.

"Send Talato and Candiorno ahead if you want…"

"Blunders and dragonheats, no!" General Sako said. "We need all three of you to fly out there at once."

"Very well," Faso said. "Bellroot looks marvellous by the way. He really seems to like his new suit of armour."

Hastina unclipped herself from the railing and strode up to the console. "What did you just say, Faso?"

"I said that Bellroot has a new coat of armour. That's what I've been working on all this time here. It's lucky I know the prototypes well, because it's not easy to work fast under these conditions."

Hastina's face had gone red. "Who ordered this?" she asked.

"It was my idea, of course…"

"I said who gave the orders?"

"Well, General Sako—"

Before Faso could say anything else, Hastina whacked the microphone with the butt of her spear. She turned to the general, her fists clenched around the shaft, the whites of her knuckles showing. "Once again, you directly circumvented protocol, General Sako. It appears you never learn, and you will face court martial for this."

"Are you asking me to step down?" General Sako asked.

Hastina glared at General Sako. She twisted her spear and I noticed that green glow again in her eyes.

"*Hastina,*" I said in the collective unconscious. "*Remember yourself.*"

She blinked again, then took a deep breath. She turned slowly to face the window, and she stared out at the battlefield.

Another missile traced across the sky, knocking into a Grey and downing it, rider and all. Another black dragon emerged from the raging ocean after it had fallen. Dragonheats, we needed to attack that barrier as quickly as possible, otherwise they would turn all of our soldiers into dragonmen, and we'd have nothing left to fight with.

"You know full well that the battle is lost," Finesia said in my head. *"But I can offer you and your partner dragonseer a truce. Come to us, and we will not destroy your friendly fleet immediately. I'll save you the honour of doing that, much like you did in Ginlast... My Fallen Executioner. How does that sound for a title?"*

I gritted my teeth. I wasn't even going to answer her. Instead, I summoned up a dragonsong in the collective unconscious, and used it to give the dragons a little bit of courage. I then modified the notes a little, to order more dragons to charge the barrier. A hundred surged forwards and bathed the strange shield in a torrent of amber flame.

But it wasn't enough to break it. We needed more.

"When do we get to test our technology out?" Faso said from the strange speaker system.

"Soon, Gordoni boy, soon. We're just waiting for the helmet to be delivered here, which Dragonseer Wells will then use to give us a tactical advantage."

"But Pontopa won't be able to use her dragonsongs effectively to control the dragons. I've not yet had time to create the interface control box she'll need to pilot Velos remotely. I need more time..."

"At least I can watch and provide some feedback. Lieutenant Talato, are you patched into the speaker system?"

There was a pause. "Yes, ma'am, I'm piloting Bellroot."

"And Candiorno?" I asked.

"I'm here, ma'am," he replied. "On Velos."

Hastina had her spear braced against the back of her thighs, her fists clenched so tightly around the shaft that I could see the whites of her knuckles. Her shoulders heaved, and I could sense in the collective unconscious how she felt about all this.

A clanking of footsteps came from the staircase behind me. I glanced over my shoulder to see the junior officer that I'd sent down, carrying the helmet. He gave me a slight bow, then handed it to me.

"I hope it helps, ma'am," he said. I gave him a curious frown, wondering if at his young age he could possibly know what was at stake here. I lifted the helmet to my head, and a sudden memory flashed through my head of Wiggea wearing this thing in the brig, sleeping so innocently as he emanated his soft snores.

"*You really don't want to do this,*" Finesia said in my head. "*You dare to anger me now, and you cannot imagine the punishments you'll receive when I eventually win you over to my side.*"

But I'd had enough of her voice. I lifted the helmet on to my head, and my mind went silent. I breathed a huge sigh of relief. I felt around for the dial that lowered the slats on my helmet and I turned it.

Now, it was time to get this battle on the road.

34

ON THE VISOR-SCREEN of my helmet, I could now see the inside of the Gileas One supercarrier through Velos' eyes. From the open hatch open above him, a haunting green light filled the room that danced in sync with the explosions outside.

Bellroot stood beside Velos, Talato seated at the front of his armour. This wasn't golden like Velos' armour but instead had a burnished silver colour that complemented his citrine scales well. Hastina's dragon had his head craned to the ceiling as he watched the sky intently. He clearly was anxious to get out onto the battlefield and test this armour out.

Talato's eyes were focused on a point above Velos' head where I knew Candiorno to be sitting. She wore a gas mask – I guess there were quite a lot of secicao clouds surrounding the Tree Immortal, and they needed to be prepared.

"Dragonseer Wells, does it work?" General Sako asked.

"Affirmative. I can see everything."

"Then we're ready to launch?"

"We are," Admiral Sandao said, and his voice took on a more commanding tone. "Saye Explorer to Gileas One. Launch the coloured dragons and the dragon automaton, and get the Rocs ready. We're going to hit that barrier with the best we have."

The night above Velos was fringed with green clouds. I felt the floor buck, and it took me a moment to realise that it was the Saye Explorer, and not the Gileas One dragon carrier that rocked.

"We've been hit," a female voice shouted in the vicinity – I guess one of the lieutenants at the controls.

"Dragonheats... Damage report," Admiral Sandao said.

"The projectile went down the aft funnel, sir," another lieutenant, this time male, said. "The damage control teams are already working on it below deck."

"Were there any casualties?" Hastina asked.

There came a crackling sound, as if someone was speaking over a talkie, but the voice wasn't very clear. Then from the bridge, the same female lieutenant who'd announced the hit said, "Negative, ma'am."

"Make sure no one dies down there," Hastina said, her voice strained. "Because that green fire can turn them into black dragons. If that happens, get them tossed out to sea before they turn. We can't afford having one of those things aboard our ship."

"Affirmative, ma'am. I believe this fire's under control. No one's going to die down there."

"I'm not sure we can hold much longer," Admiral Sandao said. "We need to consider a retreat."

"Let's just give our technology a chance," General Sako said. "I've seen what these Rocs can do. They took out a whole flock of dragonmen near the Southern Approach. With such advanced weaponry... Just maybe we can change the tide of the war."

As General Sako was speaking, Velos launched into the air. He was the first out of the hatch, and he oriented himself to face the Tree Immortal as he hovered in the sky. A green glowing missile whizzed past him, and he turned his head to watch it plunge into the sea.

Behind him, Bellroot shot from his compartment into the sky, and the dragon automaton came up behind him. Five of the enormous Roc automatons followed them up, launching from five larger hatches on the Gileas One. They adjusted their formation, until they had arranged themselves in a straight line, with plenty of distance between them.

I opened the slats on the visor so I could see Velos and Bellroot from our position on the bridge. Both armoured dragons and the dragon automaton glowed green, making it easy to see them and the dragons that occasionally passed in front of them.

Meanwhile, the Greys kept flying in erratic evasive manoeuvres as they tried to lure the projectiles away from the Gileas One. They'd given up attacking the barrier now, but this was only temporary. They only needed to buy us some time so we could fly in the armoured dragons, dragon automaton, and Rocs to attack the shield with maximum force.

A missile came sailing past Velos again. It hit one of the Rocs behind him on the chest. The light faded, leaving a black charmark on the Roc's plating, but the automaton seemed to have survived the hit.

Meanwhile, thousands of Hummingbirds shot out of other ships in the vicinity, and they joined the squadron. They buzzed around the two dragons, the dragon automaton, and the Rocs so fast that they seemed to form a protective shield of their own.

"We're ready, sir." The voice came from the Gileas One over the speaker.

"Very well, attack," General Sako said. "Dragonseer Wiggea, clear a path."

Hastina looked back at General Sako and nodded, then she sang a dragonsong. With the helmet on my head and my connection to the collective unconscious severed, I no longer had that ability. But it didn't matter, because I had my own task to accomplish...

The two armoured dragons surged forward, leaving a green exhaust trail in their wake. They cut across the night at astonishing speed. Soon, they reached the shield, and the dragons and automatons slowed themselves to a hover, letting the Humming-birds spin around them.

One projectile streaked out from the Tree Immortal towards them, aimed at Faso and Winda on the dragon automaton. It hit the wall of Hummingbirds, and the explosion painted the night green. Dozens of Hummingbirds must have fallen to the sea, letting out bright sparks when they hit the waves. Still, thousands remained.

I closed the slats on the visor, so I could see the barrier from up close. A green glow danced over the shield's surface, looking like the northern lights that wrap around the sky.

"Dragonseer Wells," General Sako said. "Can you see what's happening up close?"

A dial on the side of the helmet could adjust the magnification, and I fiddled with it to check that it worked. I managed to get a good view of a black dragon flying around in there, then I used the controls on the helmet to get a wide-angle view of the scene.

"Affirmative," I said.

"Good. Fire the missiles!"

"Wait a moment..." I said.

"Hold that order," Admiral Sandao said. "What is it, Dragonseer Wells?"

I had an idea. There was no saying I couldn't use secicao while wearing this helmet. It would surely still keep Finesia out. I raised the visor, without needing to open the slats, took the hip flask from my hip, and I took a large swig from it. My vision ghosted into speckled green, and the effect still remained once I lowered the visor. Now, I could not only focus in on things using the magnification on my helmet, but could also slow down time.

I zoomed back out as far as I could, until the camera on Velos projected a fish-eye view on the display on my helmet. "Now fire!" I shouted.

"You heard the lady," General Sako said.

"Yes, ma'am and sir," an officer said.

Presently, the missiles launched out of the Rocs, and the gatling guns on the armoured dragons and automatons started to whirr. They unleashed a volley of bullets that did nothing but prick the shield, creating slight indents in it like hailstones might in a pool of water, but failing to break it.

Moments later, a good two dozen missiles hit the shield, spawning thousands of smaller explosions, just as they had when we'd deployed them against Indira. They sent up plumes of black smoke that concealed the battle for several seconds.

When the smoke faded, the shield remained intact.

"Blunders and dragonheats," General Sako said. "It's as tough as a bunker. Did you see any weaknesses, Dragonseer Wells? Anything that we could exploit?"

I raised the visor so I could look at him. "Mere pinpricks. Nothing that's going to help."

"I knew it... It's impervious," General Sako said. "Admiral, we don't stand a chance here. You're right, we have to retreat."

From outside, a screech cut across the night. Another Grey had been hit, and it plummeted into the sea.

Admiral Sandao had his hand on his chin, considering. "I don't think we have a choice..."

Hastina, who was gazing out the window, turned to face both the admiral and general. "Do it. I need to go in alone..." The room went silent for a moment, and all eyes fell on her. "Finesia... She keeps inviting me in. I don't think that we can get through the shield. But as a dragonwoman... Maybe I can get through. It's worth a try, at least."

I studied her eyes for traces of green, but this time she seemed completely under control.

"I should go too," I said, and I reached up to remove the helmet.

"No," Hastina said. "If Finesia takes hold of your mind... That dream... Yol believes that there's a lot more at stake for me than you. I have to do this alone."

Another scream came from outside, another Grey fell, another black dragon rose from the dark and turbid waters.

"Blunders and dragonheats," General Sako said. "We can't stand all day and talk about this. Admiral Sandao, we must retreat."

"Very well," Admiral Sandao said. "Commander Pulan, recall all dragons, and set steering course for two-seventy degrees true. Carry mostly left to combat the storm. We're getting out of here."

A female officer in a navy-blue uniform turned back to Admiral Sandao and saluted. "Aye aye, Admiral."

"Thank you, Admiral Sandao," Hastina said. She turned to me. "I'll be okay, Dragonseer Wells. Don't come after me."

My heart was pounding in my chest, as I watched the commander walk up to the microphone and relay the commands into it. Hastina moved towards the staircase and climbed quickly. I put down my visor to watch the dragons turn around in slow motion.

That was when I saw it... A green missile surging straight towards Velos. A gap had formed in the wall of Hummingbirds as they readjusted their course.

"Dragonheats," I shouted. "Candiorno, evasive manoeuvres now!"

But though the secicao let me speed up my mind, I couldn't force my words out any quicker. Candiorno had no time to react. Within seconds the light from the missile wrapped around my vision. The display became white noise.

"Dragonheats!" I said again.

I lifted the visor on my helmet. I didn't want to say it... But I had no choice. "Candiorno, disengage immediately... That's an order!"

Unlike the riders on the Greys, Candiorno would be harnessed in. If he turned into a black dragon on Velos' back, there was no telling what he might do. "Candiorno, I hope you heard me. Disengage immediately!"

Talato would hear this, and she would hate me for it. Yet, I had to protect Velos.

I was too far away from Candiorno to see how he did it. But he heeded my orders and launched himself off Velos. The murky waves seemed to reach out like claws that wanted to pull him beneath the water.

A dark cloud passed in front of us, and so I didn't see what happened next. Part of me hoped he wouldn't arise from the waters. Maybe, Finesia would at least give him an honourable death for his courage...

I swallowed my fears, and I ripped off the helmet – it was useless now.

"*Well hello, darling,*" Finesia said in my head.

"*Just shut up,*" I replied. "*I have my friends to save.*"

She continued to natter in my mind, but there was no way that I was going to pay her any heed. Velos needed me out there, and I wasn't going to let him die.

"Dragonheats," Faso said over the speaker system. "This green flame can burn through my seatbelts, which I created to be fire retardant. Candiorno's down, I'm afraid, may he rest in peace. Meanwhile, we have to get out of here. Faso Gordoni, out."

"What about Velos?" I asked.

"He's... Dragonheats, the armour is keeping him aloft. But his wings are damaged, and he can't fly anymore. We can't save him, Pontopa. I'm sorry."

"Faso, you'll bloody well do what you can. After all the things Velos has done for you, he deserves your help."

"Pontopa, this will kill us... Winda, what the dragonheats are you doing? Don't lean out like that... No, not your harness. You need to be strapped in. Dragonheats, why now?"

Winda was also screaming something, but the beating wind muffled her voice, so I couldn't make out what she said. Soon, both their voices cut off, and I pursed my lips, fearing the worst.

More clouds forced their way into the vicinity, obscuring

everything that was happening in the distance. We couldn't see the Tree Immortal anymore, but I could feel it tugging me towards it. Meanwhile, Finesia kept shouting in my head, willing me to turn into a black dragon...

I knew I had no choice, and so I started to transform... Scales pressed at the skin on my forearms, and my shoulder blades began to tear.

"I'm going too," I said to the bridge, and my voice came out incredibly gravelly.

Both the general and admiral turned to me, jaws hanging low. Admiral Sandao reached down for the pistol at his hip.

I didn't wait to see if this meek and well-mannered old man would dare to shoot me point blank. Instead, I charged towards the staircase, ripping off the karabiner that secured me to the railing, as the scales ripped my skin apart.

I stormed up the stairs with speed generated both through the secicao I'd drunk and my massive scaly thighs. By the time I had reached the upper deck, I was a dragonwoman.

"*Marvellous work,*" Finesia said in my mind. "*Now join us. The ritual will soon start.*"

Taka, I thought... He was in danger. But then my heart went out to Velos, and I could feel him struggling in the collective unconscious.

"*No,*" I said back to Finesia. "*First, I will save my dragon, and then I shall find a way to destroy you.*"

I roared as I launched myself into the raging storm, as Finesia's manic laughter pealed through my mind.

35

THE STORM FUELLED ME, much as it had when I'd murdered Bassalhan in the secicao jungle. Green lightning flared through the clouds, and a bolt struck my back. I roared in delight as power surged through my thick veins.

Part of my mind stayed connected to Finesia. That part wanted me to follow Hastina straight towards the Tree Immortal. But now that I had torn myself from the helmet, my connection to Velos had returned.

I could feel his muscles weakening, his wings failing. In the distance, the light from his armour seemed to flicker like a candle flame ready to gutter out. Something was stopping the armour from augmenting him fully, and because of that, he was losing strength.

But he hadn't given up yet because he still had help at hand. Through the clouds, I could faintly make out Asinal Winda crawling onto him from the dragon automaton. Bellroot remained near him too, Talato astride him. Still, there was no sign of Candiorno. Had he arisen from the water? Had he also joined Finesia's side?

No doubt similar questions were going through Talato's mind, and I could only imagine the pain she was in right now, but still I knew that she'd do her utmost to aid Velos. Because that's where her loyalties lay.

"*You don't need your dragon anymore,*" Finesia said. "*You don't need any of your old friends. Once you have united with me, your previous ties will mean nothing. You will see...*"

Her words caused elation to rise in me, and another flash of lightning surged from the sky, filling me with sweet power. But the effect only lasted for a moment, as I remembered to envision the blue flame. Behind it lay my connection to Velos, my true friend...

"*No,*" I said back to her. "*My friends and family will always mean something to me. Without that, I'm a monster, just like you and Alsie...*"

As if in response to my insolence, another spark of lightning plucked at the scales on my back. Pain melded with pleasure in my body, my mind stunned. That was when I realised... This lightning didn't just fill me with power. It was Finesia's way of getting me to submit to her.

It must have been how she'd gained such control of me in the battle outside Fortress Gerhaun. She'd used the shock to temporarily sever my connection to the collective unconscious, and she'd done it for long enough to cause me to forget myself. Long enough for me to kill Bassalhan, but fortunately not long enough for me to completely lose my mind.

I focused again on the blue flame. Another flash of lightning flared from the sky. This time I saw it coming and I dodged out of the way. Dragonfire burned hotter than usual at the pit of my stomach. For a moment, I feared Finesia, and I feared what this lightning she was clearly summoning would do to my friends.

But I couldn't let the fear reign. Only two goals mattered now: rescue Velos; rescue Taka.

The Rocs sailed towards me, their long sandpiper-like beaks piercing the night. Having already spent their ordnance, they passed silently. The lightning striking my skin had augmented my speed, and this allowed me to catch up with Hastina. She looked back over her wing as I approached.

"Dragonheats, Dragonseer Wells. Didn't I tell you to stay put?" she asked in the collective unconscious.

"You did. But there's more at stake now... Hastina, did you feel it? Velos got hit. He might not make it if we don't help him."

"But what can we do?"

"Use some of our strength to help him back to the ship..." I said. *"He's weakening, and I don't think he'll make it through."*

"Then go and look after him... Meanwhile, I must get through that barrier..."

"Dragonseer Wiggea, I might need your help too. Two of us to carry him, to stop him falling into the sea... Winda's on top of him, trying to save him. But he's not got enough strength in him, even with the secicao in his armour. I can feel that... I can feel the pain in his wings."

Hastina let out a loud roar, and she stopped herself in mid-air with her wings. She used the change in momentum to bank towards the point where I could see the glowing armoured dragons and dragon automaton. Bellroot and the dragon automaton had flown underneath Velos in an attempt to push him upwards. Even with Faso's technology, neither had the strength to keep Velos aloft. On the contrary, he seemed to be pushing them back down towards the raging sea.

I had flown close enough now that I could see what the problem was. Green secicao leaked from one of the sides of Velos' armour, just below where Winda sat on the central seat. She didn't have her harness fully secured, and instead used half of it for support as she leant down with a large squeezy tube of sealant to patch him back up.

"Why do you bother with such nonsense?" Finesia asked in my mind. *"Your dragon will die eventually, and so will your friends. You will have to leave them behind, unless I choose to end your life now..."*

"You don't listen, Finesia. I will not abandon them..."

"That's sad, because the dragons at least will have to die. But, if you really need them so much, I can make your friends immortal..."

"Finesia, what are you—" I stopped speaking as soon as I saw the projectile of green light hurtling towards them.

"The fools, by bunching together like that, they have created such an easy target."

"No!" I screamed it out loud, cutting the air apart with my roar. I wasn't close enough to reach them in time and save them...

Hastina was. She tucked in her wings and took a dive towards the water, skimming the surface with her underbelly as she gained speed. As the green fireball drew closer, she lifted herself gracefully from the dive.

She launched in front of Velos and his bearers, then twisted her open wings to break her speed. Silhouetted against the growing light, she embraced the projectile. As the explosion engulfed her, she let out a cry so high-pitched it caused me to grimace.

But she remained in the sky, without falling.

"Dragonseer Wiggea, are you okay?" I asked.

"It burns a little but we're almost invulnerable... It will heal, I'm sure..."

Just before she finished speaking, another ball of green caught my eye. This time, the Tree Immortal must have put some spin on the fireball, because it now approached slightly from the right, ready to hit the dragon automaton and knock Faso off his perch.

Fortunately, I was close enough to block the projectile. I cried out, then summoned strength to my wings. Lightning flared around me again, but it didn't seem to want to strike at me anymore. I didn't have time to dive and soar as Hastina had, and it took all my strength to get into position.

I opened my wings at the last minute, and the missile hit me bang on the chest. It sent me reeling backwards, and my muscles spasmed in pain. But I'd blocked it, and I looked over my shoulder to see Faso staring up at me from the dragon automaton's back.

Once he realised that he was safe, he turned back to Winda, and started shouting at her. I didn't hear exactly what he said, but I did hear Winda scream back at him, "Shut up, Faso!"

Those words silenced him for a short while. Then came the whistling sound of another projectile streaming through the night. This time I saw it curling around from the other side, towards Bellroot and Talato. There was no way that we'd be able to reach it in time.

"*They're dead...*" I said. "*I'm sorry, Velos...*"

Just before it managed to hit its target, both Bellroot and the dragon automaton split apart. Winda righted herself and quickly buckled her harness. At the same time, the Gatling guns pivoted around on Velos' armour, and they unleashed a volley of bullets behind the dragon. He shot forwards, projectile missing him by inches.

Velos' armour then flared bright green. He roared, and I felt the strength return to his muscles. He flapped his wings and gained speed. I could still feel his pain, but I could see from the way that he flew that the secicao had given him enough strength to get back safely, luck permitting.

I watched the three dragons fly towards the fleet. Winda had dared to unlatch her harness again so that she could clamber onto Velos' front seat. As she did, Faso was screaming out at her from his seat on the dragon automaton. Bellroot flew on the other side of Velos, and I breathed a sigh of relief to see that all three now flew in a steady rhythm.

"*He'll be okay,*" I said to Hastina.

"*It seems so,*" she replied. "*Velos will live to fly again.*"

Then Finesia's voice came in my head. "*After all that drama, I've decided to let your friends go to live another day. I won't send out any more missiles at your retreating fleet, so long as you join us. Come promptly. You are needed for the ceremony.*"

I growled from deep within my chest, and turned back to face the barrier, glowing faintly against the night. Clouds had pooled around it, as early morning mist does on a lake.

"*We should go,*" Hastina said. She had also turned to face the barrier as well. I glanced over to see a green glow shining out of her narrow eyes.

Together we soared towards the shield. I took one last glance over my shoulder – my way of saying goodbye to Velos, my friends, and the ships which were now hastily making their retreat.

PART VIII

"Find a monster, and study them through the glass until you no longer see a monster. Do this enough, and you'll come to realise there are no monsters, only misguided individuals who excessively overvalue the things and people they hold most dear."

— *CRALANEIN GAO, DRAGON QUEEN*

36

THE BARRIER CALLED us towards it like a siren's song.

As Hastina and I approached it, my mind became affixed on the patterns of green light that streaked across it, passing over the surface like gentle waves over a calm lake. Lightning flared out of the clouds, and with each flash came the gentle tug of static on my scales. The air tasted fresh, as it does after a storm, even if the true storm was yet to come.

From the barrier, came voices – whispering susurrations promising a better life, a better future. It didn't take me long to realise that the voices weren't emanating from the barrier but from the Tree Immortal. And I didn't hear them in my ears, but in the collective unconscious. They seemed to belong to many, but as I focused more, I realised they all belonged to Finesia herself. It was as if she had many incarnations, and each one had its own story to tell.

But as the words took further form, I realised all the voices were in fact speaking the same message.

"One soul living through many minds – the destined evolution of the collective unconscious."

Once I'd latched on to the meaning, all the voices had become one, and I heard the same words over and over, as if on repeat in my head. By then, I had become completely mesmerised, and had lost myself to Finesia once again.

My focus remained transfixed on the barrier, and it wasn't long until Hastina and I passed the threshold. The sky suddenly seemed to flicker, and night transformed into day. The sun stood directly overhead in the sky, the Tree Immortal towering up towards it. Streaky clouds swirled around the tree, forming wispy concentric circles.

"*We're here,*" Hastina said to me in the collective unconscious. "*Our ultimate destination. Our destiny finally awaits.*"

Her yellow eyes now glowed green, but that didn't worry me. Rather it seemed the most natural thing in the world. Raw dragonfire heated my stomach, and elation surged in my chest. Satisfyingly warmed from the inside, I let out a bright green jet of flame into the sky.

"*We have waited long for this moment,*" I said. "*The past – what I and you once were – doesn't matter anymore.*"

"*Only our faith matters,*" Hastina said. "*Finesia is the ultimate fate of this world.*"

"*And we know the truths of the myths... The Gods Themselves didn't leave us out of disappointment, but because they knew that by handing the world to Finesia, they'd leave it in safe hands. Now, it is time for her to rise again.*"

We weren't really talking to each other. We were speaking for another who listened to our thoughts nearby, checking that we hadn't passed through Finesia's threshold with malicious intent. To do so would have been impossible, because Finesia had a leash on all her subjects within this realm. Hastina and I were dragonwomen, after all.

I sensed our guide approaching, soaring towards us from behind. I didn't turn to see her approach, however, for I knew instinctively that she meant us no harm, at least for now. A high-pitched trill came out of Alsie Fioreletta's mouth, as she overtook by swooping down below us. She banked upwards, braked with her wings, and turned to face us from where she hovered in the sky. Both Hastina and I used our wings to brake so we didn't collide with her head on.

Alsie addressed us both in the collective unconscious. *"Empress Finesia is pleased that you've finally seen sense. She is waiting eagerly for the ritual."*

I still had no idea what the ritual was. But it didn't matter anymore because I trusted Finesia to lead me towards a better future. She was, after all, the goddess who would inherit this world.

"Lead the way, Acolyte Fioreletta," I said.

"As long as you promise you are loyal, Acolyte Wells," Alsie said. *"That, I must ask of you first."*

"My heart and soul will remain the property of Finesia..."

"And what do you say of your crimes against her?"

"That I must do my penance, and so Finesia can do with me as she pleases."

"Then I'm sure your sense of duty will delight our sacred one," Alsie said, and she bowed her head before turning to Hastina. *"What about you, Acolyte Wiggea... What say you of your crimes against Finesia?"*

"That I am truly sorry, and I am hers to command, always..."

Alsie let out another trill, which soon turned into a roar. She spread her wings, then soared down below us. *"Come,"* she said. *"Acolyte Wells, you shall enter with me, as you are required for the ritual. Acolyte Wiggea, you shall wait outside."*

She turned, then floated down towards a wide tree stump on a raised knoll just in front of the Tree Immortal. The top of this was large enough to land on, and when she did, she roared once again, passing a swathe of fire over the bark of the Tree Immortal in front of her. The tree shuddered, and the patterns in the bark twisted into different shapes, until they eventually revealed an entranceway into the tree. Something metal glinted inside, coming from an array of cogs and gears connected to the edge of a brass platform that spanned the diameter of the bole.

Back on her stump, black smoke rose around Alsie, who

quickly converted into her human form. She wore a long white robe, with a hemline that trailed behind her as she walked. She strode inside, and the patterns in the Tree Immortal's bark shifted again, soon concealing Alsie and the platform from view.

The Tree Immortal quaked, together with the ground in front of it. The stump that Alsie had landed on lowered itself into the ground, sending up a plume of dust. Two other tree stumps rose from the ground in its place, conveniently situated for Hastina and I to land on.

As I approached one of the stumps, my claws poised, and my back arched ready to land, Hastina's voice came in the collective unconscious. "*Dragonseer Wells, now it's safe for us to talk. I can mask our thoughts for only a moment... I hope I haven't lost you to her.*"

I looked at Hastina, confusion reeling around my mind. Her words sounded unreal, as if they didn't belong to anything natural. They weren't a product of Empress Finesia... The green glow had left Hastina's eyes, and a sense of alarm surged inside me. "*You aren't a believer... You don't serve our—*"

"*Dragonseer Wells, listen!*" she snapped back, and out from her mouth came a deep growl. "*Find yourself, or I'll have to take you down before you even have a chance to enter the Tree Immortal. Remember who you are...*"

Her thoughts meant something. They were important, somehow. But what she was saying sounded like it was straight out of a dream, and not the good kind. How could I trust such impudence?

A long silence passed between us, as I edged even closer to the stump.

Hastina let out a roar, and she swooped upwards and veered in front of me. "*I hoped it wouldn't come to this, Dragonseer Wells.*"

She dived at me with an open mouth, her gaze focused on my throat. I readied my claws to bat her away. But before she could get within inches of me, another shape lunged out of the sky. A massive beast of a black dragon, even bigger than Alsie. It knocked Hastina off her flight path.

"*I'll handle her,*" Charth said in the collective unconscious. "*The Empress is eagerly awaiting you, Acolyte Wells.*"

His voice sounded dry, but faithful. Both Hastina and Charth rolled out of view, as a sense of fear rose within me. Alas, whatever memories tried to find purchase in my mind sank back down again to be replaced by Finesia's voice.

"*Come to me, my Acolyte. I feared you would forever be my Fallen, but again you've proven faithful to me.*" Her voice soothed so much that the shapes that I'd just seen – the dragonmen fighting somewhere outside of my peripheral vision became unimportant to me.

My mind elsewhere, I ran my claws over the patterns in the tree stump, swirls running around its bare surface in a similar concentric pattern to the clouds above the Tree Immortal.

"*What must I do?*" I asked Finesia.

"*Become human,*" she said. "*We will need you like that for the ritual.*"

I roared in delight. I was finally about to serve my purpose.

Black smoke rose around me, and within seconds I was human again. Once I had transformed, I took a breath of fresh secicao, the gas coming from the Tree Immortal, infusing me with strength.

The Tree Immortal looked even more massive from the ground than it had from the air. It wasn't just the trunk that was enormous, but so were the roots which soared out of the ground then plunged back beneath it, each like a wave as high as a dragon queen. One root – more levelled than the rest – formed a path leading from my stump to the Tree Immortal.

The bark of the tree had now started to shift again, the whorls turning in a slow spiral pattern. I only needed to blink, and a hole large enough for me to step through had opened where the root met the trunk.

Now in human form, I took a second breath, tasting the

secicao at the back of my tongue. This was what I had been waiting for all my life. Somehow, I knew it in my bones – my destiny was nigh.

With that thought in mind, I clambered over the root and into the embrace of the Tree Immortal, which was now completely under Finesia's control.

37

"YOU CAN'T GO to the ritual dressed like that," Alsie said out loud, and she pointed to some white robes hanging off wooden hooks that protruded out of the bark behind her. "Get dressed and remove those daggers from your garters. All you need will be provided in due time."

Her robe fell just short of touching the wooden platform on which we stood. Her raven hair hung loosely over her shoulders, from behind which she assessed me with a narrow, piercing gaze.

I didn't stop to ask what this ritual was. Rather, I was still mesmerised by the green gas that rose around me from the edges of the platform, seeping into my nostrils. It made me feel a little giddy, but at the same time relaxed me, as if right now I had nothing to fear.

We both stood on a wooden platform, inside the bole of the tree, which must have spanned one hundred paces in diameter. Ridges ran down the length of the bole. Networks of brass cogs and gears connected the platform to these ridges. These were the only sign of any machinery in here, as the platform was made also of wood and looked like the exposed top of a tree stump.

Alsie didn't look away as I removed my clothes, starting with my jerkin, then my blouse, followed by my trousers, my socks –

garters and all – and finally my underwear. She would have seen me in my nakedness in my dreams anyway, much as I'd seen her in mine. I turned, unhooked a robe, put it on, and tied the cord.

"Come," Alsie said, and she held out her hand towards me. I took it, and she pulled me towards her. With me in one arm, she reached out behind her and pressed something on the bark. The platform shuddered, then it creaked and started to descend. It accelerated to such a pace that I knew we were travelling deep underneath the earth.

Alsie pulled back from me a little, then she reached out to stroke my hair. She looked deeply into my eyes – her own ones tinted with green. "It's such a shame we have to do it this way. You have always been such a beautiful creature. In another world, perhaps you could have joined us... But you have failed Finesia too many times."

I was still completely under Finesia's thrall, my heart beating slowly in my chest, my breathing careful and steady. At the same time, another part of me was trying to break free... Blood pounded to my head, and I saw an image. I wasn't holding Alsie's hand for a moment, but Sukina's. My old friend seemed to regard me with an expression of sympathy, much as I'd seen her at the beginning of that insightful dream.

As we descended deeper into the earth, my connection to Sukina strengthened. The pressure intensified in my ears, making me more conscious of the world around me. Soon, this gave me enough strength to summon the blue flame at the back of my mind, and the hold Finesia had on me slipped away.

"*You can't leave me now...*" Finesia said. "*We've come too far together.*" Yet her attempts to regain control over me were futile because I'd already woken up.

Before I had time to act, though, Alsie reached into her robe and pulled out a dagger. She lashed out with remarkable preci-sion, stopping the edge of the blade just short of my throat. "*Finesia doesn't want it to end this way,*" she said in the collective unconscious, *"but it doesn't matter to me whether I deliver you alive or dead."*

I didn't dare move. *"So kill me. Because I will do nothing to aid this world's demise."*

Alsie's lips folded into a wide grin. *"You've done all you needed to do. You killed Bassalhan, and you took the boy to a place where we could easily snatch him from your grasp. We thought we'd lose many more dragonmen in the process... I believe the one we did lose was especially dear to you. Did you really think you could win him back over to your side?"*

"There's always light inside people... You just need to know where to look."

Alsie raised an eyebrow. *"Is there?"*

The platform bucked as we hit the base of the trunk. This gave me an opening. I clawed at Alsie's face with my fingernails. She yelped, and I spun away from her. I whirled towards the pile of clothes I'd left lying on the floor and drew my two knives.

Alsie wiped some black blood off the side of her face, then used her fingertip to get rid of the remainder. I took a defensive stance, keeping my right dagger in front of my body, the other slightly to my side. Alsie shook her head...

"You have always been such an imbecile," she said out loud.

Then, in my mind, came that terrifying high-pitched scream she'd used before to numb my senses. My head reeled, and my muscles became weak. My hands shook involuntarily, and I dropped the daggers on the floor.

Alsie charged forwards and wrapped her forearm around my neck. With her other hand, she kept the tip of her dagger pressed to my stomach. I willed myself to transform, even if I worried that through doing so, I'd lose myself to Finesia once again. But this time, I felt no strength surging to my muscles. No searing of my skin, or scales trying to push through. No wings tearing out of my shoulder blades.

"I gave you this gift," Finesia said. *"Which I can just as well*

take away from you... If you betray me any more, then I will leave you to rot in secicao's soil."

Alsie turned the dagger and kneaded the hilt of it slowly around my waist as her iron grip tightened around my throat. I wanted to gasp for air, but she'd blocked my windpipe. The dagger came to rest by my hip, the cold steel of the blade again pressing against me.

"Oh yes," she said... "This is the beginning—" Then, a sharp pain stabbed into my side.

I didn't hear the rest of what she said, as my screams drowned out her voice.

"Shut up!" Alsie said. "Will you really wail before a god?"

All my energy had been spent... My vision went blurry, my pulse throbbed in my head, and I could feel my blood flowing out from my side. I looked down at the dagger buried there.

Alsie twisted it, and pain shot upwards from my hip to my head. I soon blacked out.

I WAS unable to move anything other than my fingers, my toes, and the muscles in my face. My hip throbbed where Alsie had stabbed me. I hadn't healed like I usually did. But I hadn't died either.

I opened my eyes to see through my blurry vision a massive chamber, suffused with green light. The walls were made of bark, with green glowing vines wrapped across them. A massive fountain lay in the chamber's centre, constructed from stone, from which great jets of green liquid shot up towards the ceiling and back down into the pool in a narrow arc, sending up trails of pungent green secicao gas when they hit the water.

The floor curved in such a way, that I knew we could no longer be inside the Tree Immortal's bole. Rather, I guessed we were in a swollen section of one of the massive roots. I couldn't see any exit or entrance though. The place was sealed off tight.

The vines on the walls seemed to converge at some point opposite me, where I noticed someone trapped underneath them.

My vision became sharper, and I saw a boy's lifeless face, only the whites of his eyes showing. He was dressed only in a threadbare hemp vest and a loincloth made out of leaves and vines. Tubes ran from his body, pumping dark viscous blood away from him.

My heart jumped in my chest when I realised who it was.

"Taka..." I said, and I tried to wriggle free. But the vines held me secured to the tree bark. "Taka..." I tried to shout it, but my voice came out raspy, my throat dry.

"*So, you've awoken,*" Finesia said in my head. "*Then it is time...*"

"*Finesia, whatever you're up to, you cannot win this war. Humanity has always found a way to survive, and we will survive again.*"

"*Always such a stoic... But that's the thing, I already am the pinnacle of evolution. I bested the dragon emperor Honore and my husband Finase, once emperor of the humans, and I knew from the days I set my eyes on the Tree Immortal that it would be mine to claim. Now I am here, ready to be reborn from it in a better form. It is time for the ritual to start... Your final battle is nigh.*"

"*Finesia... You will never have any power in this world. You don't even have a body.*"

"Dear, oh dear... You really don't see what's happening in front of you..." That was when I realised that I heard her with my ears, not in my head anymore.

I looked to the side slightly, and I saw another humanoid form wrapped up beneath the vines. She was green, clothed by the vines wrapped around her breasts, waist, and torso. Her skin glowed, just like secicao, and her hair was also made of thinner vines, twisting around each other like snakes. She was as large as a dragon queen. Her lips were bark-like and cracked in places.

They moved almost unnaturally as she spoke, her voice like stone grinding against stone.

"When I drank the sap of the Tree Immortal, The Gods Themselves told me that immortality wouldn't be gifted overnight. Instead, I had to wait for someone to deliver it to me. Frustrated, I hacked the tree to pieces, and scattered its remains across the Southlands. Those remains became secicao...

"I didn't know it at the time, but this was all part of the divine plan. Since then, secicao has fulfilled its purpose. It was once the Tree Immortal, and needed to regrow as the Tree Immortal, creating the conditions across the world for it to do so. Now that the process is complete, immortal beings can thrive upon this world once again.

"The roots of secicao run deep. They reach far beneath our planet's mantle, and they've been waiting for the right conditions to grow above the surface across every single landmass. They created an environment from which I can revive, and my faithful dragonmen and dragonwomen have helped create the perfect conditions for my rebirth."

"No..." I said, but my words came out weakly. This had to be a delusion. It had to be another one of those dreams – perhaps my final one. "The Gods Themselves had no such designs. They never wanted to harm any of us. I won't believe it."

"You fool!" Finesia said. "The Gods Themselves left me as the rightful governor of this world, freeing them up to find other worlds to improve in their image."

"But the Ambassadors..." I said. "The Gods Themselves put them here to protect the world. I am a direct descendant of the Ambassador Candida. My purpose is to stop evil beings like you from ever rising to power."

"That's where you're wrong," Finesia said. "Your myths saw these Ambassadors as protectors... But no one wrote in your texts of old, what the Gods Themselves told me. The descendants of the Ambassadors, they said, would also evolve, into beasts that can become my faithful servants. One of these descendants would prove themselves in a final battle against another, and then become my rightful aide, an inheritor of the new world, with almost as much privilege as I. You have one last chance to prove yourself, my Fallen. The test to me seems futile, but fate has deemed you should be given a worthy chance. Who am I to argue against the will of the Gods Themselves?"

I could taste bile on the back of my tongue. "I knew it... All this time when you said I could serve at your right hand. It was all a ruse..."

"I needed the most gullible of all the dragonseers – the one with the weakest of minds, the easiest to influence. Thus I've brought into the final battle against my favourite acolyte the one who was most likely to lose."

A high-pitched creaking sound came from the other side of the chamber. The vines there twisted away to reveal a passage-way, from which Alsie Fioreletta stepped through in her long, white robe. She sauntered up to me, then took my jaw in her hands, squeezing it so hard my eyes became blurry. Then she tossed back her head and cackled.

"Alsie Fioreletta," I said. "Why do you fight for Finesia? Do you not have a past? People who cared about you? Don't you have something you wish to protect?"

My attempts at gaining a reaction from her did nothing to wipe the smirk off her face. She turned back to Finesia, as if inviting her to speak.

"That's why you are fated to lose this..." Finesia said. "My servant Colas, when he started experimenting with Exalmpora, allowed me willingly to inhabit his feeble mind. He raised Alsie Fioreletta as his daughter and my loyal servant, making sure she had no connections to anything most humans hold foolishly dear. Like secicao, she's only existed for one purpose. To recreate this world in my image... Now come, my most faithful acolyte, Alsie Fioreletta. Show this woman who is the rightful inheritor of this world."

"As you wish, my Empress."

"But don't forget the wishes of the Gods Themselves. Give the woman something resembling a fighting chance," Finesia said. "We need to make a show of it, on the off chance that one of the Gods Themselves is still up there and watching. I suggest Exalmpora."

Alsie strolled up to me, with a hideously inhuman grin on her face. She reached down into her robe and produced a vial of silver liquid. Exalmpora, just as Finesia had promised. Alsie uncorked the vial, and the metallic scent of it wafted up through my nostrils.

I craved it, but I had to suppress that desire, so I focused on the pain at my hip, trying to look down at it. But my head was angled in such a way that I couldn't see my body.

Still, Alsie seemed to detect where I was trying to look, and she reached out with her free hand and squeezed the flesh around the wound. I screamed out in pain and my vision became suddenly blurry again. Alsie let out another cackle in chorus.

"You resist the will of the goddess who has been with us since the beginning of time. The Gods Themselves gave us Finesia and gave her the Ambassadors and descendants of them like ourselves. There's no point trying to fight the designs of the divine."

I turned my head away from the Exalmpora, tasting bile in my mouth. "Finesia is no goddess."

"She will be soon... Reborn once again..."

Alsie squeezed my cheeks so hard that it hurt. I tried to wriggle away, but she was far too strong. She pressed the uncorked vial to my mouth and tipped it.

Within moments, the Exalmpora trickled down my throat, and I felt strength surge through me. The pain subsided at my hip, and though I still couldn't see it, I could feel it healing – the skin around the wound closing up.

I willed dragon scales to rip through my skin, so I could tear myself out of her grasp. Still, I hadn't regained that ability. It seemed that Finesia could both choose when to grant me her gifts and when to take them away.

My only defence was the focus I kept on the blue flame at the back of my mind, as strength washed over my body. I sensed something in the collective unconscious. An image –the eyes of a great black dragon, a jaw plunging towards me... I recognised the dragon, Charth. Then my heart went out to Hastina, and I sang a dragonsong in my mind, hoping it could help her...

"Your friend is lost to you," Finesia said, "and you have far more important things to focus on. For now is the time of your final battle with my acolyte, Alsie Fioreletta. The one you've been destined to lose since birth."

The vines loosened around my shoulders, chest, and neck. I gasped, only just realising how much they'd constrained my breathing.

Alsie took two long steps back towards the fountain and dropped something into it. A green, pungent gas rose up from the green waters, smelling even more sulphuric than secicao.

Alsie looked down at the rising gas and smiled. Then she removed her robe.

38

I FELT LIGHTHEADED, and my vision went black for a moment. When it returned to normal, I wasn't inside the Tree Immortal anymore. Instead, gnarly, bare secicao plants surrounded Alsie and I, their branches twisting up towards the roiling brown sky. I took a breath of the secicao, letting it fill me with strength. I was drawing off an ancient and evil power, but I had no better choice.

Either what I saw was an illusion caused by that green gas, or I was once again exploring the world of dreams. I guessed I was still awake, as I'd seen visions like this before. Secicao in its strongest forms was a powerful narcotic that rendered its subjects suggestible. Whatever I saw in this realm would probably have an equivalent in the real world.

I looked down at my body, naked just as Alsie was. Though she wore no clothes, she stood tall as if dressed it the finest coat of armour.

"The moment we've been waiting for," she said. "But I've told you along, you're destined to lose."

"Then let us get it over with," I said. "If I'm to die here, I'd rather do so quickly. But don't think I'll go down without a fight."

"Who said anything about dying?" Alsie said, her head cocked.

I only needed to blink, and she was clad in a suit of golden armour, wearing a helmet of the same colour, housing a fiercely sharp visor.

I also felt extra weight upon me, as I was now adorned in a heavy suit of armour. I couldn't see its colour because a helmet graced my head, sweat pooling at my temples underneath. The visor restricted my peripheral vision somewhat, creating a dark frame around the slit, through which I could see Alsie.

Above us, black dragons carved the sky, roaring in delight. They weren't coming close, but they had gathered to watch their two leaders battle to the death.

Alsie drew a claymore from her back. I reached behind me and slid out the heavy sword that had found its way between my shoulder blades. We both held our weapons at the ready, circling each other. Very faintly, from behind the vertical slits on Alsie's visor, I could make out the green glow in her eyes.

"Time for you to die," I said. I scuffed my heels into the dirt and charged at Alsie.

"You should be so lucky." Alsie turned her sword sideways as mine clanged against it.

I tried to overpower her with sheer strength, drawing even more power from the clouds themselves. For a moment, it seemed to work, and Alsie bowed under the weight.

But she merely intended to use my power against me. Suddenly, she turned, and my sword slid off hers. She came around in a fast, graceful manoeuvre, her sword spinning straight towards a section of exposed waist underneath my armour.

I pirouetted out of the way at the last moment, ducking slightly as I did. The tip of her sword scratched against the side plate of my armour, sending up a bright spark.

My sword now high, I hammered the hilt of my sword down

on Alsie's visor, letting out a loud clang. A sharp pain lanced down the forearm of my dominant hand.

Alsie took two steps back, then lunged at my stomach. I pulled my abdomen back to stop her impaling me in one motion. Alsie entered a defensive stance. We circled each other, and I looked for an opening.

"You fight well for someone who spent most of her training in the art of knives and daggers," Alsie said.

"Then why don't you even the odds and give me the weapons I'm most suited for. Presumably, Finesia has control over this illusion."

"You really think you can outmatch the reach of a five-foot claymore with knives?"

"I could equally well knock off your head with a bullet from a Pattersoni rifle..."

"Always such a foolish wench! The Gods Themselves didn't design such battles to be fought with dirty firearms."

"I'm guessing then that they are okay with knives?"

Finesia's voice suddenly resounded from the sky, or at least it seemed to – this had to be an illusion after all. "I never thought you to be so arrogant, with your inexperience. But then it would be good to get this battle over quickly."

The sky above me seemed to flicker, and my shoulders lightened. Two knives appeared, crossed in my hands, and my armour also vanished. Instead, I wore a long threadbare cloak with a protective layer of leather armour underneath it. The loose cotton trousers were designed for flexibility, and not for getting hit...

"*Aren't we going to fight in dragon form?*" I asked Finesia in the collective unconscious. "*That was always how the dreams you showed me ended...*"

"*You really think you deserve such a gift? You have failed me too many times, my Fallen.*"

"*I just thought there was a certain order for things.*"

"*Which I shall decide.*"

Alsie had already readied her sword at chest height for another charge. She sped forward, the tip of her blade pointed towards me. The spurs on her boots sent brown dust clouds into the air. At the last moment, she twisted her torso, and the blade slashed toward me across the outside of her stance.

Too high to jump. Too low to duck. My only option that didn't involve getting sliced in two, was to roll away from it.

I emerged from my roll just in front of Alsie, ready to thrust my blades into her throat. But she was executing a full turn at the time, and my blades glanced off the armour on her back.

She continued to swing a three-sixty, the blade coming in low. I vaulted over it, executing another roll upon landing. I spun around quickly to face Alsie, who shifted the grip on her sword. She brought it across her chest in a defensive stance.

"I'll make this easier for you, wench," she said. There came a flash of light, then the helmet disappeared from her head, showing a full-toothed grin. "Now, you have a target for your dainty knives."

I knew she was just taunting me. It didn't matter whether she wore the helmet or not. She wielded her sword so well that I had no chance of striking a lethal blow there. I had to hit low first if I had any chance of winning this fight.

I wiped some grit off the side of my mouth, then I charged. I crossed my knives together, to deflect Alsie's feint. Then I ducked and got ready to land a blow to her exposed mid-section.

But she was already in the middle of executing a perfect downwards strike. I raised my weapons at the last second. My knives clanged against her sword, and our blades locked.

Steel grated against steel as I pushed forwards with all my strength. To my surprise, Alsie yielded, allowing her blade to get close to her chest.

Some light glinted off something near Alsie's midsection. I dared glance down, and horror surged through me. She'd shifted her grip to use one hand to execute her final manoeuvres. Being a dragonwoman gave her the strength to do this with what would usually be such a cumbersome blade.

Now, she wielded her claymore only in one hand, using her superior dragonwoman strength to keep the weapon aloft. In her other hand, she held a dagger. She thrust this at my stomach, and she hit her target true.

Pain lanced through me, starting at my stomach and blossoming outwards. Alsie cackled out loud again, then she charged forward, pushing me back.

I hit something hard, and the pain flared even stronger in my stomach.

Now that I was finally defeated, the chamber containing Finesia revealed itself to me once again. The dagger Alsie had plunged into me was actually a wooden stake that had me pinned to the inner bark of the Tree Immortal. Two gnarled wooden branches, the size of quarterstaffs, lay on the ground in front of me.

Vines started to entangle me, and I was soon completely restrained. I wanted to die. But my gut told me Finesia wasn't going to let that happen.

This, after all, had been all a part of her plan.

My vision went dark for a moment, and my mind wanted to black out. But a part of me wouldn't let it.

"*As dictated,*" Finesia said. "*You've lost... Now, Alsie will become my aide, and you will stay here. Yours and your surrogate son's blood will complete me, the blood of humankind melded with the blood of the Ambassadors. Isn't fate a beautiful thing, my Fallen? You spending eternity here stuck beneath the earth, whilst my aide and I claim the treasures from above.*"

I tried to say something, but the pain made it impossible to think. The vine around my forehead tightened, pulling my head back and forcing me to stare up at the massive green form of

Finesia. Below her Alsie once again wore her robe, and was prostrating before her empress.

While before, Finesia's skin had been a pallid green, now the colours that surged across it were more verdant. That same dark oily spectrum that streaked across the skin of the black dragons also washed over her body.

From the vines stretched across my stomach, I felt another sharp stab as thorns protruded out of them and pierced my skin. They sucked the blood out of my body and carried them across the inside of the trunk through the network of vines, towards the body of Finesia that the Tree Immortal had grown. Another tangle of vines carried dark blood towards her from Taka's direction.

"Auntie Pontopa," Taka's voice came in my head. *"You're there..."*

"Taka?" I tried to turn my head to look at the boy, but the vines had me secured too tightly. *"You're alive."*

"You shouldn't have come, Auntie... You should have left me here."

I tried to swallow, but my mouth felt so dry I couldn't move my throat muscles. *"I couldn't have left you... I promised Sukina... Your mother."*

"But now we've messed it up... That's Finesia. It's how I've always seen her in my dreams."

The Empress had gained even more colour, and her skin now looked almost human, except still with a slight green tint to her complexion. The vines peeled away from her, allowing her giant form to walk freely. Only the vines around her breasts, loins, and stomach remained. These warped, and wrapped around her, transforming into a short and radiant dress of golden silk. The vines coming from her head also thinned and took form, creating a full head of wavy platinum-blond hair.

"Your empress has awoken," she said, and her voice boomed around the chamber. "Acolyte Fioreletta, let us complete the transformation."

I wanted to scream at her, to tell her that we would find a way to stop her, that she couldn't win. But more vines quickly wrapped around my open mouth, gagging me.

Finesia looked down at me, disdain in her dark eyes. It seemed she had nothing more to say to me.

A plume of black smoke rose from around her feet. Alsie stood up, and black smoke also rose around her. Soon, two dark clouds had enveloped the both of them. The one around Finesia grew much larger than the one around Alsie. The clouds soon faded to reveal two dragonwomen.

Alsie looked the same as I'd always remembered her. But Finesia's dragon form was twice the size of any dragon queen – large enough to best any one of them in fair combat.

Finesia, still in her dragon form, tossed her head to the sky and let out a roar that shook the inside of the Tree Immortal. She spread her wings and flew upwards. The tree bark writhed, to create a massive opening that let her escape into the main bole.

Alsie watched for a moment, then followed behind her. She said nothing to us, either out loud or in the collective unconscious. The opening into the bole proper sealed shut behind her, trapping us in this gloomy place.

"Is she in your head anymore, Auntie Pontopa?" Taka asked me in the collective unconscious.

"I heard her a moment ago..." Putting word to thought was hard right now, with the pain flaring through me.

"But can you hear her now?"

"I can't..."

"I think she left when she separated herself from the Tree Immortal."

"She—" Come to think of it, something had changed... I didn't have to keep Finesia out of my head anymore. I didn't have to focus to make sure my mind was my own.

But still, with the pain in my stomach, I was in a far worse state than I was before.

"*So that's it...*" I said to Taka. "*Exiled underground. Left like this for eternity, to go mad.*"

"*I'm sorry Auntie,*" Taka said. "*The way that I treated you back at Fortress Gerhaun... And then how mean I was to you at Gahl. I was wrong. You were never a bad person. You were never the monster... I saw you fighting Alsie. I saw how you fought for something greater than yourself.*"

My breath caught in my throat. "*You did what you believed was right,*" I said, and I closed my eyes, at least hoping to get some sleep.

I don't know if I managed to get any, before a massive creaking sound caused my eyes to shoot wide open. There came a loud crash, and a large section of bark blew out of the tree where Finesia had previously been attached.

From the hole this created, water came flooding in.

39

THE WATER HAD ONLY JUST BEGUN to tickle the skin at the bottom of my bare feet, when a black dragon rode the torrent of water spurting out of the hole. For a moment, I thought that Finesia might have sent one of hers to finish the job. Then I heard Hastina's voice in my head.

"Dragonheats, I don't know why you masked your minds for so long – if you did it yourself – because I've only just managed to find you here." The channel was open to both Taka and I in the collective unconscious.

Before I even had a chance to respond, Taka spoke, and he did so out loud. "Dragonseer Wiggea... You made it... You're here to rescue us."

Hastina, in her black dragon form, landed in the water pooling at the base of the chamber. Black smoke rose from around her taloned feet, and she soon emerged from the fading cloud clutching her spear in both hands.

She turned to Taka, and with swift motions of her spear she cut the vines away that tied him against the tree. Taka fell to the ground, stumbling for a moment.

"Take a robe, Taka," Hastina said, then she turned to me and strolled over.

While Taka picked up one of the robes, now soggy, from the ground, Hastina looked me up and down. I groaned, and wanted to say something, but my mind wasn't so sharp and so she got in the first word.

"What the dragonheats did you do, Dragonseer Wells?"

Instinct wanted me to shake my head, but it was still restrained. "What exactly did you see?" I asked. "What happened up there?"

Hastina's jaw tightened. "The top of the tree exploded, and then two black dragons came out from amongst the falling branches. One of them was twice the size of Bassalhan. I've never seen anything like it. At the same time, the barrier suddenly vanished, and the black dragons left to head north."

"Finesia..." I said. "That dragon queen is Finesia..."

"What?" She turned her spear towards me, pointing it towards my neck. "So this was your plan all along."

Taka ran over to her and pulled down at her arm trying to lower the spear. Hastina nudged him away.

"Stay out of this, Taka," she said.

Taka narrowed his eyes, then stepped in front of her. This time, he managed to shove the spear away.

"No, I won't... Auntie Pontopa is our friend – our ally. She did everything she could to stop Finesia being reborn. But they only needed my blood and Auntie Pontopa's blood... She and Alsie fought with sticks and stakes, and Alsie won."

"Why the dragonheats would your blood do anything?" Hastina said, her hand on her chin.

"I don't know..." Taka said, his voice sounding strained. "It was part of some legend or something. Please, Auntie Pontopa is in pain. Can't you see?"

As they spoke, the cascade was pushing away more bark away from the hole, great pieces of it floating on the rising water. It came up to my calves, where the salt caused the scratches on my skin to sting. It would hurt even more, I was sure, when it got as high as the wound in my stomach, where the stake was still embedded.

Taka seemed more worried about my plight than Hastina, because he stepped forwards, and pulled the stake out of my stomach. My vision went suddenly blurry, and I saw red for a moment. The pain caused me to yelp out, but I didn't scream.

"Please, Dragonseer Wiggea," Taka said. "Let her free. We're in this together, remember?"

She nodded, then cut rapidly at the vines that entangled me. Some of her slashes grazed my bare skin, but I had enough adrenaline pumping through me that I felt no pain. Taka scurried away, splashing up water behind him.

I touched the wound at my stomach, then looked down to see it had already started closing up now that the stake had gone. It was as Finesia had promised – I still had my 'immortality' – so long as no one ended my life using the weak spot at my throat. But why hadn't Finesia also taken that away? Somehow, I doubted any of her other 'gifts' remained.

Taka returned with the second robe, which was stained with dark blood. I nodded to thank him, then I put it on. It was soaked through, but I preferred this to my birthday suit.

"What happened to Charth?" I asked Hastina.

"Dead." she said. Then, when she saw my shock, she lowered her head. "He told me in the collective unconscious that he wanted to die; he asked me to release him much like Wiggea asked. There was no turning back for him."

"You mean to say he let you win the fight?"

"I guess there was still a part of him left inside... From what I heard of him, Charth was always strong."

I gritted my teeth, and I looked up at the hole. The water had reached my knees now, and it was rising fast. A boom came from above, and then another hole opened up. More fragments of bark were getting tossed down by the cascade.

"The tree is collapsing," I said. "How far underwater are we?"

"I don't know," Hastina said. "Just stop wasting time, transform into dragons, and we'll fly out of here."

Taka let out a whine, and I tried to will the scales to me once more. It was as I'd thought. The ability had left me. I still felt weak, and a little dizzy from having been drained of blood, and no doubt Taka felt the same.

"We can't transform," I said. "Finesia leached that ability out of us."

"But Finesia gave us that ability in the first place..." Hastina said, sounding confused.

"I guess it was on temporary loan." I shuddered as the realisation came that Finesia could drain power off any one of her dragonmen. I couldn't even imagine what she might be capable of in her new form.

The ground underfoot quaked, and more bark showered down from above. There must have been at least a dozen jets of water coming out of the walls at this point, and the level now came up to our waist. A sliver of sunlight streamed through one of the holes, refracted by the water. It provided enough of a glow in here to see the ceiling.

Hastina looked up at the sky, and a roar came out of her throat as black smoke concealed her. The water rushing around her washed the smoke away quicker than usual, and she lowered herself to the water.

"*I really hope there's a way out of here,*" she said in the collective unconscious, "*because this chamber is completely submerged.*"

I pointed to where Finesia had left the chamber. "*Finesia and Alsie went that way to the tree trunk. Reckon you can rip your way out?*"

"*But if it leads to the bole, then some of Finesia's guards might still be up there. I came in underwater for a reason.*"

"*That's a risk we have to take,*" I said. "*Can you do this or not?*"

"*I can try,*" Hastina said. "*Jump on. We really need to get out of here.*"

I didn't want to hang around another second either. I let Taka rush up Hastina's tail first, and he took a place straddling Hastina's neck. Hastina didn't have a steering fin, and all Taka had to hold on to were the grooves in Hastina's scales.

I clambered up after him, dangling my legs over Hastina's shoulders and using Taka's waist for support. Hastina took off from the water, her tail whipping up a spray behind her. She headed straight towards where Finesia and Alsie had entered the bole. Taka tensed up when she grabbed hold of the bark with her claws. But he held on tight.

The bark seemed to peel away easily, and it didn't take Hastina long to rip a hole into the bole with her teeth, and she flew through. I looked down to see the wooden platform we'd arrived on, far below us. Above us, the tree bark had crumbled, creating an opening through which sunlight streamed.

Hastina spiralled up towards that opening, and she emerged into a blue and sunny sky. There was no sign of any black dragon guards. They had no doubt flown north with Finesia, to unleash terror upon our lands.

As we flew further away, I saw how The Tree Immortal was flaking away into pieces. Green strands of it stretched out across the water, getting tossed up upon the roiling waves. Seeing it like this reminded me of the history that Finesia had recited – how she had hacked the tree apart due to her madness of being left alone.

I couldn't help but wonder if history was repeating itself. Was our civilisation doomed to make the same mistakes over and over? If so, who or what could stop her? Or had Finesia now found a way to succeed at what she'd failed to do in our distant past? It seemed that we'd discover the answer to these questions soon. The first thing we needed to find out was where she planned to strike next.

To the west, the sun glinted off some distant ships, now stationary. Hastina let out a squeal, and she headed towards the two fleets where our friends and dragons, I hoped, were waiting for us.

40

"BLUNDERS AND DRAGONHEATS, YOU SURVIVED," General Sako roared up to us from the railings of the Saye Explorer's quarterdeck. "Taka, Dragonseer Wells, you're alive!"

He had watched us approach from behind his secicao pipe, while able hands worked around the ship, fixing what equipment had been damaged in the battle. From around us came the sounds of hammers clanging against metal, punctuated by the occasional hiss and grind of a steam-powered circular saw.

The sea was still a little choppy, but it had calmed immensely with the departing of the black dragons and the removal of the protective barrier around the Tree Immortal. From this distance, it looked quite a spectacle, still glowing as it peeled away.

I wasn't in the mood for any bantering, and by the looks of it, neither was Taka. I just felt incredibly drained and wanted to sleep.

Hastina seemed to instinctively understand our exhaustion, probably detecting it in the collective unconscious. She lowered us gently to the deck, and I clambered off first, barely able to stand when I made it off her tail. Clearly noticing how much I was wobbling, General Sako strode forwards and provided a shoulder for support. He offered Taka a hand to help him down from Hastina's back.

As soon as Hastina had enough room, she transformed back to human form behind a cloud of black smoke. She stepped out of that cloud before it even faded away, handed her spear to General Sako, then took hold of mine and Taka's hands.

"If you'll excuse me, General, I need to get them to the sickbay."

General Sako's jaw dropped, and his pipe fell out of his mouth. He caught it against his chest, not letting go of the spear with the other hand.

"I thought they were invulnerable," he said.

"They are," Hastina said. "But something changed in that massive tree. Their physiology might be different now."

"What happened?" General Sako asked, but Hastina had already whisked us too far away from him to reply. I felt secretly grateful to her for that, as at the time I really didn't have the head for conversation.

Hastina took us below deck, through the corridors, towards the medical room. When she opened the door, out wafted the smell of oil and antiseptic. The room contained eight beds, seven of them occupied. Doctor Forsolano was inside, with a couple of medical officers. As soon as he saw us, he ordered a sailor with a sling over his arm to vacate one of the beds, leaving two next to each other free for me and Taka.

"What happened?" Doctor Forsolano said as he felt my and Taka's foreheads with the back of his hand. "In fact, don't answer that. Lie down before you say anything. You're both incredibly pale."

Taka took the free bed, and I let the sailor gather his things from bedside cabinet before I took the other. He saluted me on the way out, then walked towards the door with a limp in his step.

"They've lost a lot of blood," Hastina said to Doctor

Forsolano. "I think they'll need a blood transfusion. I presume Admiral Sandao has a roster of blood types on deck."

Doctor Forsolano examined us from over his glasses. "Of course, of course. I'll get to it... But yes... Could you get that roster for me? It could come in useful."

"Of course," Hastina said, and she hurried out the door.

That was when I heard some commotion from outside. It was Faso – I'd recognise his voice and manner of speaking anywhere. "What do you mean, I can't go in. He's my son. I need to see him, for wellies' sake. Hastina, you must have a say in the matter..."

I was too tired and didn't have the energy for dealing with him. He was someone else's problem for now. I turned to see that Taka had already closed his eyes, and was fast asleep, breathing softly.

Just before I slept, my mind reached out to Velos, and I felt his emotions the way I used to a long time ago, before Finesia started to occupy my mind. My dragon was well, though also in pain from his injury. But I could sense that he would also live to fight another day.

Feeling placated by that fact, I let myself drift off to sleep.

I AWOKE, feeling much better for wear. I had a headache, but I knew that I was safe and warm. Doctor Forsolano sat at the doctor's desk in the middle of the room, reading some papers with medical information on them and complex charts. He turned his head and noticed I was awake.

He stood up, walked over, and felt my forehead with the back of his hand again. "How are you feeling, Pontopa?"

"Better..." I said, and I looked down at my tummy, opening my robe slightly so I could look for a sign of the wound. There wasn't even a scar.

But there was something different about me. I felt purer –

there was no better way of describing it. For one, I didn't have the sense of Finesia inhabiting my head anymore. I also knew in my bones that I couldn't transform into a dragon. In all honesty, I was happy to lose both things.

"Did you give me a transfusion?" I asked Doctor Forsolano.

"I did. You were easy, Type A. But Taka... Well, universal donors are great until you have to give them blood."

I smiled. "I heard Faso wanted to visit."

"I let him in after he had calmed down a bit. Taka woke for a while, and they've already had a heart-to-heart."

That was something I hadn't wanted to miss. The moments that Faso showed his humanity seemed rare. "How long was I asleep?" I asked.

Doctor Forsolano looked at his pocket watch. "A good four hours, I'd say. You know how it is... From what Hastina and Taka have told me, you needed the rest."

The hatch into the sickbay opened, and Hastina walked in. She had her spear with her again, which she deposited by the door, propped up against the wall. From beside me, Taka yawned, and he lifted himself up in bed.

"Is it time for us to leave now?" he asked.

"Leave?" I asked. Dragonheats, I had missed a lot.

Hastina nodded. "We received a telegram from the Masked Regent. She wants us over at Slaro Palace as soon as you're able to travel."

"Why? What happened?" Dread rose in my chest. "Please don't tell me Finesia has attacked already."

"Not yet," Hastina said. "But we all fear she might soon."

"Then what does Valpeonia want?"

Hastina scowled and glanced over at her spear. She, turned back to me and took a deep breath. The scowl melted from her face soon after. It was as if she was trying on a new personality and wanted to lose her fierceness.

"Not much can be said in a telegram, you know," she said. "We're just going to have to wait until we get to Slaro Palace."

In that case, I wanted to get there as quickly as possible. I swung my legs around on the bed, and I lifted myself to my feet. I still felt a little dizzy, but I didn't want anyone to see that. "I'm ready now," I said.

"Oh goodie," Taka said. "Another adventure." He was already on his feet, and he sprang towards the door.

"Taka's coming too?" I asked.

Hastina nodded. "The Masked Regent asked for all of us."

"Then we should take Velos, Bellroot, and the dragon automaton, surely."

Hastina shook her head. "None of them are fit to fly right now. I'll fly you myself."

On that note, she waltzed out the hatch. I followed her up towards the quarterdeck, with Taka trailing close behind.

HOURS LATER, Hastina, Taka, and I approached the Slaro Palace throne room where Valpeonia – my biological mother – sat. The room had been cleaned up since we'd last seen it. It also smelled of myrrh, as if there'd been a recent funeral. Valpeonia had nothing on her head, though she wore the same flowing black robes as before.

"You lost the mask?" I asked her.

She nodded. "We can't lie to our people about the future we have ahead of us. Moving forward, we have to be honest about who we are. From now on, there will be no masks, no lookalikes, no rightful heir to the throne. The population will know who Taka really was, and the crimes that both King Cinis committed during their reigns. While you've been away, I've been discussing with members of the press about how we're going to reveal this to the public without causing riots. They're much more cooperative than I thought they would be, which is good. Anyway, enough of that. Tell me, what happened?"

I took a deep breath, not wanting to relive it. But if what

Valpeonia said was true, then she would be temporary ruler, along with Cralanein, until we found a better solution. I guessed that Cralanein would still be kept secret, despite what Valpeonia said.

I explained everything as quickly as I could, trying to leave out as little as possible. But I found it difficult to talk about the details of what happened at the Tree Immortal, and so I skimmed over the gruesome parts, as well as the condition I'd discovered Taka in. At the end of it, Valpeonia reached out and offered me a handkerchief. I'd failed to notice the tears in my eyes, and for a moment I let them flow.

Valpeonia lowered her head, remaining seated on Cini's former throne. "You've been through quite an ordeal..."

I looked over at Taka who was staring at the exact spot where Taka used to play while King Cini III held court. Perhaps Taka had been kind of wishing that he'd become king. I made a mental note to explain to him later that being dragonseer is probably a lot more fun.

"It was worth it," I said. "I saved Taka and kept my promise to Sukina."

Valpeonia gave me a smile that looked almost like one of pride. It was perhaps the most emotion I'd seen from her since I got here. Then, the features on her face darkened, and I already knew what was to come next.

"We will need to prepare for an attack by Finesia... I'll send word to all the dragon queens to watch out for her and for anyone to report when we learn of her target."

I looked down at the floor. "What can we do? We can't win this war..."

Valpeonia gave me another smile, this time a sly, knowing one. "That's where you might be wrong."

I blinked away the disbelief. "What do you know?"

Valpeonia indicated the secret passageway down to the underground caverns with a cock of her head. I had been so wrapped up in explaining the situation that I'd failed to notice that the entrance was open to them, letting out a bitter draft.

"There are some old friends of yours with Cralanein," she said, "whom I think you'll be happy to meet."

CRALANEIN WAITED for me on her ledge, her head lowered to the floor. She looked as if she was half asleep, or at least about to fall asleep. I had probably been lucky to get to her in time, because once a dragon queen enters a slumber, it's hard to wake them up again for quite a few hours without significantly irritating them.

Hastina had come with me, on Valpeonia's orders. But she didn't approach Cralanein, instead waiting at the side of the ancient dragon queen's ledge. Torchlight flickered around us, filling the entire cavern with a soft warmth.

I hurried over to Cralanein, and she raised her head to my hand so I could touch her nose. Once I'd made physical contact, her voice came in the collective unconscious.

"Dragonseer Wells, you have changed. You seem more sure of yourself."

"I lost Finesia from my head. Though I can't say I defeated her."

"Still, it sounds like a victory of your own. Now show me what you saw."

Much as she had when she showed me the visions of her past, I showed her exactly what had happened when I had entered the Tree Immortal. Alsie knocking me out on the platform, waking up completely restrained, fighting and losing the final battle against Alsie, surviving somehow with a stake through my stomach as Finesia revived herself using mine and Taka's blood. The images rushed through my mind, even more vivid than I remembered them.

When I had relived everything, I gasped for breath, as if I'd been suffocating. My heart pounded in my chest, and I could feel my blood coursing through my veins. *"We've lost,"* I told her. *"She's too powerful now. Finesia is reborn as a god, and one who cannot be beaten."*

"Is that what she would have you believe?" Cralanein asked.

"What reason do I have to believe otherwise? Please tell me, because Valpeonia thought you might have found another way."

"Not I," she said. *"But three old friends of yours have."*

"Who? Come on, I've had enough suspense for one day."

"Remember the three old men you met beneath the Pinnatu crater? You ate oatmeal with them by the fireplace above the lava lake."

"You're kidding," I said. *"No... They were underneath the volcano when it erupted. They can't possibly..."*

Cralanein lowered her head slightly, but not enough to break contact with me. She shifted her body out of the way. My mouth dropped open when I saw the three old men, framed by torch-light – the anthropologist, the biologist, and the linguist.

The story will conclude in Dragonseers and Immortality, coming 2023.

SUKINA'S STORY

The Sukina's Story novel tells the story of how Sukina came to be a dragonseer, which you can download by signing up to my email list.

I send emails approximately twice a month. You can subscribe at http://chrisbehrsin.com/sukina/.

ACKNOWLEDGMENTS

I'd first like to give thanks to Wayne M. Scace for your incredible input, as well as Carol Brandon for your extremely thorough proofread. Your work has been invaluable to me, and it has helped improve me as a writer.

I'd like to thank my lovely wife, Ola, for everything that you do. Thank you also to my parents for all their help and support.

A big thank you to everyone on the ARC team for your patience, feedback, and encouragement that you've given me through this series and my other books.

Last but not least, thank you to all readers of my works. I really do appreciate everything that you do for indie authors and the reading community.